AF225848

Jason Bitzer has been a lifeguard on the beach since 1999—working the last 10 years on Oahu's dangerous North Shore where he was awarded the Mayoral award for lifesaving merit in aiding in the rescue of professional surfer, Evan Geiselman, at the world-famous pipeline. He cut his teeth writing as a contributor to Vice Sports as well as writing feature scripts, such as '*In Deep*,' which made finals of various screenplay competitions such as the California Film awards. Looking to challenge himself in long-form storytelling, he wrote his first novel, *ISO: In the Wake of Technology*. The story encapsulates Hawaii's role in global affairs while showing what it would be like if the islands were cut off from the world during a major military conflict.

To Pat and Jim Bitzer, for always letting me follow my own path and trusting in my madness. To Roberta, James and Numa, for being my foundation.

Jason Bitzer

ISO: IN THE WAKE OF TECHNOLOGY

AUSTIN MACAULEY PUBLISHERS™
LONDON • CAMBRIDGE • NEW YORK • SHARJAH

Copyright © Jason Bitzer (2020)

All rights reserved. No part of this publication may be reproduced, distributed, or transmitted in any form or by any means, including photocopying, recording, or other electronic or mechanical methods, without the prior written permission of the publisher, except in the case of brief quotations embodied in critical reviews and certain other non-commercial uses permitted by copyright law. For permission requests, write to the publisher.

Any person who commits any unauthorized act in relation to this publication may be liable to criminal prosecution and civil claims for damages.

This is a work of fiction. Names, characters, businesses, places, events, locales, and incidents are either the products of the author's imagination or used in a fictitious manner. Any resemblance to actual persons, living or dead, or actual events is purely coincidental.

Ordering Information:
Quantity sales: special discounts are available on quantity purchases by corporations, associations, and others. For details, contact the publisher at the address below.

Publisher's Cataloging-in-Publication data
Bitzer, Jason
ISO: In the Wake of Technology

ISBN 9781645363460 (Paperback)
ISBN 9781645363477 (Hardback)
ISBN 9781647505394 (ePub e-book)

Library of Congress Control Number: 2020910434

www.austinmacauley.com/us

First Published (2020)
Austin Macauley Publishers LLC
40 Wall Street, 28th Floor
New York, NY 10005
USA

mail-usa@austinmacauley.com
+1 (646) 5125767

Table of Contents

Foreword

I have been writing since I was young; music lyrics to punk songs, short stories of travel I had imagined but had not yet experienced. I have a slight dyslexia, which has always hindered me releasing my writing to the public as my words have not always translated from my thoughts correctly. It has gotten better through effort. When I was young, I had vision problems and my mother who was a Special Ed. Teacher had noticed it. She had put me in an eye training program to correct my issues. Once I was through the training, I never had to wear glasses even through my adult years. So, moms, pay attention to your kids. You never know how big of an impact you will have on your kids later in life.

My father was an avid science fiction reader and I would grab his Isaac Asimov books when he was through, which consequently led me to writing *ISO: In the Wake of Technology*. Through my mid-twenties. I was a professional Bodyboarder and change was my constant. I would travel non-stop, almost as if to be running from something or chasing experiences, whether it be in the surf or on land. I wrote through my travels, fiction and non, until my wife and furthermore my daughter Numa came along, I had never thought of releasing anything to the world. However, like everyone, I will not be here one day and thus decided to release dribs and drabs of my writings so Numa would always have a piece of me to reflect on. I practiced, first with a script during my wife's pregnancy dedicating it to my daughter and then some non-fiction for VICE Sports. However, I wanted to tell long form stories and incorporate real life issues, to find some resolve in the major issues the world, and my surrogate home of Hawaii. *ISO: In the Wake of Technology* was born from really nothing other than the frustration of how the world treats itself and, especially, Hawaii. It's a testing ground for everything bad in agriculture, but holds the richest soil in the world. It is a society based on Aloha, but holds the Pacific's greatest military installment. All the things that make you ponder what are we really doing with our world and where will we end up if we keep complacent and let the powers that be push the power envelope. Even with *ISO: In the Wake of Technology's* worst case scenarios, I still have hope for the world and human spirit. That's truly what this book is about. Cross racial lines, power struggles, and battles over resources to benefit the greater human good. We are all on this big blue marble in the sky together and nowhere more so than on a remote pacific island do you realize you rely on you.

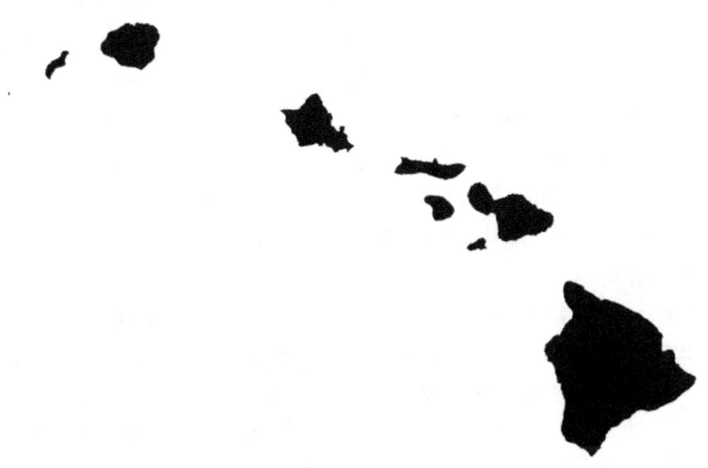

Introduction
A "Island Chain" of Events

When the event happened, the island was in its own world, a daily fight to be a part of some idyllic dream of living in paradise. Who had time to worry about war? Hell, most people needed two jobs to keep the lights on. Most of Honolulu's Hawaiian residents had more in common with Manhattanites than they did their Tahitian ancestry. Skyrocketing cost of living, the Pacific financial hub centered in Honolulu, a housing crisis, and corrupt politicians. The who's who of socialites could be found at any given political fundraising dinner. At this point, the blue water was the only thing left masking the island as a paradise and that could be quickly ruined by city rain runoff.

World War III was an inevitability everyone had accepted back on the mainland. Between bi-partisan rhetoric, a road blocked senate born from an aggressively progressive left fighting a highly regressive right. Washington was divided and weak. But, hey, we stay on Hawaiian time. That's for the busy bodies in Washington to chew on, not us islanders, the politicians and wealthy knew the score but the day to day people were as surprised as they were during the Pearl Harbor attack. Somethings change in society but keeping the common man well informed was still status quo.

Hawaii was part of the machine, even if only through complacency. The military industrial complex was just too fine-tuned. To the residents on island, their activity was just a news blip on their phone, but the military kept the island economy running with new crops of grunts spending their government funded cost of living check at businesses island wide. It's like they could bomb a small city, drop a base complete with strip mall anywhere in the world and get the boys back on Hawaiian leave in no time. Drones were delivering hellfire missiles or your groceries, depending on what side of the hemisphere you were living on. Oahu had all the benefits of being a part of the US empire, but somehow tried to hold the notion it was separate from its capitalist manifest destiny pouring east.

Everyone knew Hawaii was never without fault, both locally and in the bigger picture. We just felt removed from the equation. Yes, the economy was driven by the military bases operating on our islands. However, it never felt like we were truly under the thumb of Washington. It was more like an absentee landlord. The US played war games on our shores, but the generals couldn't even pronounce the street names. The RIMPAC military exhibition was a way for the US to invite the world to a US-owned friendly paradise where they were reminded who was carrying the big stick. New weapons were put on display and Generals postured, showing off their resources, but they paid their bills and provided a lot of people in the private sector with wealth beyond reason. However, for the masses it was a daily struggle also known as the "service industry." Paying bills by making the tourists happy, going home to an overpriced one-bedroom studio that faced a mall or a prison. The odd rainbow sighting keeping everyone's hope alive in pursuit of that Hawaiian dream.

The mainland's grumbles about which way the US was going, or which candidate would steer us to the promised land, seemed like an "us and them" conservation. However, in reality, mainland influence had overtaken the Hawaii of old, chipping away since the state's shadowy annexation. Hawaii's culture did see a renaissance, but it was from the minority and was ceremonious at best. "Kill Haole Day" was no longer staple at high schools across the state. The assimilation of the new Hawaii was in full force. Too busy with social media and pop culture to care, teens played the role of good Americans island wide. Hawaii became such a melting pot over the years that true Hawaiians and their hopes for a "Reinstated Hawaiian Nation" became a talking point at barbeques. A mute topic, hampered by big business and insider land acquisitions and corrupt heads at the Office of Hawaiian Affairs. There was more Micronesians living in Waikiki than Hawaiians in the entire state at the time it all went down. The plantation colonies of the 1800s spawned generations of families from the Philippines, and Micronesians were given green cards in trade for Washington's use of the Marshall Islands. That's the least they could do for using their atolls as bomb testing grounds. Who could blame them for trading one poisoned island chain for another?

However ceremonious it sounded, a reinstated Hawaiian nation did have a ring to it and, considering the sad state the US left the islands' resources in, I am sure the uncles holding signs at the local beach park couldn't do any worse. Living in a place where ninety-nine percent of the population is dependent on the next boat to arrive for their survival is a weight that everyone felt. The true King of Hawaii became the Matson container. For a few lucky locals, there was one benefit. You could buy a seat as a well-paid blue collar longshoremen. They did pretty well for themselves, until that last container changed everything. Shit, no pun intended, we only had enough toilet paper on island to last three days, a reality not taken lightly. It wouldn't be long before we were, literally, heading up shit's creek. The truth is the day the shipping lanes halted, bullets became our island nation's new currency. The Bible thumping missionaries warned us the world would throw their gold and silver into the streets, however, the bullets stayed right in the chamber, for now anyway!

After the event, the construction cranes crossing the Waikiki skyline looked like birds of prey with fire and chaos brewing below. If you look back at Hawaii's "modern" history, at least since the missionaries arrived, there has been one haole-instigated fuck up after another. Somehow each event leading to the next chapter of Hawaiian history. For example, on January 20th, 1900, the Black Plague hit Oahu. It was rampant in Chinatown. Chinese families hid bodies under superstition their souls would be in limbo if they remained in Hawaii. The Dole regime decided to light a "controlled" fire at select homes. The fire Marshall didn't adjust for the prevailing trade winds switching to the southwest Kona winds. Half of Nuuanu burned. The fire raged for seventeen days, and the island was changed again forever. The plague was halted by the burn, and Washington commended Dole's regime by giving them control over Hawaii due to their "Board of Health's" and a haole lead fire department's "success." A true Banana Republic, born from the fuck up of the decade solidified by revisionist historians.

The irony Hawaii holds is immeasurable; one debacle after another, saving one side of the coin and destroying the other in the same breath. However there are three sides of the coin, the edge that it rarely lands on, but when it does, boy o boy things do get shaken up. Who's to blame really? I'm walking contradiction, a quarter haole, quarter Japanese, and the remainder Hawaiian. I wouldn't know which side of my face to slap. We're all at fault allowing this tinderbox landscape to exist. A single Matson container and a USB drive is that all it really took?

The General's Account

That first flash, man oh man! You've got to give it to them Chinese, they know how to play the game. Why destroy a perfectly good military base? Just take the power source away, wait a few weeks and replace the flag, voilà, China would have a new home smack dab in the middle of the pacific. I think the US heads of state thought China was just going to play Koi, leaving the heavy lifting and threats to North Korea, that semi-retarded junkyard dog of a country China kept in its back pocket. Dumb luck is all that saved our base. The redundancy of the Marines plus some equipment not hooked to any network. Thank God for Ulupa'u Crater, that glorified storage unit. It's almost comical. The Chinese were using our money to buy Hawaii lands at the highest rate seen from any foreign country in history. Years of US dollars stored in their banks had to flow back to its source at one point. Land acquisitions were their first way to get a foothold on island. Running legal businesses, financial firms, and acquiring visas for their "businessmen." I preferred to call them spies, but hey, I am old school. They were even selling cheap nik-naks to our military commissaries. They tracked the Malware payload back to a USB thumb drive shipment. They were US Navy Logoed thumb drives used as giveaways for recruiters at events. What says join the military better than a free USB drive, right? Unknowingly, we used them on base as giveaways with $50 purchase at the NEX. I knew the marines shouldn't have been sharing a base with the Navy. The virus went from a point of sale computer to industrial controls within six hours. A nineteen-year-old tech caught it an hour before the event, but it looked like it was your typical credit card scam searching for card numbers in the commissary checkout machines and retail computers. How it jumped ship into our communications and operations network we will never know.

My guess is when the World Monetary Fund and the US FED Department pulled the rug out from under the Chinese yuan, forcing deflation, plan B was put into play. The Germans call it a "Blitz." The US coined it "Shock and Awe." However, when the Chinese copy another nation, they really outdo themselves. I mean, an attack on each continent simultaneously; they started with cyber-attacks on bases nationwide, then EMP's on assets they want to adsorb, they brought Hawaii back to the stone age. Tactical nukes in every major city. It makes me think there still is a bit of Mongolian blood running in their gene pool. Hawaii is not the most secure location on the planet, something we all figured out after the attack on Pearl. A bullseye in the middle of the vast Pacific Ocean.

They had Russian support on the NATO front. The Pacific turned into an afterthought on the US military priority list as the strikes poured in. Insert any cliche you want, "foot in mouth" or "bit off too much to chew." The US could have held court to any of a number of sayings, none more apropo than what a local civilian construction contractor said after the attack; "Brah, I told you, de's fakas was gonna get it one day." He was quickly dismissed and base privileges revoked, I assure you, but, hey, as far as the military goes, we knew we had it coming. The school bully always gets what's coming to them.

We knew the EU would one day break down. After the Brexit, it was like a house of cards placed in front of heavy tradewinds. Europe was dealing with a migrant population like the world had never seen, and they could not even defend their own borders. The flood gates had already been opened.

The attack was worldwide. Intel came in right before the lights went out. One hundred million enlisted Chinese servicemen made this feasible. NY, Tokyo, Sydney, San Fran, LA, London, Frankfurt, Paris, and Washington all took strategic nuclear hits and, I can assume, other NATO installations were hit as well. US ports were flooded by stealth ships and air support. If you were to wake up that day, not aware of the past ten years of geo political dealings, you would have been in shock. In reality, years of military sequestering brought on by a ghastly US national debt owed to China made their Commie Capitalism play on the US nothing short of military/economic genius. Our far right current leader couldn't spend fast enough to secure our shores, all he did was poke the sleeping giant. In chess and war, it's not the move that wins, it's the position that set up the end game. We were ripe for the fall, played on all fronts. When their currency manipulation failed, they just blew down the weakened front door. Perfect timing, eight years of military pandering to the masses. We were weak. The country was divided and squabbling, ripe for the picking. Even my post at Kaneohe Marine Base was sequestered to no end. Hawaii got off light, in reality, compared to the mainland. The news could barely cover it. They struck once and hard. The total opposite from our US Military strategy of ongoing, nitpicky conflicts. It was like, "Guess what? We're here! One billion strong. What the fuck you gonna do about it?" This was not a sanction-driven, long game agenda. This was it, game over. Russia would be lucky if the Chinese let them hang around, they might be in their own self-created gulag soon enough.

A tech working the Navy Satcom in Kauai picked up the scent of Chinese boats just before their systems were halted by the Malware jumping networks. They launched missiles back towards Oahu and Kauai shores, systems were down, and any back-ups were shut down from the EMP hidden in a shipping container at Pier 19 in Honolulu. Just after the first strike launched, it pulsed leaving all systems down. Our navy is positioned on southern shores of Oahu, almost all of it was obliterated. Kauai's Barking Sands missile silo was hit hard. They were able to launch anti-aircraft missiles, but once the tracking was disabled they all just sputtered out into the Pacific. One US Pearl Harbor bound ship was hit, and half sunk right at the mouth of the Harbor. A Chinese cruiser ran aground on the reef off the coast of Waikiki, which looked like a futuristic tourist attraction off Queen's Beach near the Duke Kahanamoku statue. Soldiers poured onto the streets and, soon, a land battle began. Cops, military, and armed locals fought back.

Three boats made it to shore ten minutes prior to the first EMP strike; one at Sand Island, one at Pearl, and one at Kaka'ako. The boats at Kaka'ako had the least troops onboard. We assumed they anticipated little backlash from locals. China's one flaw was not reading up on Hawaii's massive ramp up of private gun ownership in the past decade. Locals might hem and haw about US policy but the second amendment was going strong in the islands. Before all the hoopla of mainland school shootings, AR-15s were Hawaii's go-to weapon. Most serial numbers had been filed off, or the lower receivers made in DIY 3D printers just outside the law for a rainy day. It rained lead that fateful day. From the apartment buildings, casings littered the streets. Kaka'ako through Pier 14 on Nimitz was our open gate to keeping the invasion at bay. Paratrooper from the Chinese wave dropped in near Kalihi valley and were met by troops and locals as they hit the main highways.

This time at Pearl Harbor, the attack was much more thorough. Our ground forces subdued Chinese troops within two hours of them hitting Pearl, but they shut down the harbor by sinking a dummy boat at its entrance, there was no way to get our ships out in time. There was no air offensive after the EMP. All but a few Chinese war ships remained. Sand Island took the longest to secure, due to the terrain of the shipping yards. Containers made for good bunkers. The enemy was trying to recover their device. We assumed it to be hidden in a shipping container. It was crucial for our boys to secure what supplies had docked that morning, half of which were destroyed in the battle.

From what we know, and this is guess work, there could still be one of two more Chinese offensives lying in wait somewhere on Oahu. There was a blip of radio coms triangulated over the southeast valleys near Nuuanu and Maunawili. Chinese banter was picked up right before the device went off. There is, really, no way to tell how many troops and what weaponry they do or don't have. To an old special forces hard head like me the enemy known is always less scary than the one unknown. I would rather know I have a thousand men bearing down than to worry if it is ten or ten thousand at my front gate. We can work with whatever recon they give us but right now our eyes are all we got. The issue now is how do we organize to find the fight when we have not even begun to get resources to the civilians. The remaining half of the containers will need to be manually busted open with crowbars. The longshoremen equipment was rendered useless, and distribution, well, that's going to be another security nightmare for our remaining troops. It's like chess versus checkers at this point, back to basics and the rules of leverage. What do we have that the islanders can use? The longer we don't provide resources to the public, the quicker a de facto government can be established and chaos can thrive. With no contact to the mainland, we're our own entity. Even if the public does not know it, I do. We are now an armed autonomous front in this US failed state and former island nation. If, and when, the population chooses to turn on us and what is left of our military, we will need a plan. For me, personally, well I just got a promotion. What's that saying, "A tragedy not capitalized on is the only true tragedy?" I am the highest-ranking officer, top in the chain of command, incident commander numero uno. Oorah! Welcome to my island!

Kanaka Maoli (Culture Reborn)

They did us a favor. I know we lost a few bruddahs, but it couldn't have come quicker. The mainland and the rest of the world have been using our islands as a mobile outpost for everything from military installments to tourists ruining our resources for a quick romp as a "native." Our culture was almost lost. Our language and agriculture both vanished from the land. An opportunity to live Pono has been given to us from Akua. A return to the bloodline and new rule of the Ali'i could be upon us, where ancestry and lineage to King Kamehameha will mean more than a statue in Waikiki and the Kanaka can establish their birthright. The Reinstated Hawaiian Nation began with a flash and if need be, we will secure it with a BANG!

Strength in Numbers

We have always survived by sticking with our own. We are all family. This is a tragedy, and we plan to do our part, but with all the uncertainty you can be sure the Micronesians will stick together. We were organized prior to this event, and that does not change now. If progress is dependent on a vote and or force, we are here for our people first. The US brought us here under the Compact of Free Association treaty. This is now our home, for better or for worse. We traded our land for the "American Dream." The Hawaiians did not have that choice, but now we are all in this boat together and I hope we can get along in this post-event island landscape we have been handed.

Nurses Filling Hearses

Resources were limited and beds were scarce. We needed FEMA to set up cots at all the major hospitals in the parking lots. As bodies came in at Red Hill, we knew there were going to be more casualties than we had ever seen. Without electronic equipment working, there was no way to shock patients that were coding. Defibrillators were not working, and all we had were manual drip IVs to administer pain meds. We ran out of syringes fast. If there was a pill available, we would have to grind it up and put it into some water for the trauma patients. The big worry was a week from now, cholera or another epidemic. We were already at capacity. Staph infections at hospitals were common already, and MRSA had us on our toes prior to the attack. With every hour, the equipment became more unsterile and our job was becoming harder. Once the Board of Water Supply pumps failed, they shut down supply to the Red Hill facility. We were dead in the water, and a lot of the men died from dehydration before the wounds. We received the lion's share of the military casualties, and we got word Queen's Medical took in civilians that joined in the ground fight as the Chinese pushed ashore. By the time transportation was cut off by the EMP, local Honolulu hospitals were already flooded. Even the hotels and beach parking lots became makeshift wards with police, firemen, and lifeguards attending to the wounded the best they could.

Chapter 1
Awakening

There were these long white clouds in the sky. If you didn't know Oahu's weather, you would have thought jetliners were buzzing the crests of the Koolau Mountain Range with Contrails so visible conspiracies theorists would have a field day. Spring was in full effect, unpredictable variable winds and humid air were the norm as we rounded out May. Locals and long-term transplants all understand that Hawaii does have seasons, contrary to what Mainlanders might think. Tourists are notorious for saying "must be nice, same weather every day of the year, 85 and sunny. How can you get sick of that?" The truth is, the devil is in the details. The rainy season is mainly fall through spring, which also brings the surf. It is, somewhat, dry May through August with minimal ocean activity. Lilikoi, or what mainlanders call passion fruit, produce in the spring. The only way a tourist would know that is if Leonard's Bakery was selling lilikoi malasadas. They only offer them in June, and the lines are as wide as the tourists. Birds migrate, winter storms come and go, leaves even fall, you just would not know it if you're on a ten-day holiday.

That day had strange signs and signals all over it but locals, even residents with Hawaiian blood, have lost touch with the nuances of the island's nature. There are more injuries due to cell phone use than fishing or diving these days. The birds were giving us signals. Heck, my dog was even nervous, but, with all the technology floating around who would know if it was not just to the beehive so to stay, a transistor exploding from overuse or something else was happening. All assumptions were pointing to the device being on island well before the attack. According to Doctor Lightfoot, it's pretty hard for a device of that size not to give off a signal from its magnetic field prior to a pulse. I guess they did not perfect the device but, hell, it did the job.

About five minutes before the island went dark, Poi, my mutt of a dog, went hiding in the valley. This is not altogether strange, but he was never a get-up-and-go morning vanisher. Even though a boar in the rut would get his attention, he would never leave the property without us. All I remember was Poi digging out and soon after hearing the first hum which grew louder. The power went off, and we just assumed it was a brownout with the air conditioning use heading into summer. Oahu has become over populated and the infrastructure overloaded. Then we all heard it again at 12pm and 6pm. This time the hum was deafening. After that, came the attack.

Doc said a device large enough to knock out the island's grid needs to charge and pulse more than once to make sure it worked correctly. HECO's electric workers had been out since the first hum, trying to get the grid going, but only a few of their trucks were operable from the pulse. Turns out the Chinese tapped into the main transformer on Nimitz Highway and ran a line back to the container through the sewers that connect from Kaka'ako Park all the way to the airport. This means they had men on the ground, or someone was getting paid for something they did not fully understand. My guess is Chinese developers on the Kaka'ako waterfront were just a guise to lay cable to execute the grid attack. All that matters now is that it's June 1st. The last ship came on May 26th, and the natives are getting restless.

Doctor Barrington Lightfoot was an Englishman whose lifelong goal was to immerse himself in academia. Finding himself forty-two, on the Board of Oceanic Research at the University of Hawaii was the last thing he would have anticipated in his early years at Cambridge. A work/study program brought him to the Midway islands to study the effects of plastic waste on the migrating bird population culminating on the island. On his return trip, he stopped with his fellow researchers on Oahu, boarding at UH for the week. He, consequently, fell in love. Not only with the island but a researcher named Julia Berry whom, since her divorce earlier in the year, was doing private contract research for the government on Kauai's Barking Sands Navy installation.

Prior to the event, Dr. Lightfoot spent his time scaling up an aquaponic project for mass use called the Kapu system. The system's end goal was to produce high yield food off renewable energies. Ha'a Klein's family estate funded the Kapu system project. Being a prominent figurehead in both Hawaiian politics and philanthropy, Ha'a used his resources well in the eyes of residents. Considered a voice for native Hawaiian people, he spearheaded the project to get Hawaii's food security on track. He aptly named the system. The Kapu system of historical Hawaii was the religious law of Hawaii's people. It held court over every aspect of life. The rules applied to anything in day-to-day life and were based that everything came from the Mana or spiritual realm where things gained their power. So, whether you were caught stealing from another man's Auwai (fish pond), or were wondering when you could hunt animal, the laws of the Kapu system all applied. He felt so strongly about.

Funding for the modern day Kapu System came from the Klein family endowment. It had been funded well, but was not Ha'a's vision. However, he was close to a sustainable Oahu and, possibly, Hawaii. Using only small amounts of land, it could provide the islands with fresh fish and produce in a closed loop system, with little to no waste. They had formed a work/study coop with the University of Hawaii and the Hawaiian prison system at Halawa and OCCC facilities. Students mixed with non-violent drug offenders to help with research. Some of the convicts tended the fields better than the botanists. I guess all the years of growing Pakalolo was as good as a UH degree when the rubber hits the road. Ha'a's land and the program was heralded as a success for its social impact. The project was rounding the corner to the finish line when the EMP sent Hawaii into the dark ages.

The major issue was making it scalable and, with the soon to be starving masses, the race was on to bring the Kapu to the people. The last harvesting of crops and moi fish from their onsite Kapu system was scheduled two days prior to the event, meaning the Klein Estate had food produced and fish in the pond that could last them for weeks if they could keep it chilled. However, as the estate's residents looked down on Honolulu, if they dry the fish, whilst burning, their safety net was more of a bullseye thea a nest egg.

Ha'a sits down with Gordon weekly, as he liked to call upon his researchers to present their findings to the Klein estate's board as a tool to lobby the fund towards renewable energy, sustainable agriculture and aquaculture. HECO (Hawaiian Electric Co.) who was bought by a mainland NEXTGEN in a highly scrutinized sale as HECO was a public utility and a monopoly. The once-monopoly utility in the islands had regulators force a sale on the grounds. NEXTGEN would adopt sustainable outlets to offset Oahu's highest cost in the nation's kilowatt rate. They dotted the lines of a contract with the Klein foundation to adapt and create a Geothermal system using steam generated turbines as an energy source. This was to complement Oahu's solar and hydro efforts as they came online.

The Big Island had been tried and tested, but there, volcanic activity was always at the surface and changing, whereas Oahu's tectonic plates were deeper and its volcanoes were not active. Deeper drilling led to higher cost but a safer playing field. The funding the Klein Estate provided had them a lot closer than years prior. The military had been knocking on the door of the Klein Estate research lab for years. The military and particularly the marines had Kaneohe marine corps base or K-Bay, which housed a geothermal test area at Ulupena, was the only viable platform the Ha'a and his group were without a major source and had been testing off a small site on the Klein Estate near Kualoa Ranch. This was enough to power a closed loop system on a 12-acre estate but not for an entire island. Ha'a and the board wanted to control their system, for the people and for financial reasons. Making it a government affair, after all the ground gained, was not in their plan. However, the ever-pervasive General Hayden had been trying to pull the technology under their control to complete the puzzle.

Military grants to the Hawaii Dept. of Education were offered at $1.3 billion dollars alongside other concessions to the Klein's research program. However, the estate took up an agreement with NEXTGEN during the HECO privatizing sale to avoid being in the department of defense's pocket. Ha'a decided a low cost per Megawatt agreement with NEXTGEN could offset the rising cost of living and inflation for Hawaii residents. If he didn't make this deal, he felt a monopoly in energy and unregulated pricing would occur. NEXTGEN was becoming privatized with very little government oversight. NEXTGEN was obligated to fund a Hawaiian student grant program as part of their deal with the Klein trust. The program's recipient would gain a full ride to a Klein board chosen school of the sciences. The grant would allow Hawaiian students, if qualified, to study abroad for free if they committed to coming back to Hawaii to work and better the society of the islands. Ha'a's dream of a sustainable Hawaii was in reach before the event. Post event, the Kapu project was not a dream.

It was a necessity and necessity is the father of all creation.

Hawaii still had the ghost of HECO's past, with Big Oil pumping petroleum 24/7 through pipelines off of Ewa Beach shores. NEXTGEN had been pumping non-stop, until the event, to keep up with the high demand of Oahu's exploding population. One refinery built in 1951, and the other in the early 70s, barley made the quotas needed to keep the glitz of Waikiki and Honolulu lights on. Hawaii's refineries could not accept sulphur rich crude, so the addiction of the light and sweet higher-priced crude was at an all-time high. Ha'a Klein wanted to be the islands' petrochemical addiction rehab specialist, using the trust as a giant Betty Ford clinic through Kapu System. However, he knew the grips of addiction on oil was as bad as the meth epidemic hitting the islands and the dealer, Big Oil, truly was only stopped by the disaster. Tankers lined up to the horizon sat moored, post event. The lifeblood, both fueling and poisoning the island, was left frozen in time.

The Klein family trust was the second biggest landholder in Hawaii, with the military being numero uno. Ha'a and the Klein Board of Trustees, unlike the military, had committed their resources to the betterment of Hawaii's residents both native and non. All profits were going to the public in the form of community projects, botanical gardens, playgrounds, schools, transportation, and sustainable farming. Public land use was the priority, and it made them butt heads with K-Bay's General from time to time. Especially when it came time to negotiate government leases for off-base training grounds or cleaning up ordinances on Klein leased properties.

It became the largest US-based trust and hedge fund in the world, just under the Fonseca fund managed for the Saudi royal family. The land trust, alone, produced a real estate portfolio that was worth trillions, and their liquid assets from land leasing was on par with Manhattan's and Moscow's biggest land barons.

They supported the Polynesian Voyaging Committee to recreate how Polynesians reached Hawaii by sending crews across the Pacific on traditional canoes of old. Ha'a was wealthy beyond any need or want, however he committed to his father's path of a hands-on Hawaiian teacher and cultural advocate. He felt his greatest accomplishment was becoming a navigator. He piloted a second mission to Tahiti and one to Easter Island to track his ancestors' paths. He became a rescue swimmer, a master diver, a certified lifeguard, and a boat captain all to limit the risk for his all Hawaiian crew. He helped build each sailing canoe that went to sea, and continued to with Kapu his teenage son. Kapu was set to voyage at the end of his senior year of high school this month. As a father/son team they have won titles in Surf, Paddle and Freediving, Kapu was recruited by the Harvard crew team to paddle. As well, he was offered a tryout for the US Olympic Crew Team but had not committed due priorities on island. He was waiting until he made his first trans pacific voyage before future planning. The father and son duo were in the public eye, in a positive manner, understanding their responsibility to the people of Hawaii being tied to a great amount of land and resources. Their ocean escapades further perpetuated their commitment to Hawaii centric school of thought. The need to secure sustainability much like the Kapuna ancestors of old. The only thing that slowed down the Kleins was constant in-fighting with Kamai, Ha'a's bullish cousin who was the main heir to the trust until Kapu was born. Ha'a was born when his mother was forty which was rare for his generation.

Kamai was the older cousin who felt the family's positions were too diplomatic and Ha'a threw softball solutions at hardline Hawaiian problems. Kamai was the head of a sub-movement, the Reinstated Hawaiian Nation. He felt the estate's financial gains should be used to aggressively move towards a reborn, autonomous Hawaiian kingdom of old. Although he had no control over any of the estate's funds, he did carry the Klein name and clout to organize Hawaiians and he focused on the ones living in the government allotted homesteads.

A small community of "forward thinking" transplants became opponents to the Klien estate. Silicon Valley money flowed into Hawaii with an agenda.

These heavy hitting elite wanted Hawaii to be the next Silicon Valley, with tech and renewables as the platform to unite them on both sides of the Pacific. The fact that all things could be tested well in Hawaii, both agriculturally and in the technology sector, made it a great place for big companies to roll out new products and services in their new island bubble home. The negatives of this were when they impeded on the people and their rights to land usage, health, and the pursuit of happiness. Which, in terms of "Big Agriculture," had become the locals' boots-on-the-ground turf war. Big companies like Syntan Inc. and Movado, the two biggest in their industry, had been leasing from the smaller estates and even tapped into government used lands to test their GMO seed crops which utilized Hawaii's fertile soil. Tech companies were testing things like self-driving cars and electric public transit ridesharing. Big Ag was a huge force, but Big Tech was picking up the slack by saving energy resources and, until the EMP came into play, technology was a benefit to Hawaii's future. However, the winds of change had started to howl. Isolation had always been a blessing and a curse for Hawaii. Oahu's soil was the gold rush of this century, and the price and stakes were high. Ever since the days of sugarcane and pineapple plantations, the "Aina" had taken a heavy lashing. Arsenic plagued most of the agricultural lands on Oahu and, furthermore, all of Hawaii. However, this was manageable. Plantations and the land could be partially remediated by replacing topsoil. However, groundwater would feel the effects for generations to come, and no public utility had a chance in these areas as far as wastewater was concerned. The entire North Shore was still a giant leech field, with no sewers and rivers being polluted perpetually. Ha'a's dog, Poi, was now blind in one eye from drinking well water on their North Shore property. The Haleiwa estate was acquired in hopes to give it to the Department of Education after an environmental impact statement was finished. They would summer in Haleiwa while the plans were drawn for the property to be donated. The land still remains dormant, as the soil was deemed toxic. It just so happened that Movada Co. had been prepping a parcel next store on an old military site that was being subleased to them from the US military, they started planting before they finished a full ordinance purge of the property. When the trade winds picked up, traces of their DDT-based pesticides could be found a mile away at the local high schools in air sampling done by the Klein Estate. Isolation was a key reason they were putting so much money into Hawaii from Movado, it was an insurance. If it all went wrong, a monoculture melt down, a plague on plant life, they could simply light a match, keep it to Oahu. Shut the pacific gate and cut their loses, little did the public know we were all part of the experiment. A modern-day Quarantine sponsored Big Ag.

The Kapu program was something that could cure the woes of living on a poisoned island. The estate's money was something that was a blessing for the entire population. It did, however, come with repercussions from Big Ag's iron fist. Ha'a's son had been approached, on his way home from school, two months prior. A man in a button-down shirt, looking more like a Secret Service agent than an agricultural rep. The man was looking for Kapu's father, stating to Kapu they had an appointment. He asked if Kapu could let him on the property. Kapu alluded the man by telling him he was going to a friend's, and that someone at the gate would see him in. The man waited until Kapu made his way home, but Kapu knew he was being followed and went through the Old Pali Road gate disappearing into the valley. The following day, a note was placed on the Old Pali Estate fence. Kapu suspected it was for his father, and grabbed it. Upon opening it, it read more like a death threat than an opportunity for a business meeting. "We are waiting and watching in lieu of your decision to lease us the Klein estates properties on the North Shore. Your board has stated interest, we are aware of their of limited use to your prior plans ."

Kapu showed his father, and Ha'a's reaction was very blasé. "I don't need to lease them anything. I would rather it sit open to the public as a reminder to the people the Aina is for them, not Big Agriculture, even if it can't be donated to the DOE. These mainland businessmen have lost their privilege to my ear."

Kapu had asked if he worried about the Big Agricultural companies. Ha'a replied, "I worry a dollar means more to people than clean food. I don't concern myself with men in tight slacks with self-appointed worth. I suggest you don't either, Kapu. I suggest you worry about the hearts of the people that should be stewards of the land, which you are one of." Even though the Kleins had more money than they could ever spend, he knew it was not real, it was not what really provided life, he knew once you take it all away, the world could do nothing with money but burn it to keep warm. The lands were the wealth of Hawaii and he wanted it to be accessible and used for the island's people.

As the project moved forward, it seemed to be a split between refining the aquaculture and its need for a more stable power source. Dr. Hind felt the power source of geothermal could be used on a more dynamic scale than just powering a food resource. He felt that a military collaboration was the only way for success. However, when you put "Dr." before anyone's name, it seems like the "God gene" embeds itself without consent. Dr. Hind loved his titles, and grew to dislike sharing any limelight with college Gordon. The military only exacerbated the scenario. Dr. Hind was on his way to producing Oahu's largest geothermal resources fueled by ego alone, with the General providing him with side funding for a new site on Kaneohe Bay.

Ha'a approved a test of Dr. Hind's prototype unit on military land, however it was by necessity and not choice. It seems one of the two only viable sources of water for geothermal electric was on the dormant volcano at Kaneohe Marine Corps base. It's proximity to a water source allowed for safety and steam generation for turbines. Also, the base was a secured micro city which could test a sizable grid. Dr. Hind's success spawned adoration in the science community, as his low-cost Geothermal product powered the military base perfectly for a duration of three days before being shut down. The General immediately asked Washington for appropriations to install a permanent unit as a backup generator to their primary system. However, the research and development had been funded and registered under the Estate's NGO and all future relations and partnerships would have to have Ha'a and the board's approval of their proprietary information first. All equipment was removed after the three-day trial, leaving the power lines and grid wiring into the bases transistors and back up.

Battery secured in the crater. If Big Agriculture wasn't enough, now Ha'a had the federal government in line for the estate's biggest achievement. With no approval for a secondary site, the geothermal system had been off the grid for months prior to the event. The only other large, sustainable renewable energy was located on the north side of the island near the very remote Waimea Valley on a wind farm sitting just above the valley. This made its feasibility a huge undertaking even for the estate's deep pockets. Stryker Road, a military bypass, had been made connecting north to south-facing bases and training grounds. It was built to allow easy access to training sites in the valley. They had used it as an emergency exit during rockslides, when the mountains in Pupukea shut down the roads below. No one ever drove down Stryker without a military escort or at least their eyes on them. A huge amount of legwork, manpower, and funding was still yet to be in place. The aquaculture that was supposed to complement the system was a much easier transport and could run off the backup generator until a renewable source could be tapped. For now, the estate's ranch on the east side of Oahu was the home for the full scale aquaponic set-up, but this was held in secrecy. This side of the program was currently run off a main line utility on Heco's now offline secondary grid. The fish would die unless the outflow system or "Auwai" could sustain the waters that needed to be oxygenated. Ha'a needed to get his team out there within two weeks, or they would lose the island's biggest chance at survival. Days remained until his project turned into Hawaii's own Dead Sea.

Chapter 2
The Delegates

It had been three days since the event. It seemed all parts of the island were having issues with looting and regaining order. Only a quarter of the military was still operational, with one-third having been eliminated in the battle and the remainder unaccounted for, assumed dead, or AWOL to take care of their own families. Martial Law was in effect where the military was operating, and people were making their own rules elsewhere. Ha'a was well aware that something needed to be done quickly. The resources were going to disappear, and the distribution methods were nonexistent. Hanalei, his wife, had suggested that Ha'a take a ride to Waikiki and see what was still left of the government buildings, and what was being done in the state's capital. She was aware of the security issue for her family, so she asked Ha'a to call on his good friends, Kamalei Asato and Jimmy Nakamura, to put together a security convoy. He had boarded with them at Kam schools in high school. The brothers had been mixed martial arts fighters that had trained and competed on a world class level. Afterwards, they were invited to train local military in hand-to-hand combat. They had always stayed in touch with Ha'a after their high school days, and came to the estate for family gatherings. Ha'a sent out for them to put together a team of four to go with Ha'a, and four to go incognito following the group into what was left of Honolulu. The goal was to make contact with any government officials still left, police, and or local groups organizing. Most notably would be the Micronesians of who had been rumored to have made a move to secure the beach front hotels. Micronesians have been known to have a hold on the hotel unions in Waikiki as they made up a large portion of their labor force. Directly after the event, within two days, they had kicked out the majority of the traveling tourists and had taken over the rooms for displaced locals.

Since the event rendered all cars useless, the first thing that Ha'a noticed was a makeshift bike rickshaws moving through Kalakaua Avenue. It was reminiscent of 1900s Waikiki. If there weren't hotels where taro plantations used to be, you could almost think this new Hawaii was a blessing. However, the reality was that there were over 750,000 people still on the island needing to be fed. Ha'a knew this was an issue, and that everyone would need to work together or there would be a new war over old problems once the food ran out.

The trip took all of six hours with stops through Nuuanu, then Chinatown, Kaka'ako, and finally Waikiki. The crew noticed that the most heavily hit was Chinatown. Whenever there was a disaster on Oahu, Chinatown always was the epicenter. During the plague, it was ground zero off pier 19. During the Pearl Harbor attack, unexploded ordnance were found on sidewalks. Knowing that something could go wrong at any moment, it was an uneasy adventure . Even public buildings were thought to have had ghosts from various murders and incidents that happened over the years.

With no plan and the sun setting, the group had taken refuge at the Halekulani Hotel. One of the security crew had, previously, worked at the hotel. Running night operations for the hotel, he knew how to access the panic room and security hall with no electronics needed. The crew entered from the parking structure, undetected in the dark, so as not to give signs to their presence. Under normal circumstances, a group of men of their size would have no worries. The rumors that had been spread that Waikiki was under new rule or, even worse, no rule was something that they had to take seriously.

When the sun rose over Mt. Kaala, the crew had already started their walk towards the old labor union hall where they had assumed they could find the Micronesian community leader. To stay within the element of surprise, the group barged into the hall from the back entrance, surprising everyone. Ha'a was the first to speak. "Everyone remain seated. We have come to see what is going on in Waikiki. Who is in charge?"

A short lady stood up, no more than 5'3" wearing a mumu dress and holding a clipboard. "Ha'a, that would be me," she said. Nia Edei, the one who spoke, was the head of labor relations for the Micronesian people. She held the role as chairman of the board for her local consulate in Pahoa Valley. Somehow, with her small stature, she commanded the respect of the men encompassing their community. She was a scrappy, hard-working 40-something-year-old Chuukese woman who immigrated from the Marshall Islands twenty some odd years earlier. She graduated from the University of Hawaii with her Political Science degree and a chip on her shoulder. She knew her island's history, and the USA's method of operation when it came to occupation in the name of military might. It came as no surprise to Ha'a that she was still in control of her people and, furthermore, all Waikiki hotels.

She was the one who, single-handedly, organized the labor strike of thousands of hotel and restaurant workers in the Waikiki area. When wages did not meet living standards with Hawaii's abnormal living costs, she brought the state's tourist industry to its knees. This feather in her hat not only captured the attention of the Micronesian community, but minorities in general now look to her for organization and ideas for the future. It seemed natural to Ha'a that this would be the post event scenario as well. He approached her as if seeing an old friend.

"So, Nia, long time since our debate class at UH Manoa, huh?" He went on. "I guess there's not much to be debated now. Pretty much every aspect of the US government is in shambles." His group moved closer to the main boardroom table. She never seemed to have a worry on her face. Little did Ha'a know, but outside the door there were 15 large men that could do battle with whatever his group brought to the table. If someone were to yell for help, it would be a swift departure for Ha'a's group. After reviewing most of what was going on, Ha'a came to the realization that all seemed to be fairly well organized, considering government operations had ceased. The elephant in the room was an issue with the tourists. Nia had gone along with a vote in which all tourists who were previously set to depart the island would be placed at the Honolulu Zoo construction site. Being that there was no accommodation for the departing tourists, something had to be done. There was an unoccupied, covered extension to the zoo that was under construction. It was being used as a makeshift camp for six thousand plus tourists that had previously occupied the main strip in Waikiki and had a scheduled departure the day of the event. It mimicked a large internment camp of old, similar to what Japanese Americans saw during World War II on Oahu. Rations and water were given, children were allowed to be with their families in a separate area, couples remained together and all were given cots sourced from the Diamond Head Crater FEMA warehouse, where some workers remained active. It held communal showers, using brackish irrigation water that was set up for landscaping. The water was pulled from the Ala Wai River. It used a gravity-controlled pump valve, for pressure, that was in place. If it didn't rain for a couple days there wouldn't be enough downward pressure to run the showers, and we could only assume people would get frustrated as tainted river water was better than nothing. When the cots ran out rattan beach mats from ABC stores became sleeping areas. Nia had lived near the FEMA staging warehouse based at Diamond Head. She orchestrated the workers to help start the facility right away but, without compensation or a structured top down government management system, she could only assume operations would falter without her own crews managing it. A plan was in place to secure the hotels and move displaced local families into any empty rooms. Secondly, once locals were secure they would move the in limbo travelers to the zoo.

Ha'a felt uneasy about the scenario. One reason was because it was unmanageable and, two, because it was unfair to hold innocent people against their will. His ancestry, although Hawaiian, did include Japanese. His father was once held at an internment camp during World War II. His mother was 70% Hawaiian and 30% haole. His father was 50% Hawaiian and 50% Japanese. His father entered a special regiment during the war. He was pulled out of an internment camp under the AJA (Americans of Japanese Ancestry) program which placed him in The Nisei Provisional Infantry Battalion, later known as the 100th Battalion. They fought during the Battle of Midway after they were trained in Wisconsin. Ha'a did not agree with many things in the US past, but his father instilled in him pride in being a Hawaiian/Japanese American. One of the main things his father took to heart was America's right to due process, and all that was gained in Civil Rights Movement. Therefor Ha'a felt Nia had made a grave mistake entrapping the tourists. Thinking they could succeed in controlling one population while they still were figuring out how to feed their own was a bad idea. However, there needed to be a starting point, and war times have never been easy for anyone. Knowing that Honolulu has always been the epicenter for both food distribution and markets, as it held the largest population in the state, there would be no way of making decisions without Nia and her people's blessing. The two had made a pact knowing the future of Hawaii was dependent on cooperation from every organized group.

From there, they formed a plan to meet every Monday at the labor hall and, before the next meeting, would both reach out to delegates from the Japanese and Filipino communities across the island. Nia would reach out to her contacts on the West side and in the Kunia plains. The Filipino community always had been the backbone of Hawaii's agriculture, and it would be an alliance that would lead to the success of the hopeful new Oahu. When there are no markets for cash, gold, and silver, agriculture becomes the new vehicle of wealth. Ha'a would take the lead in reaching out to the Japanese community, knowing he would have to deal with the remaining Yakuza element holding down the docks. He knew he would have a daunting task as most Japanese businesses in Hawaii had ties to Mr. Yakimura which, in turn, meant they had ties to the Japanese mob. He was the largest foreign national land holder in the islands. He had done the majority of his purchases through the Kimura Holdings Corporation. Everything was owned by Kimura Holdings, besides his home compound at the top of Aiea Heights, which was held outside the corporate structure in a land trust. He once stated in a Japanese business magazine interview, "Every fortress has a weakness," and, so to protect his family's interest in Hawaii, he separated the compound from the business structure and hired the local Yakuza as security. He had never nationalized to the US, and would leave to Japan every few months when his business visa needed to be renewed.

His home resembled a military base. Guards could be 25 to 40 deep, on any given day. He legally employed the security through his corporation, however, all were in Hawaii on working Visas as Japanese nationals as well. Distrust kept any no Japanese from working for his companies. He had been in many legal battles over discriminatory hiring practices in which he had lost, paid fines, was forced to hire diverse employees by the state and, subsequently, fired the local employees just to be sued and go through the process all over again. All of this to keep his business secure and out of reach from anyone outside of his camp. He imported popular Japanese products to Kimura's and sold them at a premium. Kimura's was a membership-based grocery wholesaler, and assumed to be the washing mechanism for the drug money coming out of the various night clubs he owned under another shell company, Abuni LLC. Abuni was a one-stop shop for tourists and party groups, mostly from Japan. Basically a tour group for debauchery on the streets of Honolulu in which the Yakuza and furthermore Yakimura held court over.

Ha'a had a relationship with Yakimura. His father, always being an honest hard-working businessman, commanded respect from his Japanese peers. Mr. Yakimura always had opinions about how Mr. Klein ran his business. At times, he would scold him for allowing diverse employees at his businesses, feeling he would ultimately create confusion by trying to allow cultures to mix and work alongside one another. Ha'a was brought up with the mindset that his multiethnicity made him a representative of everyone on the island versus one portion of his heritage taking center stage. His father felt one's work ethic and humility were the true measure of a man, not his features or skin color.

Nia and Ha'a came to the conclusion that they would each need seven days to reach out to the delegates from each demographic they had ties to. The goal was to figure out if the agricultural systems were still operable and would the work force be in place for harvesting wasn't going to be enough to feed the masses. With the Kapu system not quite to scale, there was a long road to food security. Transportation, warehousing, and distribution would be the next steps to getting food to the people without creating riots. This is where Mr. Yakimura came into play. However, there was no way to keep the military out of the equation. He was their only real shot for keeping the food secure without handing it to the bases. With no combustion engines working, a transport system would still need to be set in place. The rail lines were finally finished, after the years of construction, but no electricity meant no trains. So, the next step would be to find a manual system that could transport produce and perishables across the island. There was a need to get it from Kunia's West side plantations to Honolulu as well as to the East side. The North Shore had ample farmland, which could be a self-sustaining area, depending on how organized the North Shore was amongst the chaos.

Nia pointed out that Ha'a's team were lucky to have made it unscathed to town, as they were only able to secure parts of Waikiki into parts of Diamond Head. Chinatown was not under their control, and was an open landscape for the former drug dealers and criminals that continued their stranglehold, groups of hoodlums looking for resources in the pier area carried, and still had, ample ammunition after the initial fight. There was, also, a rumor that the local gangs had taken over a stockpile of arms that the military had abandoned when the Chinese ship ran aground and forced US troops back up Nuuanu.

Ha'a decided that the information given, even if secondhand, was enough for them to avoid the area until they had a need to go to the docks. They would make their way, with what remained of the day, back to old Pali Road. Leaving the labor hall at around 2:30pm meant that they would be traveling the last half hour in the dark. Ha'a was okay with this, as he knew the back roads well. Still, hitting Nuuanu Road, which was at the crosshairs of Chinatown and Pali Road, provided a possible dangerous scenario. Even though it was two miles from the pier, it gave the group a worry. The last time they passed this area, they were cloaked in darkness, in the middle of the night, and dusk hadn't really even begun to settle.

The group had made good headway and were on time, leaving about 30 minutes of light by the time they reached the border of Chinatown and Nuuanu Road. To get back to the old Pali Road was another ten minutes. They would have another thirty minutes, with a straight shot to the estate's safety. One of the crew noticed a pharmacy dimly lit by the setting sun off in the distance. Ha'a suggested a quick pitstop for medical supplies, toiletries, and things their families may need over the next few weeks until more stability came into play. Ha'a, knowing the risk being that this was right on the border of Chinatown, also knew that they were forty minutes away from any medical supplies once they ran out at the estate.

The crew voted to make a quick pit stop, for no more than a few minutes, at the pharmacy. As they approached, they noticed a window was already knocked out, most likely, during looting directly after the event. Since they were not sure what was outside or inside, they divided the teams up into two, two men groups. One team would watch the other two teams, from both sides of the building, through the windows. Each team would have a member keeping manual time. Since there were no working watches, they would manually have to count back in their head when 10 minutes was approaching. Ha'a went in with Kamai, and Kapu split the pharmacy run with his friend

Harold. Both were still in their late teens. Their baby faces gave them an innocent, doting look.

The sun was about to set as they entered the Long's Drug Store. The team split left and right, looking for medical supplies. Ha'a and Kamai came across some leftover canned goods. The store looked like it had been ransacked by a mob. Shelves were bare and knocked over, however, Has found some leftover first aid kits behind the pharmacy counter. The kits were piled in a frenzied manner, as if looters had just exited the building. Outside, the two teams hung by the entrance and the broken window, patiently nearing the five-minute mark. One of the crew noticed a dim light in the distance, almost looking like the hue of a bonfire, but it was moving down the road. A strange coloring and reflection, bounced off the glass windows on the buildings, it seemed to be getting closer. With his partner counting back to eight minutes, Harold called into the store, "Come on, guys! I'm not sure about what I'm seeing, but I think we need to go." As he said this, the first team of Ha'a and Kamai came barreling out with a minimal amount of supplies stuffed into a first aid kit.

Just as they made their way out through the hole in the glass, the group spotted the shadow of a person coming around the corner, lit up by what seemed to be a camping torch. Kamai stuck his head into the broken glass hole in the store window. "Kamai, Pau already. Let's go! We get company." Turning back again towards the light, they noticed the others gesturing to make a run for a gas station across the street. The shadow of a large group seemed to be moving a substantial structure down the street. The group barreled out the front entrance, both holding the medical kits, one in each arm. Upon seeing Kamai and Ha'a run to the gas station, they noticed that the other group chasing them did not see them leave the building. Kapu and his friend hammered towards the bottom of the Pali Road. As soon as they started across the street, they heard shots fired and hit the ground on the highway median dividing them from the Pali. Both groups, Ha'a's and Kapu's, were now under attack, dodging stray bullets flying towards the gas station and, also, towards the boys. Harold made it to the tree line with Kamai and, as they dove into the bushes, Harold felt a pinch unlike anything he'd felt before. Harold had been hit on the side of his right thigh, and now was separated from the group. The other six men moved from behind the nearest building across the street, dodging fire from the opposing side.

They could only imagine that these were the ones trying to protect Chinatown and the pier, where food shipments were stored. Ha'a's team could assume they would be seen as a threat. Slipping into the tree line, the two made their way onto a path that they used to hike as kids. The Old Pali Highway Trail led them to safety. They made their way through the thick brush, by memory alone, catching their clothes on tree roots and slipping on wet leaves along the way.

The boys ended up camping for the night, and mending Harold's wound. The bullet had cleared Harold's left thigh. He felt he could make the trip, but needed to stop the bleeding first. Kapu took a chunk of Hawaiian chili pepper flakes out from his backpack, and mashed it into Harold's open wound. He screamed until he passed out. The injury would add time, so there was no need to rush. Around midnight, they were awoken to the sound of rustling in the bushes, along with lights beaming from inside the brush. Frozen in fear they both hid low in the bushes , fearing the thoughts of it being Hawaiian "night marchers." The folklore states if you stare at them, they would take your lives. Kamai noticed that the language coming from these large beings wasn't English or Hawaiian. As a student at Kam schools, he'd learned his second heritage's language, Mandarin Chinese. In recent years, many Chinese tourists had started arriving from Beijing and Hong Kong. The dialect was new to Hawaii but, slowly, it had become a familiar sound flowing from tour buses. What Harold heard didn't sound like the same Chinese language the people from Hong Kong spoke, but he felt like they may be in for an unpleasant encounter no matter what the language.

Kamai tapped Harold, as is if to say don't move. Unknowingly, he hit Harold's leg. Grimacing in pain, Harold grabbed and bit a stick to avoid making noise. The boys continued to look on as over a dozen Chinese men, outfitted in army green camouflage, carrying what looked like M4 76.2x51 passed by. Harold joined ROTC at Kam schools, and could spot an M4, but it was odd as the Chinese often used Russian AK's, not M4 rifles. The boys assumed that their lights were only working because they had protected their gear upon arriving in Hawaii, or had parachuted down after the effects of the EMP. Either way, the boys were not alone and were outmatched from every angle.

The following morning, Ha'as men debriefed over breakfast at the estate. Discussions about what they saw, and a plan of action, took place. Kamai felt this would be the perfect moment for them to reinstate the Hawaiian Nation. Most agreed, but were under the realization that their numbers were too small to create anything that would last. Ha'a felt that the new Hawaiian Nation should not be a blood-based organization, but give equal rights to everyone currently on the island with new rules making a quality of life that would excel for everyone who survived the event. There was some resistance to this notion, as many present were over fifty percent Hawaii blood and felt it would be a lost opportunity to bring Hawaiians into a culture renaissance.

Around midday, just after lunch, the crew headed back east over the Pali, away from the estate, leaving Ha'a to think. They spotted twelve military men and the general coming up the road. Kamai commanded Kumu, the second youngest of the group, to circle back and alert everyone at the estate. The crew vanished off the road, and followed the switchback over the Pali mountains towards Kaneohe. The men were armed, so it was best to alert Ha'a before they were at the gate.

The military men were greeted at the gate. The General did not hesitate to let them know why he was there. Their goal was to see where the Kapu project had left off, and if there was anything that they could do to assist it getting it operable. The Military wanted to get the grid back up and running. Ha'a expressed his appreciation for the General and his men having come all this way, but a decision on when the next test of the system would be done was not known. Ha'a asked the General not to visit again until the grid was back up and running. Current resources and food distribution should have been both side's priority, and Ha'a made sure that the military didn't forget it before the meeting was done.

The General assured him that they were conducting food distributions at the gates of all bases with what resources they'd secured from what was left over in the commissaries and the Navy Exchange. After military families were secured, the Marines would be distributing rations to the public. Ha'a asked how they were able to get to the containers and transport them. The General relayed they had not yet figured that out, also that Pier 14 had been secured by rebel forces, gang members to be exact, and they held over half of the perishables and non-perishable goods which had landed prior to the event. The General felt that the only secure area for rationing would be the bases entrance or Aloha Stadium, as all other structures would have easy access for looters and riots and all FEMA rations along with what was secured would be routed through these choke points as he called them.

Ha'a agreed the military needed to intervene with food distribution, but revealed nothing of his own plan. He kept quiet about his plan to meet with the other delegates, and continued the conversation focusing on what the military was doing for the public and what he could do to support. He internally felt that the General had never given him a reason to show the military their cards. In Ha'a's mind, it would be a worst-case scenario to involve the military in his vision of a new Hawaii. After their years of mishandling Hawaii, giving them any more power could be fatal to Ha'a's plan. Ha'a asked the General how they planned to deal with the tourists currently being held at the Honolulu Zoo. The General stated, "To be honest, Ha'a, we just learned of this issue. We've been so busy securing food and taking care of base security, that we didn't know there was a holding pen for the remaining tourists. We've been told there's something similar happening at the airport. We placed strike teams in place to monitor and provide security if needed." He continued, "From the last I heard, the situation was manageable but they were only a few days into it. There could be unrest between the tourists, with lack of resources a revolt is not out of the question. It's not ideal. If the lack of food won't get them, the sun exposure will."

The General thanked Ha'a for his time and insight, then rallied his men and started to make the trek back east over the Pali Highway at dusk. Kapu noticed that there were 25 additional men waiting just outside the gate, having emerged from the brush, that he and his father's scout had not previously noticed. Understandably, the General and his men needed security, however, not letting Ha'a know that these men were in their midst was just another sign of mistrust. Unfortunately, an EMP only fries electronic devices, meaning all manually triggered weapons were still intact. The military held the lion's share. Ha'a did not have access to any form of relevant paramilitary weapons compared to the scope of what the leftover military still maintained. Ha'a knew the only way to have the plan work was to involve the Yakuza. This meant a meeting with Mr. Yakimura was unavoidable, and would have a different tone than organizing the other communities.

This wasn't a commercial operation to feed the masses like Costco. With no currency, besides bullets and canned food, all new food items would need to have an ethical and logistically friendly distribution method backed by a neutral party's security force. If the military provided this infrastructure, there would be no way to ensure a neutral existence and that food would not be used for their power. Although he knew they were in a precarious position, there was nothing else to do except to organize the influential groups to be able to have an alternative to a military state.

Ha'a was not altruistic about his position and laying ground for a new government. However, giving the power back to the people, while giving them a secure food resource, would be the best option Hawaii had. All true Hawaiians, and those who paid relevant attention to the culture, knew that living Pono was always a precursor to survival. Living Pono meant that everything was in harmony with the land. The Aina, or land, provided resources and it is the people's responsibility to take care of the Aina. Hawaiians knew better than to bite the real hand that feeds them, and that was the Aina, not the US Army. Since the 40s, it seemed that sustainability was disappearing and dependence on foreign oil with shipped goods and Petroleum based electricity was creating a dependency on the Western system. Ha'a knew if there were ever a land that could sustain its population, it was Hawaii. The

Kapu project was a throwback to an old Hawaiian way of using fish ponds in a sustainable ecosystem to feed its people. Mixed with new technologies using Aquaculture/Aquaponic hybrid systems, a closed loop method was as ready as it ever would be.

In older days, Hawaiians lived in a caste system. The Monarchy delegated who tended the land. Commoners, or the "Kanaka Maoli," were not entitled to land ownership, but were given the responsibility to tend the land for all the people. None went hungry, and everyone was treated equal. The Kanaka Maoli, or the Monarchy's subjects, all worked and had a job, be it a farmer, fisherman, land worker, or other. Everyone provided for the society and the kingdom. The goal, now, would be to do this without any form of caste system in place, each one to one's ability and each one to one's need. It still sounded like Utopian, or Marxist, if you put it on paper but, hey, they were on an island with no room for the perpetual growth paradigm capitalism called for. Plus, when bullets replaced dollars as a trade worthy currency, something had to give before anarchy set in.

The Hawaiian Monarchy went awry when they placed trust in the missionaries. Much like the ill-fated Native American Indians it did not take long for the newcomers to overstep their boundaries. Puritan values don't mix well with what the newcomers considered heathen gods. At the time Hawaii Kanaka Maoli were motivated by a sense of nationalism and God-like ideology of the Ali'i and the Kapu system. It was different from what we would call communism but did reflect the more becoming values of Marxism. Efforts were in place to support the whole Hawaiian nation, but there was a defined class of royals based on bloodline, backed up by the Ali'i's island style socialism, everyone having a shared responsibility in their survival and a strict set of rules with harsh punishments. The son of King Kamehameha, Liholiho, decided to allow men and women to eat together at a feast attended by high chiefs and several foreigners. Also known as the 'Ai Noa, this act alone is thought to have made the Kanaka sway from the entire Kapu law system. Hawaii lacking a sense of true North and the Kapu system's cultural compass swayed to the ways of US business leaders and influential visitors. The US took away Hawaii's sovereignty, and replaced it with a Democratic capitalist way of life eating away the old ways year after year, campaign after campaign. The Kapu system fell once the Kanaka saw these visitors. Ha'a felt that in a multicultural Oahu, reverting back to a government based on bloodline would cause backlash and fighting for land grabs that would be hard to regulate off hearsay of one's lineage. A reformed and updated Hawaiian governmental policy was the goal, but not at the sacrifice of excluding the land's people, new or old. The reinstated Hawaiian Nation would disagree but, he assumed, they would understand his points and the urgency to organize the major players on the island for the good of all people. As any rational person with Hawaiian blood would think, it was their birthright, and a great opportunity, to reinstate the Hawaiian Nation, but what does that really look like in this new world, post-event.

If your station in life was dependant on your birthright, and your birth right left you at the top of the heap, it is human nature to put a system in place to backup your rights. Ha'a, however, felt a flag is only as good as the strength it represents and, if the people of Oahu were divided on one side of the fence or the other, the unity would break down at some point leaving the remaining de facto US military back in control. In a divided society, might almost always makes right and the "fear of the other" is always exploited.

The General left knowing Ha'a had his own agenda. He felt disguising his intention would not gain him a foothold with Ha'a, so he presented his plan as to a T. Too many years of US deception to create power and strength had been in play for the military to continue the charade. In this new Hawaii, politics were useless. Bullets and rations would be making policy, not diplomacy and glad handing. The General had a stockpile of weapons, and manpower to use them. He did not want to resort to a massive use of force, but he let Ha'a know it was on the table if things got out of control.

Kaneohe Marine Corps. Base had a decommissioned hydroelectric system called the "H Buoy." It had been placed in a munitions bunker, months prior to the event, at the Base of Ulupau Crater at the Northeast most point of the base. It was operable, but getting it into position, manually, was an issue in itself. The H had been taken out for repair after a season of giant north swells knocked it loose from the grid cable that powered a storage battery inside the crater. The Kapu project was more sustainable at the estate for now. The General felt the Power Buoy station could give the island a jump start, and bargaining chips to get the public under control quicker than the estate could do on their own. With the current state of affairs, any opportunities to show stability and safety could be a leadership campaign of its own. The General promised Ha'a would be rewarded with political appointment. Ha'a thanked him for his offer, and left it on ice, stating, "This land is bigger than just myself, General. I thank you for your visit, but I have some discussions to be had with the board." This was a way of buying time. Ha'a didn't say no, and a maybe left negotiation open to the General's interpretation. The estate board was not known to show up to meetings regarding the Kapu project, even when their cars were running. The likelihood of them showing now was non-existent. Ha'a would be making executive decisions from here on out.

Ha'a decided that his group would make their way to Mr. Yakimura's residence at first light the next day. Knowing, now, that they may be in future conflict with the general, it made it imperative to acquire a safe storage and distribution facility. The food and rations were only as valuable as their protection. The plan was for a 24-hour turnaround. Until there was a secure platform for the Kapu project's expansion, there needed to be resources to warehouse and distribute food recovered from shipping yards and/or coming from harvested Oahu farms.

Ha'a awoke 45 minutes before the rest of the group, and checked his equipment for the trip. He had loaded two 9mm clips holding ten rounds each for his Glock, a utility knife, four packages of Ramen, and two sets of clothes for the hike, which he wrapped inside of his windbreaker to waterproof it inside his bag. After his morning coffee, near the backyard pond, he woke the rest of the crew. The group was comprised of all the same men from the last mission, minus Harold and Kapu. With only a six-man crew, they knew they wouldn't be a threat to any gangs, but just in case they needed to make an escape the other crew members prepared with whatever small arms were available. They were not so worried about what lay in front of them when they met with Mr. Yakimura. More concerning was that they would be moving through thick brush to cut down road time, and then forced onto the urban streets of Kalihi, controlled by the MWH Crips, an offshoot of the famous LA Crips Gang. The property stood on the top of the hill just below the Likelike Highway, looking down on Kalihi. If they followed the H1 highway, they could exit through the valley and meet the front gate with minimal time on the visible streets.

Kalihi was known to be one of the most dangerous and gang occupied areas of the island. It was at the base of a beautiful mountain where the boys high school, Kamehameha Schools, is located. Nonetheless, they knew ever since Kam school days, the streets below were inhabited by various groups such as the MWH crips and smaller rival gangs. MWH stood for Mayor Wright Homes, and if they lucked out and didn't run into the MWH crips, there were Kuhio Park Terrace gangs and smaller gangs such as BHB (Bad Hawaiian Bloods), Pinoy 808 (comprised of local Filipino transplants), and SOS (Sons of Samoa). There could be trouble from many angles during their escapade through Kalihi.

The two major planned housing communities MWH and KPT held over 6,000 low-income studios and one-bedroom tenement-style apartments. Police avoided these projects due to gang relations, and only S.W.A.T. operations would enter with warrants to conduct drug raids and systematic checks. It was a rat-infested, dangerous group of apartment complexes that bordered both urban and tropical surroundings, making it easy for criminals to hide and hard for authorities to keep tabs on the goings on. It was run like any ghetto. There was a leader for each region and each gang held their turf, and each apartment building could have a new Gang boss holding court. This created order within the region and, unless you broke the rules, you were, for the most part, fine to do as you pleased. However, only Kamai had any ties to the projects, with his estranged uncle living in the area. Kamai's uncle was let out of Federal prison on drug charges. He did a short bid at Halawa Prison, which was two miles from MWH, before being sent to Arizona when he was sentenced for selling meth inside the prison. His friends would fly a drone at night to his cell window and he would pull a bag full of Meth, Black Tar and anything an inmate would need to pass through another day in confinement. He ended up selling to a plant that was working for the Department of Corrections and did five more years on the mainland before being released on probation. With a record and no job opportunities, he disappeared into the MWH.

The group could bypass most of the danger by hugging the outskirts of the project in the brush. Traveling through Kalihi after the event couldn't be safe for anyone, and it was best to assume the worst. They would be seen at one point but, hopefully, less likely to be engaged if they traveled the streets mid-day. Having weapons provided some protection but also made them a target if a gang got wind of them. It is hard to hide a 30 ought 6 bolt action rifle or a tactical shotgun when you're wearing boardshorts. Handguns were sparse. Only Ha'a had a side arm. One could only assume, a housing project full of gang members meant others may be armed in the area.

The first two hours of the trip, the group saw nothing more than people going about their business within the apartments and properties surrounding the H1 Highway, a few odd looks from families watching over the perimeters of their properties. The view of cars frozen in time along the H1 Highway was mind boggling. You could grab any car you wanted in this giant abandoned car lot, if they only started. Most of the cars had been stripped of any valuables that were left when the EMP went off. The crew could see thousands of cars littering the street. Looking further past the highway into Pearl Harbor, they could see a devastated landscape. Skeletons of ships scattered along Pearl Harbor, battered and blown up tanks in clear view from the H1 at the entrance to the base. Only one ship seemed to have remained intact. It was pointed in the direction of the Harbor's mouth, and looked abandoned.

It was nearing dusk, and the crew were getting weary from the walk. As they came to an off-ramp, right near the base of Kalihi, they hooked back towards the brush to get out of the line of site of the adjacent buildings. It was uphill hike to the base of the Likelike where Yakimura resided, and arriving at night could be seen as a threat. They did not want to risk being fired upon at

Yakimura's gates. Ha'a decided to hold up in a park with good tree coverage. Kamai asked Ha'a if he could pull two men to explore the Oahu Gun Club & Munitions he knew was two blocks over. It was Oahu's biggest gun club, famous for having an array of inventory. If it was manned, maybe they could barter or, if not, they could scavenge. Ha'a decided against it, as there was no room to move any new equipment and providing security for that type of mission was out of the question. If gang members were running the show at the gun store, the risk would be too high.

That night, while the crew was sleeping under a Banyan tree deep within the district park, Kamai woke Teddy and said, "Let's go. Teddy, let's go see if the store still got ammo. We'll be back in an hour." Teddy was game, because he was the only one without a weapon on the team. The two took all of 15 minutes to get to the shop, just off H1 Highway exit 20A, at the base of Kalihi. It was dark, but they could see men sitting at the door. Two had red bandanas, and the third wore a black leather biker jacket with a "MWH Clique" patch on the lapel. Kamai tapped Teddy on the shoulder, " How's dat Blalah over der." Blalah was a pigeon term for badass and the man in the jacket fit the term to a t.

The three gang members had gone down the alley to the back door as Kamai and Teddy watched. The two circled back to flank them through the other alleyway. Kamai slowly trailed the MWH crew, and signaled for Teddy to follow when it was clear. There was a storage shed with two cots and a hammock. The gang members entered one at a time, one stayed out front as the other went in. The final one laid in the hammock outside the locked gate, while the other two went further back to the store. Kamai signaled to Teddy with three fingers to show him the number of men standing guard, then hand signaled 1 and 5 as he pointed to his watch. Teddy understood. They would bum rush the gang in 15 minutes, hoping the two men in cots would be asleep. Kamai pulled a ream of duct tape from his bag, and showed it to Teddy from across the way. 10 minutes into their wait, they noticed a man keeping watch from inside a car parked across the street. He was dozing off, but they knew the man was checking his rearview mirror periodically for anyone coming up the street. Kamai, also, started to think that the keys may be on the inside and the guard up front was just there to warn the others. Kamai knew that, more than likely, the rounds and weapons were not in the shed but, hopefully, the keys would be.

Kamai and Teddy viewed their watches as they struck 12:00 pm, Kamai pointed at the guard, and motioned like a director would call action. As Kamai reached the man in the car, he put his hand over his mouth and nose. Teddy, simultaneously, hit the lookout with the butt end of the small shovel he had been carrying for camping. They duct taped his mouth, then took a zip tie from their bag to secure his hands. They searched his pockets for keys with no luck and placed him in the dumpster. With no keys, they had to make a new plan. Knowing that they were going to be in the daylight soon, Kamai and Teddy knew they would have to chance it and get back to camp fast. A small window atop the back entrance looked to have just enough room to sneak into the building, but noise would be a factor for the guard they spotted across the street. So, they decided to split up and, if the guard awoke to the sound of the glass breaking, Teddy would knock out the guard and zip tie him in the car.

Kamai climbed to the top of the fire exit to shimmy in the window. Teddy placed himself next to the passenger side front wheel. Kamai jumped onto the windowsill, and then looked over to see if Teddy could see him. Teddy pointed two fingers at his eyes and then back to Kamai. With that, Kamai signaled a 3,2,1 count and broke the window. The guard shuffled a bit, but did not wake. Kamai slid through the window, disappearing from site. Kamai had positioned himself on top of a wooden beam, which had chicken wire around it. A barb had caught his right boot forcing him to pull a knife from his belt and off his top lace. Kamai noticed there was a storage box sitting on a pallet that held stacks of loose rounds. Only a few scattered weapons were seen leaning against the pallet. The guns looked as if they were ready to be fired, not just part of the storage. Finally clipping the wire off his boot, he started to shimmy down a vertical beam. Just as he'd gotten his waist over the ledge, a wooden truss broke sending him falling onto the pallet below. Kamai bounced off the floor, setting off a round from a rifle leaning against the box. Teddy heard the round, and so did the outside guards. Teddy tried to punch through the window, and hit the headrest, as the guard opened the driver door sending Teddy rolling onto the sidewalk. The man in the car ran down the back alley and into the dark. Inside of the building, Kamai was in a frenzy, he grabbed the rifle, a few boxes of shells, and a Glock 9mm handgun he had seen on a pallet. Jumping back up, top the pallets to escape, shots were fired and Kamai was forced to jump back down behind to dodge fire.

Another shot was heard from outside, and then three more, but not in Teddy's direction. Kamai shot the lock off the door, and escaped through the front. He grabbed Teddy, and they sprinted towards the brush line as they heard yelling from the back of the building. Before hitting the camp, Kamai pulled Teddy aside, handed him the Glock and said, "We need to get our stories straight."

Teddy asked, "What happened anyway, Kamai, I'm not too sure I know the real story anyhow?"

"I fell off the pallets, and a round went off from a rifle resting against some pallets of ammo." Teddy replied.

They decided to tell the crew they bartered some camping gear for the rifle and ammunition. When day broke, there would be no hiding the new weapons so best to keep it simple and see if it would blow over.

Ha'a noticed the gun as Kamai kneeled down to a camping burner to brew coffee. Ha'a yelled "You no like listen, do you? You want to start a war? We got enough issues on our hands."

Kamai looked at him with disdain, like a toddler getting scoldings from his dad. "What, Ha'a? We bartered for them. There's nothing to worry about."

"I never got cut trading with anyone," Ha'a said while looking at Kamai's ripped fatigues and tear in his boot. "Enough of this. Let's get up the hill. We need to get back home before dark."

The group packed up and made their way into the brush. They followed an old trail Kam schools students used to cut school. The group took a side trail to cool off by jumping in the Kalihi ice ponds. They remembered as kids cutting class themselves to sneak over to the ice pond, the goal was to hang out until the second bell, then sneak back down to the road and catch a ride to surf while everyone was in class. Dead wind made the hike more difficult. The heat was stagnant. Kamai and Teddy caught the worst of it with their new ammunition adding weight to their already arduous trip.

As they approached the complex, Ha'a got a feeling they were being watched. They knew there were guards. Mr. Yakimura was notorious for being cautious when it came to security. Not without reason, he was one of the richest foreign nationals in Hawaii, and was heard to have kept large stockpiles of cash and arms within the compound which he used to run the Yakuza payroll. When your CPA carries a sidearm and carries a handcuffed briefcase, you can assume there are other trust issues abound. Trying to avoid a grandiose entrance, Ha'a asked the group to fall back as they got close so as to not pose a threat. Ha'a was allowed into the complex with Mr. Yakimura's blessing.

Surprised at the lack of security, Ha'a only saw one guard with no visible weapon. Ha'a was put at ease, until the man nodded and asked, "Are they with you?" Ha'a turned to see his group tied, hand and hand, with AR-15s to their backs.

"Yes, they are. We're here to speak to Mr. Yakimura."

"Why all the gear? You think he enjoys surprise armed visits?" A voice came from behind the fence.

"Ha'a, come in. Leave your friends outside." Yakimura's reputation preceded him with his ominous voice piercing the compounds walls. The group besides Ha'a remained outside with armed guards watching. Ha'a was blindfolded and walked down a tunnel, turned a few times, then spun, then told to walk again. Ha'a was able to keep his senses, however, and calculated he made two rights, a left, a right, spun 360, and went straight for nearly 300 yards before turning sharply to the right, hearing a sliding door shut behind him.

When he was finally unblindfolded, Ha'a was in an outdoor courtyard, with a Japanese Bonsai tree garden, and koi ponds bordering its pathways. In the middle stood Mr. Yakimura, feeding his fish. "Aloha, Mr. Yakimura. It's been a long time."

"Konichiwa, Ha'a. Yes, it has." After a brief pause, Yakimura enquired, "What brings you here? Should I be concerned that armed men are roaming my property, well, ones that are not on my payroll?"

Ha'a breathed deep to calm his nerves and responded, "They are with me for my protection on the streets, not as an aggression towards you."

Yakimura nodded. "Understandable. You should be forewarned that my guards are on watch in the valley 24/7, and your friends are not the only ones roaming my property line." Ha'a shook his head and replied. "I can imagine you have been on your toes, but I don't know who the others are, I promise."

"Owning a food storage business in a crisis makes you a target," said Yakimura matter-of-factly.

Ha'a paused and started the conversation again, "Have you rationed out any goods yet to the public?"

Taking a more stern tone, Yakimura interjected, "Ha'a, I'm a businessman. Does it say 'F.E.M.A.' at my gate?"

"No sir," responded Ha'a.

"The military can, surely, purchase my goods for a price." Ha'a nodded again. Yakimura continued, "But to answer simply, no, and I have no plans to open up my gates to any outsiders. It has worked for me all these years. I do not plan to change my ways now."

Ha'a looked out at the back part of the property, where 50 trucks stood next to loading bays with large sliding doors built into the mountainside. His facility was purchased from the US Government in the 70s. During the gas crisis, the economy and fiscal budgets were low, and the Military started selling off lands that were not in use and/or were in debate with the Office of Hawaiian Affairs.

The Office of Hawaiian Affairs considered this land to be bordering historical land that looked over a fertile valley used by ancient Hawaiians. Also, if the government were to keep it, they would have to do an ordinance clearing. Mr. Yakimura purchased it with the liability, and never did a clearing. He would joke, "I got a free minefield out of the deal." The US Government sold to the Yakimura corp. in 1975, and Mr. Yakimura turned weapons silos into efficient cold goods storage facilities and the warmer bunkers held his illegal gaming machines and card tables. Yakimura would send produce trucks filled with various illicit gambling machines or supplies for impromptu to card games to be held in the back of Chinatown restaurants. It was hard to catch the gaming as you could not just search a produce truck at a restaurant without probable cause. Yakimura's team was in and out moving shop and strong-arming businesses for use of their property after hours. Since the mountain kept the storage areas cool, his refrigeration costs were lessened and, since the government broke ground first, he did not have to associate with OHA's request for further land inspections as he keep the outside lands the same with the exception of his house, security cameras, and storage upgrade. One thing was impressive, more than the others. He installed more checkpoints than the military had prior and since it butted a mountain side, all Yakimura had to worry about was what was in front of him.

Ha'a knew that the task of making an ultra-capitalist like Mr. Yakimura use his empire for the greater good was a real task, unless he had something to trade. He quickly decided it was crucial to sweeten the pot. "Mr. Yakimura, I have given this some thought while making my hike to your property. We both know trade is our real working capital in this new Hawaii. My goal is to unlock its people from the former military stronghold, and give back the land to its people. I understand there will be blowback and compromise. I am willing to give you the Klein Estate's Kunia land in return for storage of what is able to be harvested. We will require security for the Kapu project, as well. Right now, it is situated at my home. We will not use the warehouse as a distribution method, but for storage only. We can utilize the Kamehameha school campus as a distribution point, and would just require security to move the goods to the campus and from the fields. We can use the estate's horses, attached to your flatbeds, for transport to and from on distribution days."

Just as Ha'a finished, a shot was heard from outside the grounds, followed by a flurry of machine gun fire. Ha'a was reblindfolded and, along with Mr. Yakimura, was rushed to a safe room where they waited out the quick fire fight. Outside, Ha'as crew was held up just outside the gates, with thirty plus MWH members carrying various weapons.

"Yakimura, we had an agreement. You like renege with us, you not gonna like da terms."

A guard shouted over from the gate, "Don't fire! I'll get Mr. Yakimura." The guard explained to Mr. Yakimura the situation, and what the MWH claims were. Ha'a, still blindfolded, was rushed to the gate. Yakimura opened up a slide in the gate, and started to speak. "We have changed nothing. What is the accusation?"

Kasian, their leader, yelled back, "These two men, here at your gates, robbed my men last night and shot at them."

"My men don't leave the compound unless I tell them too."

Ha'a blurted out, "It was my men. They acted against my orders." Mr. Yakimura looked back in anger. "Your men brought this to my gates? You need to make this right Ha'a was rushed off to the gate entrance still blindfolded."

Ha'a spoke up, "Yakimura has no connection to this. My men worked against my orders. We will give you back what is yours, and make it right."

"Yakimura, open the gates and give us these men, or our arrangements are withdrawn," demanded Kasian.

Ha'a still blindfolded turned to Yakimura, "Let me fix this. They'll kill my cousin, if not me, for my father, let me fix this." Yakimura gestured to the guards to send Ha'a out to the MWH men.

Ha'a's blindfold was pulled, and he could see a small army of men wearing red with weapons to spare. "I understand my men have done wrong. There is only so much I can do to repay, but we are here only to plan the next step for the people of Hawaii and need unity to help everyone. Unfortunately, my cousin does not understand this."

The leader of the MWH crips shook his head. "Huh? We don't care about everyone, we care about the MWH Buleh."

"The man who robbed you is my cousin. I can offer you food in return for his life. We will provide MWH the first drop off of our acquired resources. Your buildings will be allowed access to food and goods first, before we open it to the public. In return, you can keep Kamai who robbed your store as collateral on my word. We need security, and MWH is part of Yakimura's Sword. This was a mistake that needs to be corrected. Together, we all can benefit."

Kasian replied, "If you make good on what you say and we get access to food by the end of the week, he will be alive. Right, boys?"

The collective gang members yelled out, "RIGHTTTT!!!"

Ha'a asked Kasian, "Can you provide us safe travel through MWH, to make it back from Yakimura's property?"

"No one will mess with you. You should have come to us first, dummy."

Ha'a nodded in agreement, admitting, "MWH's reputation had us worried. We felt we needed to meet with Yakimura first."

"Brah, Yakimura's got the hill, but you don't get up the hill without the streets. We run the streets. Your cousin will be waiting for you when you get back on Friday, but don't bother coming Saturday unless you're planning on picking up the body." Kamai was pushed inside the gate. Ha'a and Kamai locked eyes. Ha'a re-entered the gate as Yakimura addressed him. "Ha'a, I have extended my last olive branch to you. You make good on this, and on your agreement with me. If you don't, you should consider yourself unwelcomed here."

Chapter 3
No Rest for the Windward

With a quicker journey home behind them, due to the MWH pass, a new task of getting food back within a week was hanging over Ha'a's head. He was aware he had to meet with Nia, but was not sure what would be their next move, knowing there was still the element of the Filipino delegates and the group of workers they controlled. Their cooperation was essential to gaining access to what was left of the current harvest. Ha'a had not spent time with his family, and his thoughts were clouded by the stresses the island faced. He felt the best option was to put it aside, and think the way his father taught him, all those years prior as a boy.

"Son, if your head is clouded by fear, you cannot control your mind. You need to enter the water to flush the fear away. It's the best medicine for us. Akua will guide you by just being in his creation."

Ha'a asked his son, Kapu, if he would like to go on a day adventure in Waikiki to canoe surf. Kapu was apprehensive, but loved the idea of getting in the water even though he overheard his cousins talking about the encounter Ha'a had near Chinatown. Also, his father was not being clear about where his uncle Kamai was, and why he didn't return with him. Nonetheless, they decided it would be a good thing to get in the ocean, even though Hanalei was not sold on them traveling away from the estate. The two set off by themselves, avoiding Chinatown completely and not making stops.

It seemed as if things on the streets of Kapahulu were very similar to prior the event, minus power. The homeless were still occupying the beach parks, and there didn't seem to be any fighting more than what you would see on a normal day at any Honolulu's beach parks. The surf was showing as they approached Waikiki, and Kapu's mind turned to the waves. It was midday and the local beach boys hang out near the Duke statue. Ha'a stopped on the way, to see if they had energy to go for a wave. They said they had been up all night, scavenging near the docks, but could use a rinse if they got the canoe. Ha'a and Kapu went and grabbed the six-man canoe they stacked at the Royal Hawaiian Hotel. The beach boys helped launch the canoe and Ha'a let Kapu be the steersman, the beach boys providing the muscle to paddle into waves. They caught four waves, before saying goodbye, offering them the canoe to use and watch over. It was the first time they ever saw the beach empty of tourists in Waikiki, and they felt as if they were the new Kanaka of modern day, as if there were no worries in their new Hawaii. Ha'a had, quickly, snapped back to reality when he saw a band of trouble makers working their way through the sidewalks of Kalakaua. He decided to stop at the statue, and asked his friends what they were doing.

"Those guys have been going room by room, looking for food and valuables in the rooms of the tourists being held at the zoo. They finally made their way down here. They don't seem to care too much about the surf, I'll tell you that." Ha'a knew the stark reality was grim. There were less and less resources each day, and there were no transportation methods that would get resources and new crops to the people. It reminded him that humans are bound to their way, and Yakimura was bound to his ways, which would leave him always in a better bargaining position. Ha'a cut their adventure short, and decided it would be good to visit Nia on their way out. He wanted to see if there was any progress, on her side, with the Filipino delegates.

Nia was found in the meeting hall, but was alone. Ha'a knocked before entering the room this time. "Hi, Nia. This is my son, Kapu. We came back to Waikiki to get in the ocean, but I felt the need to see if there was any progress."

"Ha'a, my team reached Kunia, but it's not good. Two-thirds of the crops burned in a store house that was hit by an incoming missile meant for Schofield Barracks. The workers had gone through half of what was left, themselves, and some areas were looted. We need another source, something more functional."

Kapu chimed in, as if he was a wanted part of the conversation. "What about Nalo?" Ha'a looked at him as if to say, 'Know your place.' Kapu continued. "Waimanalo, there are massive farms there and, with no trucks, we could use sailboats to move the crops to each side of the island for distribution. We could float goods to all sides of the island, and the Kunia crops could be used to feed central island at Yakimura's. North Shore should have resources of their own, and dry goods could be moved by boat as well from what's left at the pier."

Nia chimed in, "Well, it is not the worst idea, but who is going to reach out to the people in Nalo and see what remains?"

Kapu retorted, "It was my big mouth that brought it up, so I guess I could scout it out from the backside of the Koolau Summit. If it's safe, we'll circle back, regroup, and hike in from the Kailua side, as a group, through Norfolk Pass."

Ha'a looked at his son baffled at the assuredness of his son, shouting back at him, "WELL, I guess we have nothing to worry about then!" Ha'a looked back at Nia, "We'll meet later this week, as planned." Ha'a smirked. The group finalized some details and parted ways.

"Dad, I know I can make it to the ridge undetected in three hours from our house but would you let me bring the Ruger .22" Just in case I see a boar. Maybe I can hunt on the way back. Plus for protection, it would be nice to have."

Ha'a replied, "Son, that's your rifle. I would not have given it to you if I didn't trust you, but use the ammo sparingly. We can't just run to the store and buy more these days. The sad fact is, those bullets could be our only currency fairly soon, so no pot shots on a distant sow. OK? Also, if you shoot a sow, remember stay off Old Pali Road. You know, they say Pele may stop you." Kapu smiled, happily, as if he was looking forward to the hike or, more so, the hunt.

When Ha'a and Kapu arrived home, Dr. Hind was seen reading in the estate's lounge. Kapu had noticed an odd look on his face as both the Dr. and Ha'a's eyes met, a mix of nervousness and assumed deceit he had grown accustomed to spotting when dealing with haoles. He always gave people the benefit of the doubt, but his instinct was built into his DNA and had been correct more times than he liked to admit. Kapu had opted to alleviate the air of tension with a welcoming half hug and pat on the back.

"Hey, Doc. What's new? Any progress with Kapu on your end?"

"Well, Ha'a, that's the thing. Barrington and I have hit a crossroads with the present situation. We have a security issue with the system, and I feel the entire project should be hosted at K-Bay at the Ulupau Crater site. The base provides us security from looters, and they have the P Buoy system already in place which could create the energy while the thermal site is tested."

"I don't think dividing our resources in food production and energy is a safe and productive way to secure the system in this hostile climate."

Kapu took a second to ponder what was just spoken. "You make a good point but trusting a de facto government with the people's one true hope for the future does not seem like the best strategy either, Doc." Kapu said and went on, "Listen, are you and Dr. Lightfoot getting along in the lab? I know there has been a rift in the directions you both wanted to go with the project before the event, and don't want that to be a deciding factor on your decision making. You both are indispensable in your work to the project." Ha'a had said this with a bit of sugarcoating, to give the message some ego incentive to Dr. Hind.

"Frankly, Mr. Klein, I do not see myself working alongside him, or anyone appointed, any longer. If this does not happen at K-Bay, I will be taking my work to the base."

"I understand, Doc. We are living in a different world. What a big difference two weeks can make but, before you cut and run, can you give me a week? I have a secure place for Kapu that is right on the cusp of being a viable place to move the entire project. I can't disclose it in full detail, but it is ready and utilizes the Halawa Aquifers as its water source."

Hind looked intrigued. He knew the issue with K-Bay was tainted water. The radiation that could be coming their way, from a multitude of nuclear strikes around the Pacific, meant that a clean water source and sustainable filtration system for the aquaponic system was a must. It, also, had to be containable, preferably underground or built into a mountain side so as to create a controlled convection system that would reuse wastewater and clean it through a natural reverse osmosis steam from the geothermal pumps. Barrington had the notion that if they used a thermal energy to power the entire system, as they planned, it would be a closed loop. The steam would generate the turbine that would power the system and, in the same method, purify and recycle the water. Where else on the island would have an accessible feature to capture steam heat from the lava? Dr. Hind looked skeptical. He couldn't pinpoint a location from his knowledge of the island. Dr. Hind shook hands with Ha'a, "One week, based on good faith."

Ha'a had a notion to go right to Dr. Lightfoot, and see what was going on in his absence, but then course-corrected to check in with Hanalei whom he had only seen briefly over the course of the week. He found her near the estate's fish pond, which was stocked with Tilapia she was feeding. It was a game for the kids to take bamboo fishing pools and catch dinner once a month. They would invite the neighborhood kids to a "catch and release fishing tournament." Whoever caught the most in a half hour would choose the dessert for that night's neighborhood dinner. There had not been any sounds of the neighborhood children since the incident, and she had only seen her own son for all of an hour since he left back on his mission to Waimanalo.

"I miss the sound of people coming and going, the gate being open, and getting visitors. It's so quiet and eerie without people stopping by." Ha'a, in an attempt to bring himself back to weeks prior, looked out over the property and imagined a backyard party with the cousins and neighbors coming and going. "It seems like a backyard party is just a memory. This week went by so fast, but I feel like it took a year off my life." Hanalei started to understand the pressure her husband was feeling. He was not only worried about their safety, but the island's existence as a whole. "There's just so much happening,

Hanalei, and there is nothing I can do to keep a lid on the chaos this island is heading into."

She gazed back at him. "Ha'a, none of us can control what is out of our control, but I do know you are good at controlling what is in your reach. Don't look past what you already have in motion. It was enough before this happened, and it will be enough now. However, I do have a bone to pick with you."

Ha'a looked down at the ground like a shamed dog. "What I can't figure out is why you sent Kapu out on his own to Waimanalo. It's dangerous, even without all this going on."

"He's not alone. I sent him out with Harold."

"You mean the one that got shot the last time you went to town? He's like a portagee bullseye, just asking to get in trouble."

Ha'a replied, "I trust Kapu. I trust him like my father trusted me."

She smiled. "Glad to hear it. Didn't your father always send your cousin with you to spy?"

"Ya, but he was working for me. I got him all the ladies, so he was in my back pocket."

She playfully smacked Ha'a in the back of the head.

Meanwhile, in the MWH, Kamai was being put to work searching through the projects with a team checking abandoned apartment houses for usable goods and possible weapons. One of the men roaming the halls felt it was a good time to bring up the elephant in the room, or why there was a Hawaiian/Portuguese roaming amongst five Micronesian gang bangers. "So, what? You Hawaiians, you no like us? You think you better, one island no better than another, huh? What? We not Polynesian, just write us off lidat huh? Ali'i my ass! Look like one Portagee punk to me."

Another one of the crew yelled back, "You know we get more Aloha in my islands, so much Aloha it got us all buss up. We invite everybody to our islands and look where it got us, right dead center in da happy Hawaiian ghettos of MWH."

Kamai shrugged, knowing what he was in for. There was a lot of truth to what these guys said. Micronesians were looked at as the islanders' black sheep. They didn't have a place in Hawaii yet. Even in a haole-centric society, with all the big business and real estate owned either by Japanese or haoles, the Hawaiians cultured was always revered. Envied by transients and second generation non-Pacific Islanders alike, it was like it was okay to take over the lands but, hey, as long as they still worshiped Duke Kahanamoku and sipped Mai Tai's at the Outrigger, everything was alright.

Kamai looked over at a short, stubby gang member. He had a fish hook tattooed under his eyelid, not a Hawaiian one you would see on cultural tattoos but like one you could buy at Walmart in Anytown, USA. It looked as if the tattoo was pulling his eyelid down and to the side, almost explaining his sunken-in eyes and shady demeanor. He pulled a 9-volt battery from his pocket, put a piece of wire to either end, and placed a cigarette on the tip of the exposed wire.

"Dis one still get juice. You like one smoke? Pele lit this one himself, Hawaiian," he said, taking a poke at Hawaiian folklore and the God of Fire.

Kamai, in effort to fit in, was quick to respond, "Ya why not. We might not be around too long, anyway, the way things are going."

"Speak for yourself, Buleh. We MWH out here in the gutters since day one."

Kamai laughed. "You could use a lighter, though. So, where you learn that trick with the battery?"

"I was in prison up in Hawala. Did a stint in Arizona, at Ultramax, as well. When we couldn't find an outlet, we found ways with batteries. It's kind of tricky, but nicotine will get you to figure things out, ya know?"

"So, how did you find a live battery with the EMP frying everything? You figured everything would be used up by now."

"Dis one was in a parking garage, three stories down, under our building. I broke a few car windows, and found it in a radio playing static in a Toyota."

"What? You found a working radio, and you took the battery for a smoke? Where the fuck is the radio?"

"Frick, bah, in the Yota. I no need hear da news. We all know it's fucked out here, was all static anyway. What you want that shit fo?"

"I like static, but you show me this Yota, I'll get you one case of them cigarettes you like."

"Deal, Pele. We go tonight. Wait for boss man to crash out, take about 15 mins, we pau."

"K Den."

The men continued their patrol, and day turned to night. Everyone turned in early because of the lack of light. Kawiki pretended to sleep and kept near his cockeyed ghetto tour guide. They waited a few hours, until there was snoring heard, it was hard to tell in the dark who was asleep and who was killing time on the floor. They made their way out the door, and down the hall, towards the emergency stairs. "Bah, this one long hike, just to let you know. I not like the dark either."

Kamai said sarcastically, "What? I thought you was one MWH crip, scared of the dark, ha."

"Eh, you like me find this damn radio or what?"

"No worry. I got something for light when we get closer." They moved slowly, but methodically, through the stairwell reaching the subterranean parking level. Kawiki put his hand on the door to open into the garage. "Hey, let me see that battery."

"What? You no gonna waste um on the radio. That's for my smokes, bu. Not happening."

"Nah. I got some kerosene, toilet paper, and squeegee. Can light 'em up for a minute so we can see which car is which."

"Ah, smart, you Hawaiians. Just make sure I get that battery back, k?"

"No worries." Kamai soaked the squeegee and sparked the toilet paper with the wired battery.

They were off to the races, walking at a good pace looking at the back of each car. They wrapped around the first corner, and spotted a grey Toyota 4Runner with a military decal on the back license plate. "Das the one. See? Easy. Right there, should be in back seat."

Just as they got into the car, the kerosene started to run out and the light dimmed. Kamai rummaged in the back of the car, with no luck at first. Then he checked under the seat, feeling first a roach trap then a small rectangular shaped box. "Bingo! Got 'em." Kamai came up with the radio, and an emergency first aid kit stored under the seat.

"K, Pele, we out then. Gimme my battery." Kamai reached in his pocket and grabbed a nine volt, but not the one he was given earlier. It was a mirror image Duracell he had pulled from one of the apartments when they were scavenging.

"Eh, you no forget," as the gangster paused, Kamai got worried he was on to the battery switch. "Pele, I smoke Marlboro Reds. I no like you come back with one carton of Kools. Dem menthols gimme the shits." The two laughed, and made their way back upstairs undetected.

All the while this was going on, Kapu made his way to Mariners Ridge area all on back trails. He and Harold were on their way to the summit that looked over Waimanalo, known as the Dead Man's Catwalk. As it got dark, Kapu got a small fire going and they started talking about what they heard the last time they were in the woods. Harold asked. "What, you think that was one army or just hunters?" Kapu looked at him, as if he could not believe he was hiking with him again. "Harold, when do you ever see Chinese hunters? Plus, everyone knows it's not a good idea to hunt pig on the Pali Roads. They were something else."

"You tell your dad yet."

"Nah, he got enough going on. There were only ten of them. Anyway, who cares? They'll starve unless they go to the streets. They don't know what's what out here, anyway. They see one boar and shit themselves."

"If we see them again I'll worry, but let's just get to Nalo town, okay."

Back at the estate, Ha'a was viewing the best methods to get the remaining crops in Waimanalo distributed. He had made a promise to the MWH Crips that they would be taken care of first, but that was to be by ground transportation. They also had to decide how find a proper sailboat that could tow a makeshift barge alongside it, to get supplies to the rest of the of the island. He thought about the General, and knew the supplies they had rationed were going to the military bases first. There were thousands of military families still on island, and Ha'a could not imagine there was much being given out to the public at the base's gates. The security issue alone, and possibility of rioting, made him think the General was just paying him lip service. Praying his son would find good news on his return, he decided a trip to Kaneohe Bay to sequester a ship was there next move. Ha'a's family had boats they kept in the bay, but none could be used to move any large quantity of goods across rough waters. It was a near 227 miles circle island trip with good winds. The sail would take over 12 hours, normally. Add the weight of produce and a security team, the distribution could take up to five days to hit each of the four locations they wanted to bring food to. Not to mention there was the ground distribution to Yakimura's facility if was to uphold his agreement. That was a totally different animal that Ha'a had not forgotten. Since Ha'a was aiming to be back by the night to meet with Kapu, and see what he had found, a bike provided the best transportation. No groups, no security, just a quick visit to K-Bay to see what was left. It would take about an hour, each way, by bike plus time on the water checking boats and, possibly, a test sail.

Kapu had reached the summit, overlooking Waimanalo, that morning, the first view was that of Rabbit Island and Makapuu to the right. He could see all the way to Kailua's Mokuluas twin islands. There was a small east swell and light Kona winds coming from the Southwest. It was mid-morning and already hot from the lack of trade winds. They would have to hike a few ridges east of the lookout point. What they were after was not a scenic view, but a vantage point on what remained of the local farms. They, cautiously, made their way from ridge to ridge. Kapu was the first one to notice and state the fact that the winds were in their favor. "Harold, brah, if the trade winds kicked in right now, we would go flying into oblivion."

Harold replied, "No shit ah, but at least we would have one mean view on the way down." Kapu would have smacked the back of his head, if he didn't fear knocking him off the slim spine of a trail they had chosen. There were a few ways to get where they were going, but they chose the quickest and most out of site. The two had been on a lot of hikes, but had never needed to take this route. The two arrived at the midpoint, above Waimanalo town, directly on top of the Job Corp. building, which used to place people in need of work with would-be employers. They noticed that there was a group of a dozen men outside the building, and they were armed. It seemed odd that a random building had armed men outside. They noticed, as they scanned the ridgeline, that bordering Job Corp. were two large nurseries. The "Sunshine Farm" and "Promise Land Farms" bordered each side of the Job Corp, and they could only assume what they were seeing was staging for security to protect the crops at the farm across the street. When they looked further, they noticed there were men in fatigues and looked as if they were guarding checkpoints. The boys could not tell, exactly, what was going on, but those men were not Hawaiian homestead locals running the show.

As Ha'a made his way across the Pali, looking over Kaneohe Bay , he could see a distinct line of dark clouds following the coast from Northeast to Southwest nearing Kualoa. It was not a fast-moving front, but a large one that he assumed would be upon him at one point that day. He made it to the docks, in under two hours, with help from the H3 bypass road that leads to the Marine Corps base. He passed a few servicemen at the turn off, but neither him nor the guards gave it a second thought. K-Bay was a term used for both the base and the harbor. Many of the Windwards side elite came to play when the trade winds died. It is home to the world-famous K-Bay Sandbar, where you could dock your boat, have a beer, and get punched in the face all before noon. It was a spot where locals, and Marines had clashes on most weekends. MPs and local authorities really had little presence, and local playboys liked to smack up out-of-line jarheads from time to time, even sending their rented boats from the Marine corps base adrift on occasion. Beautiful, nonetheless, K-Bay and the Sand Bar made for an interesting scene in Ha'a's youth.

The family estate had donated to a maritime program that invited trouble youth aboard the "Kaikea" sailboat to learn their Hawaiian culture, and take them out of troubled home lives. He felt reconnecting youth to their heritage on the water was a good way to instill pride in their Polynesian culture, and steer them away from the island's pitfalls. The "Keikea," or "White Cap," was a 96-foot sailing yacht that could hold up to 20 passengers or, more importantly now, tow a lot of food around the island. He did not feel as bad taking this boat, as his family trust had paved the way for the program. He borrowed a dinghy from the dock, and made his way out to the mooring. The boat looked like it had just been refinished, looking white and shiny and new. He shimmied up the side ladder, and jumped aboard. To his surprise, a young boy holding a knife was there to meet him. "Who you, brah? You like one knife in your neck?"

Ha'a backed up slowly. "No thanks. I'm part owner in this boat. I'm a supporter of the sailing committee. My name is Ha'a Klein."

"You one of those check writing noseeums?"

Ha'a replied "What's a Noseeum?"

He put the knife down and took a step back. "You are write a check think you doing good but you no see 'em." The boy paused. "You know this boat no belong to you, brah. We run the ship now. You didn't get the memo? Your check bounced, uncle. Beat it."

"Who's we?" Just as Ha'a said this, ten 16–18 year old boys came up from under the cabin of the boat.

"We, as in us, brah," another youth said, as he clanked an aluminum baseball bat on a metallic cleat tie off. "You come up here thinking you one Hapa haole pirate, you got another thing coming."

Ha'a took two steps back. "Look boys, I'm not here to take the boat, but I think I could use your help."

"Why we gonna help you, 'cause you wrote da checks? We been running this boat for two years now. It's all we know, and now it's ours."

Ha'a thought for a second. "Wait, are all of you from the program?"

"Ya, why? You shoulda known we thugged out before you got on this ship, uncs. Brah, you the one with the foundation and all. We the new pirates of K-Bay."

"Well, you're Hawaiian Pirates then, huh?"

"Yup, we all got the bloodline."

"Well, your island needs you. They're going to starve."

"Not us, bu. We got enough hooks to keep us fed for a lifetime. We know where the fruit trees stay in Kahaluu, and can go where we like."

"That's the thing. The rest of the island don't know how to live off the land, too many soft people on this island, but that doesn't mean they should starve."

"So, what you need us for den?"

"We need to get the last harvest of crops to the people around the island, and I need a ship and a crew."

"What you offering? We get everything we need on this boat, brah."

"Not everything," interjected Ha'a. "I don't see one Wahine on this entire boat. That's the one downside to an all-boys program, huh, unless you boys like go Mahu at sea?"

"Ah, you. We get 'em, uncle. How you gonna help us with that, anyhow?" another boy shouted. "U Sounding kinda creepy, if ya ask me."

"No, dumb dumbs. I mean if you help the island get feed, all you boys will be heroes. You'll be a part of our new island history."

Pono, the first boy Ha'a encountered on the boat, chimed in, "I like that. Hawaiian heroes. Chicks like heroes but, wait, can we still be pirates?" The boys laughed.

Ha'a nodded his head, as if to say you can be whatever you want. Just as the boys started to warm up to the idea, the storm Ha'a had seen earlier looked as if it was making its way down the coast and was going to the reach the harbor soon. The winds picked up side shore out of the Northwest, and the rain line was visible. This made Ha'a think of his son. Ha'a hoped that Kapu and Harold were done hiking, and had returned to the valley, and were off the ridge for the day.

Kapu and Harold had lunch on the ridge while monitoring the style security below, clocking their movements and positioning. It seemed there was a guard switch on the 2-hour mark. One guard would check in and another would head back to the Job Corp. building for R&R. The only time Kapu and Harold noticed a lapse in security was when a guard would go to the bathroom. They used a signal system, taking a torch and placing it aside a large mirror, to sign over to the other guard he was going to use the bathroom. The boys thought that if they could lock the guards off duty in the Job Corp. building, then shut off the bathroom signal, all they would need to do is lock the one guard in the urinal and they could trick the final guard to come down from his post and subdue him. They made a few notes, and watched to see if any reinforcements showed up. It seemed these soldiers were autonomous, and had their routine down. No other guards or higher-ranking officials showed up. Kapu and Harold decided to head back the way they came around midafternoon. As they packed up, the first clouds started to burst over the Olomana Hillside. They could see there was a storm headed their way. The mountains always had clouds coming and going so it was not a cause for alarm, but they knew at any moment the mountainside's local weather could change. The light winds had them at ease as they started their hike back.

The boys were ten minutes into the hike, back on the narrow spine midway between their lookout point and the trailhead, when Kona winds out of the Northwest came rifling off the ridgeline behind them. Footing was not the best, and Harold was wearing a beat-up pair of skate shoes with no treads. Kapu was barefoot, opting for a more painful trek but better footing on the gravelly surface. They decided to tie a rope to each other's backpacks, so as to make a makeshift harness, in case someone was to fall. They were doing well, reaching the summit of the first spine. Then, the rain started to fall. Harold was caught off guard and suddenly slipped, tumbling forward, which pulled Kapu down with a forceful tug of the rope. Kapu slid on some loose rocks, which left him dangling over the side of a heavily vegetated cliff. He held one hand on a root, and the other on the rope, as Harold regained his balance.

"Shit, Kapu, hold on!" Harold walked forward which allowed Kapu to slide one hand up over the cliffside, still holding onto the rope. Then, he let go of the rope, to prop his other hand shimmying back up over the ledge.

Once settled, Kapu and Harold both sat and looked at each other. Kapu was pouring with sweat, and Harold looked like he saw a ghost. The rope had been tied correctly on Kapu's end, in a flying bowline, so it would tighten as it was pulled on. Harold's end was in a lasso, but the final loop was not cinched down. "Brah, where you learn to tie knots? If pulled any harder, it would have been 'Aloha, sayonara, dats all folks!'"

"Sorry, Kapu. Sorry, brah."

"Brah, we're done with this ridge. That storm is going to get heavy. We need to circle back, quick, and find some shelter near Olomana." The boys returned to the long route, planning on making their way back across the Pali, making their way towards the Norfolk Trail. It would add hours to their return, but they would hike inside the canopy of the tree line. As they neared the Pali they started to lose daylight. Kapu knew the remainder of the hike by heart, and felt he could continue with no light.

As the daylight slipped away, they were getting tired. Kapu and Harold were getting hungry as their ration packs were holding next to nothing. Harold started to complain, and wanted to stop. Kapu didn't want to break their pace, Harold would hum songs to keep his mind from giving out on him, but Kapu was hearing something besides his humming. "Brah, what is that?"

"Just the last song I heard on the radio, before there was no more radio."

"Not you. Shhh, I hear 'em. Think it's the Chinese, again?"

"Let's get off the path, now. Follow me." Both boys jumped into the bush line, and lay in wait to see what was coming their way. There were fifty Chinese military men walking in cadence. The boys didn't move. A group of twenty soldiers stopped approximately ten feet from Kapu and Harold, at a downhill switchback that had a clearance on the side. They broke down their gear and started to set up camp. They built a fire and put down their weapons. The boys just stared at each other. They heard a radio come on, intermittently, and were baffled that the Chinese's equipment was still working. The boys were thinking they must have gotten here after the attack. The Chinese troops had guns, lighters, radios, pop-up tents, flashlights, and other electronic gear all in working order.

As the men fell asleep, the boys started to quietly converse. "Kapu, let's bail. We can't sit here all night," whispered Harold.

"Brah, don't be one panty. We can take some gear, and hide the rest."

Harold responded in a hushed but anxious tone. "Kapu, you're nuts!"

He went on, "You want to leave them armed? Leaving fifty armed men headed to the Pali? Not good, they are headed towards our home." Harold agreed. The boys, first, took the platoon's weapons and moved them a good distance to an old cave were Kailua high school kids smoked weed and drank beers after a hike through Maunawili. Right off the path the cave lay hidden by the overgrown forest. Within one hour they had moved all the gear with the exception of two QBZ-95 Chinese assault rifles, a set of night goggles, and some rations. There was a walkie-talkie left that Harold wanted to take. Kapu grabbed it, and took the battery out.

"Later, when out of earshot," he told Harold.

"What if their satellites work? They might triangulate us, using GPS, right to our house."

"You're right, bud. So, why keep the battery?"

Kapu replied, "It looks like one of those police radio batteries, a generic Chinese version. If we find a scanner, maybe we find out what's going on elsewhere. Also, that screen had a dozen blips on it. Might be those other giants we seen the other day, da big night marcher Chinamen Sole looking ones."

Kapu and Harold ate the stolen rations, and returned to a high pace. They tempted fate once again and now that they had their gear they didn't need to worry about another hostile run in. They were close to the back entrance of the estate from the smell of plumeria trees. Kapu stumbled, as a Kukui nut hit his leg. He looked around, and with no sign of the tree. Then Harold flinched, as one whizzed by his head.

Ha'a appeared from behind a large Ironwood tree. "Boys, you guys not the best at staying out of sight. I heard you in the brush off the road, snuck behind you, and been listening to you two knuckleheads bullshit for the last hour."

"So, you hear this dumb dumb humming too then?" Kapu proceeded to tell his dad the whole story, from the Job Corp. building and the two farms being guarded to running into the Chinese on the hike back, about the hidden guns, supplies, and ammo. He pulled the radio from his bag, and relayed the issue with keeping the battery in it. Kapu's mother, who had overheard the tail end of the conversation as she gardened on the Perimeter of the estate, flashed a look of concern in Ha'a's direction. Kapu showed his father the gear, and explained the location of the other equipment. Ha'a and the two boys entered the backdoor, and Kapu dropped the battery on the kitchen counter next two the night vision goggles. "Dad, these guys are for real. We thought there was only a few of them but, this time, we saw at least fifty men."

"What do you mean this time?"

"Well, I saw a few similarly dressed men when we hiked the Pali road, from the first trip to town, but these guys are different, Dad. They're huge, muscles on top of muscles."

Ha'a sternly replied "Why didn't you tell me this at the time, Kapu."

"You seemed like you had enough to worry about, and there were so few of them. I figured the valley would have given them enough to deal with."

Ha'a again spoke, "Everything is a threat these days. If we have an unknown enemy in our valley, we are in jeopardy."

Kapu shamefully replied, "I was wrong to not tell you, but at least we know which way they were heading now and we know they are not armed."

"So, what would you do now, Kapu? You left men in the woods with no food or supplies, hid their equipment, and in hope of what? That they starve out there?"

"What do you think we should do, Dad?"

"Well, leaving them to starve is not an option."

"We could bring them to the base and they would be treated as POWs."

"How we going to do that?"

"Good question. Well, we have their gear location, radios, and the night vision gives us an element of surprise."

"We might be able to use them to load the ship, Dad. More hands make light work."

"Good idea, but you think it's ethical, Kapu?"

"I'm pretty sure they would shoot us if they had a chance, Dad, so not really worried about making them do some work for the island's good."

"That's reasonable, but the logistics are too hard. So, we go tonight. Take a nap boys, then go get your uncles and bring them here. We'll leave at 6pm, hike to the gear, and then look for the Chinese convoy by turning on the radio. They might even come for us. Harold, you think you can translate radio comms?"

"Maybe. I'm a little rusty, but I can get the jist if it is Mandarin or Cantonese."

"We need food for two days. We'll take the roads back to the Base to drop them the Chinese troops off, and then head to K-Bay to sail the boat with the gear to Waimanalo."

"What about the guards at the farms? I think they're military, Dad."

Ha'a responded "Could be, but better we confirm before we start a civil war. We're not organized enough to deal with the General and what's left of the military. I'll see if I can get something out of him when we go by the base."

"Dad, Harold's uncle speaks Mandarin, too. You like see if he wants to help?"

"If he wants to help translate, that would be great. Harold is a bit flakey, better not to depend on him only. Take the bike and go see if he wants to tag along. Bring some bread fruit and lilikoi from the yard for their family."

Harold scurried off. He wanted to organize first, before taking a nap. He was starting to feel the effects of the overnight hike.

Chapter 4
Momentum

Kapu awoke to his father speaking with the neighborhood uncles. They were surprised at what Ha'a was asking of them, but they knew if these Chinese soldiers were this close to their homes, it was a threat they had to neutralize for the safety of their families.

"Kapu, come over here." Kapu came running over, ready for action. "I need you to hang back. All of us will be gone, and we need you and Harold to stay back and here to watch the estate and check on all the aunties while we're gone. It might be more than two days before we return."

"But, Dad, I know where the gear is."

"Kapu, you think you're the only one who has ever cut school and hung out at Maunawili Falls? I know where the smoke out cave stay, boy. It's five minutes from the waterfall."

Kapu opened his eyes wide and grinned, as if to say, "Crap, the gig is up."

He gave a weapon to each of the men, and they checked their packs once more. Kapu held his Ruger in one hand as to be a part of this Hawaiian militia, even though he would not be on the frontline. The men made light work out of the hike. Having hunted pig on the trails for decades, even the oldest kept pace. They made it to the area by 7:30 pm, and found the cave in the twilight of the summer sky that had been fading quickly into the tree line. Ha'a started to distribute the goggles. Just as they were putting their gear back on, they heard footsteps. Ha'a signaled everyone to crouch down behind the bushes at the edge of the cave, making the shush sign to his lips. It was the Chinese platoon, looking as if they were searching.

Ha'a thought, *How could they be so lucky?*

They were within thirty feet of the cave. He then heard a beep go off behind him, with a light coming from one of the stolen packs. There was a transmitter on, the battery of a second radio stuffed in one of the packs, sounding as if the battery was about to die. Just as he grabbed it, a Chinese soldier pushed through the bushes holding a GPS in his hand. He jumped back as at the sight of Ha'a's men with guns drawn on him. All the men stood up, and Harold's uncle shouted, "Tíngzhǐ," or, "Stop," in Mandarin.

Ha'a fired a warning shot at a tree. Everyone halted, with the exception of the one carrying the beacon who rolled down the hill next to the cave. One of Ha'a's men fired a shot, but missed, as he vanished into the thick canopy of the valley.

"Don't chase him. He doesn't have a firearm. He won't have much luck out here, and we need to get the other men to the base by morning." They zip-tied each man's hands behind their backs, and daisy chained them together with rope. Ha'a felt uneasy with being on this side of the fence, leading capture, but knew it was the only choice presented to them. If the General got to them first, they would have been shot on site. Ha'a's men and their Chinese prisoners made a slow crawl hike out of Maunawili, and hit Kamehameha Highway at first light. The men were tired as they connected to the H3 front gate entrance to the base. A US Marine patrol saw them a mile out from the base, and signaled with white flags that they were coming back to the base and that there was no threat. The General met them at the gate with a smile on his face and a security detail. "You come bearing gifts, Ha'a! What's the occasion?"

"My boy spotted them not too far from our land. There might be more. One got away."

"Yeah, we had a feeling there were a few battalions of these slanty-eyed savages floating around."

"Eh, General, remember I'm part Japanese."

"Don't you guys hate these bugs as much as we do?"

"Getting pretty specific," quipped Ha'a.

"Feel free to call me a John Wayne-looking fuckin' haole, and we'll call it even. Thin skinned for a mixed plate, you are, Ha'a."

"Point taken, General. We're past the niceties, at this point. I have some business to discuss."

While the prisoners were filtered into a line and processed by the MPs, the two discussed various issues with the Kapu systems location. The crew ate and rested in a nearby DC7 airplane hanger, to avoid the midday sun. Ha'a sipped some ice tea, and the general on his second cup of coffee.

The General started the conversation, "Ice, I bet you been missing that creature comfort."

Ha'a replied, "If it means living on a military base I can do without for the time being."

Dr. Hind broke up the banter and relayed his security concerns with the Kapu System to Ha'a.

"It's going to be hysteria soon in the streets. What's your call? Is Ulupau Crater going to be the system's new home?"

Ha'a quickly replied, "I'm not sold on that idea just yet, Doctor. No offense, General, but the system was never meant to be a government asset or a militarized one either."

The General laughed. "There is not much to think about, Ha'a. If your son didn't stumble on to these men, you might have lost the system entirely. What if there is boats of Chinese Military in route still. You're leaving too much up to chance, and subjecting your island to becoming a fully failed state. You know what the military does with failed states."

Ha'a replied, "We have options, General. We always do."

The general replied "Sure, sure, but some are better than others."

"Are you still doing the ration distributions?"

"Well, the gates have been flooded with rioters during the distribution days. There is a bit of unrest between the different groups out here. I was hoping we could get them more organized, and I think you could play a role in this, Ha'a. The people listen to you. Haole, Hawaiian, Filipino, they see you as mixed bagged with all the answers. Coming from me it just looks like more rhetoric from the military."

Ha'a smiled. "I am glad you think Hawaii still holds my ideals valid but I can't just say everything is alright when it's not, we have our course plotted right now and we are going to stick with it, I hope you can respect that."

"Everything in life is good until it's not, Haa, right now this, well we're still good."

"Thank you for taking in these POWs, I expect them to be treated under normal rules of war."

"Yup. Ha'a, we are still running a tight ship over here. No new rules. That goes for everyone."

Ha'a understood what he meant and the men shook hands and parted ways.

As Ha'a started to walk off he turned back, "Eh general, have you ever heard of the term 'Makahiki'?"

The General nodded. "Those cultural festivals for the kids?"

Ha'a replied, "Back in the day, the king would enforce a time of peace. No war. No fighting. Games would be played, and sport was used to redirect any tension between clans. The health of the island is in need of a Makahiki. It was set up to insure crops would grow uninterrupted and to praise a higher power in Lono for a good harvest."

The general laughed. "Cute, how did that work out for you guys?"

"You know, pretty good until the GIs showed up." He paused. "What do you say we plan our own Makahiki, General?"

The General smiled, "Well, I am sure the boys on base would not mind kicking a bit of ass on the field. It's been slow since the invasion, a lot of moving rice bags around, not enough rounds fired for my boys. We'll stay in touch. Let's get something going on our current food situation first."

"I am pretty sure that's the reason we need a Makahiki, General. See you soon."

The men walked out of the base and circled back the long way to throw the guards off scent as they were heading to K-Bay. The less the military knew the better, Ha'a had decided. If he was about to take down some of the General's men at the farms, it was better not to flaunt it, as they still had a mission in front of the them. The General let the men keep their found equipment, as it did not provide much of a threat to his four thousand Marines on base.

The crew made it to the docks by noontime, and the boys were there on the docks. They had with them the 40 emptied and cleaned plastic fuel drums stored on a floating dock. "Yo, Uncle Scrooge!" Ha'a looked confused. "Ya you, Mista Money Bags! Look what the K-Bay pirates did for you!"

Still looking confused, Ha'a said, "Thanks, but what did you do?"

"How you gonna get two tons of veggies onto this ship? We need to float dat boat, bu."

"Right on, so what if we fill the containers on the floating dock and pull it behind us?"

"Das right. We got tie-downs to secure them to make one airtight barge."

"Good work. We thought we were going to be sitting knee deep in produce on this ride."

"Still can be uncs. Ten guys can stay with the barge, the rest on the boat. We stay on the boat, though. Your crew get the barge duty. We make 'em, you float 'em."

"Right on. Anybody get seasick, you just make sure you no ruin the crops, k? Keep the lids on dem drums until we get moving then air 'em out so they don't spoil." The boys laughed as the uncles started to push off their dinghies.

"Eh, we gonna bring the boat in close as we can? The motor no work."

"Pono will swim the line to the barge and tie 'em. Where we docking this thing, anyway?"

"Makai Pier. We'll come in on the right side of Rabbit Island and dock behind the University of Hawaii building, at the end, so no one sees the boat from the road."

The weather was a mirror image of the day before, but with no storms on the horizon. Puffy white clouds spanned from the tip of the Koolau mountain range all the way as far as the eye could see.

When the boys got the boat close enough to tie off the line to the barge, Ha'a started thinking. "Eh, boys, we got a problem. We gonna cross K-Bay."

"Ya, no shit, Scrooge. So?"

"Well, if the Marines on base see us on the boat, we might as well tell them our plans. We need to hide in hule of the boat until we get past Mokumanu Island."

"K, wait. You got something with the Marines? I no like having a whole base on our ass, Uncs."

"Pono, just make the boys put out fishing poles and hand lines. They will think you're just trolling for Ono."

"K, we was gonna do that anyway. Brah, you pretty haole, Uncs. Ah, nah, just kidding, but garns portagee this other ones." One of Ha'a's cousins was caught trying to untie the mooring incorrectly, and started to scratch his head. "Nevermind, you. Let us do our trip. Relax."

Kapu woke up from a midday nap, and noticed how the weather had cleared behind the house. He went out to the yard and saw his mom. "Mom, how you holding up?"

"I'm fine, Kapu. We're better off than a lot of others right now. Meat's a bit scarce, but things could be worse. The Ulu tree and the Jabong's."

"How you like me get one pig, Mom? I got caught up last, it will last the whole week."

"Is it that easy, Kapu?"

"Well, if I go check the feeders at dark, chances are there will be a sow eating strawberry guava or the grain feeder I set up."

"Okay but don't go alone, too much trouble these days."

"K, Mom. I'll go grab Harold."

"I said don't go alone, not go with Harold. That's not going to do you any good."

"He can carry what I kill, Mom."

She rolled her eyes, and Kapu was on his way. The boys headed down the valley towards Manoa Falls, stopping midway between their estate and the state park at a feed station the family had set a few weeks back. There had not been anyone in the tree stand since they set the feeder up. It was the first time anyone had been there since the incident. The boys were in full Camo with mosquito nets around their faces as the dusk sky was filling up with bugs in the valley. They hiked up the tree stand and butted up against the tree both looking opposite directions. The piglets came and went with no sow, which was strange to them. Right at last light, a good size sow came into their sites. Kapu drew his bow, and the sow dropped from a broadside shot to the heart. As they came off the stand, they saw the piglets scurry off which made Kapu a bit dizzy from the thought of taking out their mother. He fell back against the tree and had a vision of his mother in distress. Harold was put on field dressing duty. "Harold, if you hit the Tarsal gland, again, God help me I will smack your head. The family needs meat. We need to say one Pule for the sow. Pule ho'omaika'i."

Harold chimed in with a quick prayer, "Please, Lord, no piss tasting meat, those days be over please."

Harold took a pair of heavy duty shears and a razor sharp knife from his bag. He first made an incision near the Pelvis and then took the shears and cut through the Pelvic bone. Kapu hung the sow so that its hind legs dangled towards the ground. Harold made an incision near the rib cage and cut down towards the sow's anus, careful not to cut the Tarsal gland which was known to taint the meat when it's opened. The intestines fell to the ground, they took a jug of water and flushed its body cavity, they took a look for tumors and polyps in the animal as a sign of sickness before they quartered the animal. Kapu helped Harold flip the boar right side up to skin the hide. He then removed the ribs and loins. They knew they had to cool the meat so it would not spoil and with the lack of refrigeration their next best option was the cold waters of the falls. First they buried the remains, then hiked a few hundred yards to dip the meat in the cool stream coming down from the falls. They wrapped all they were taking in two small tarps, split the load between them, and started to hike back.

The hike back took a little longer, and it was 8:30pm when they arrived at the back gate of the estate. It was oddly quiet. Even with the power gone, there should have been some chatter and candle light coming from the main house. They walked back around towards the Kapu research facility, figuring Doctor Lightfoot would be reading by candlelight or still up being busy. When they passed the stables, they noticed the horses were not in their pen. They decided to investigate, but first needed to put the meat somewhere for storage. The only place high enough, where the livestock would not eat the meat, was the second story of the barn. They hogtied each end of the tarps to one another, and hung them from the rafters. Harold was rolling up the remaining rope, and saw some movement outside the barn window. There was a glow of moonlight that showed a dozen figures. He signaled to Kapu to be quiet, and they crouched near the window on either end looking down on the research center where the men entered the front door. They were put back as they were not sure who it could be. Were they friends of his father, looters that made their way up the Pali, or did the Chinese somehow track them back to the house?

Kapu and Harold were frozen in fear wondering what was done with Kapu's mom, Dr. Lightfoot, the remaining workers, and any family that had been at the home.

Kapu said in a light voice, "We can't go down there guns blazing. There could be more men inside. We don't know if they have weapons."

Harold nodded with a look of shock on his face. "Let's just wait and see. We can track their movements."

They watched as the men moved pieces of the Kapu system onto a flatbed that had been mounted to horses. The men wore blue uniforms. That ruled them out as being the Chinese.

Kapu decided they were going to need to think quick, as they looked like they were going to roll out at any moment. "Harold, go check the guest house, and I will go to the main house to see if anyone is being held there. We'll meet back behind the research building, once they leave, to see if anyone's inside. If it's empty, we follow them."

They split up and quickly searched the houses. Harold moved through the guest house and saw no one. Kapu went into the kitchen and grabbed the Chinese radio battery off the counter, which he had left there earlier the day prior. He started up his stairs when someone grabbed his pack from behind and put their hand over his mouth. "It's Kamai. Shut up, k? Low voice."

He let go. "Kamai, what you doing here? Dad said you was in Kalihi until they got a delivery of food."

"Ya, well things changed. I found one emergency radio with a live battery, been listening on and off when I was hoofing it back here. It ain't good, but there's some people on Kauai still holding on. Nothing from the mainland. Just one signal from a NOAA emergency station that some people on Kauai are using their signal."

"So, what we do now? Who are these people stealing from us, and where is my mom?"

"They took her and the doctor. They are some sort of special ops, maybe SEALs, not too sure. They know what they're doing, though. I got here just as I seen them cart off your mom and Dr. Lightfoot. Whatever that thing your Dad's been working on, they go it now."

"Brah, we can take 'em, right?"

"No chance, kid. Where's your sidekick, anyway?"

"Oh shit, Harold! He's waiting behind the research building near the Taro patch."

"Let's go, nephew. No need any more headaches."

They took off, low walking around corners, trying to spot Harold. When they saw him, he was walking alongside the cart with the broken apart Kapu system, with two guards on either side of him and his hands above his head. Kapu and Kamai moved along the tree line, and Kapu made a small bird call of a Mina to let Harold know he was watching. Harold kept his pace as the guards asked, "What's that noise, kid?"

"It's just the Myna bird in the valley."

"Must be an annoying place to sleep, huh?"

"Ya, I guess."

"Do you get used to it?"

"Ya, I don't mind."

The men thought they had captured Ha'a's son. "Your name's Kapu, huh? They named this thing after you?"

Harold responded, "It means sacred, like no touch." As he said this, he quickly grabbed a radio off the SEAL's belt and threw it into the bushes in the direction of where he heard Kapu make the bird call. The guard slapped him upside his head and pointed the gun at him.

"Eh, shit stain, you're not all that valuable to us now we got your namesake over here, so keep inline."

"Boss, gonna go look for the radio."

"Bag it, no battery. I've got a radio to talk to the command center. We're done with intercoms this mission. Back to the UCC."

Another guard shouted, "We still transferring the payload at UCC, Team Leader?"

"Correct. Back the way we came, boys." The heavily geared convoy headed left, down the old Pali Road.

Kamai tapped Kapu. "They are SEALs. UCC is the United Combat Command. It's up in Aiea Heights, at Camp Smith. They're bringing everything back there." As Kamai said this, both Kapu's mother and Dr. Lightfoot came into sight in a silhouetted vision under the moonlight. "They're alive!" Kapu's eyes started to well up.

"Why you crying, boy? Nothing you could have done. Your dad's off saving the island. He could not stop this, either."

"What now?" Kapu asked.

"You see why we need Yakimura's help? Your father bit off more than he can chew, playing savior."

Kapu yelped, "We could have done something."

Kamai replied, "You could have gotten shot. We need to organize, or we are yesterday's news. The military's still running the show. Gotta get back to Kalihi, or your father's gonna have another problem on his hands." Kapu looked up at the night sky.

"Well, we do what hunters do. We hunt, lay trap, and wait."

Kamai nodded. "Right, right. So, how we gonna trap a bunch of highly trained squids?"

"You mean SEALs?"

"Ah, whatevas." Kapu took a stick, swinging it on the ground. They heard a clunk.

Kapu followed the sound, picking up the radio Harold had thrown, and looked at Kamai. "Why fight a battle someone else can fight for you?"

"Huh?" Kamai shook his head like the kid had lost it. "You see this radio? Well, it has GPS on it. We got a battery. We know where they're going. All we need to do is get them to a location where there is only one exit, and let the Chinese soldiers do the rest."

Kapu placed the battery into the Chinese radio, and put the other radio in his pack. A screen popped up and showed three blips; two red, one green and one with an X through it. He thought that the X was for the group that his dad had brought to K-Bay, as it was positioned right on the base.

They must have trackers in their uniforms, he thought. "Uncle, you see this, there are two groups just three miles from us. We need to draw them in, near Halawa Prison."

"Kapu, you crazy. I heard all the prisoners were let out. Why you want to go near there?"

"Uncle, the last place freed prisoners gonna be is at the prison."

"True, but then what?"

"It's right near the UCC. If we can get them to cross through Halawa Valley, we can lead the Chinese there to create a surprise fire fight. We grab Mom, the doctor, and pull the system into the prison for safety in the confusion. Yakimura's men can come get it for us, if we hide it off the bypass road."

Kamai was baffled. "Just us? We gonna do that?"

"Well, there aren't too many options. They call it a false flag. I read about it for paper I wrote on the Gulf of Tonkin. The US faked an attack on their own ships then fired torpedoes at Vietnamese ships on the pretense they were first attacked. We can bait them the same way the US has been baiting the world for years. Give them a bit of their own medicine."

"And how you do that, Kapu?"

"We fire one shot at the Kapu system to get them to fall back, and throw a flair at the Chinese to blind their night vision, the SEALs will engage. The shot will get them to go for cover, and the flair will give them direction to pick up the fight. They won't have time to figure it was us. Maybe after the dust settles, but not while it's happening. We throw grenade once the Chinese are in position so they fight at a distance and don't go after the system. We light up the battlefield and, behind in the darkness away from the fight, we pull the system away."

Kamai was baffled. "Where you getting grenades from?"

"Well not a real grenade, we take a shotgun shell and duct tape it vertically so when it lands the nail will trigger the shells. I have a box of shells and nails I use as flash bangs when I dive, I take the buck shot out normally just so I can scare a shark going after my fish. We might have ten minutes to get out of there, so we should set up some markers for them to follow that keeps them off our scent. We need to move ahead of them as soon as they engage, and lay some tracks that head onto the service roads that go to H3 Highway, so they back track while we move forward towards Kalihi. You go back to MWH and see if they will help. You can assure them the food is coming, and explain what is going on."

Kamai grabbed his head in hand. "They might not be too happy I bailed."

"Either way, they're not happy with you. Better to have a reason. I'm sure they would not want the military coming their way, and will take a chance to keep them out of their area."

"K. You smart Kapu, I trust you. Kam schools was not bad for that brain of yours."

"Ha, not like I was going to West Point, Uncle, but better to know your history then get exploited by old mistakes."

"Roger dat, Kapu. The Reinstated Hawaiian Nation needs a guy like you. You got mana and brains."

Kapu looked back at a serious-faced Kamai. "Uncle, we all know the Joint Resolution of 1898 was unconstitutional. They never made a treaty with a peaceful Hawaiian nation. It went against the US constitution, taking a peaceful nation and annexing under a warring nation."

"Boy, I neva knew that why we need you."

"Uncle, I am all for a new Hawaii, but people are people. I got blood from many nations in me. We need to unite, no matter the bloodline, but that does not mean it needs to be under a US flag again."

They walked off in separate ways, deciding to meet at the prison the next morning with whatever they could come across. Kapu turned the radio off as he saw two blips move slightly in their direction besides.

Ha'a and his crew had sailed after midnight under a full moon. They set a rope tied to a piece of driftwood knotted every six feet. This was to calculate their speed and course, an hourglass kept on board for decoration was used to calculate the Dead Reckoning. A basic navigational tool the boys used in their instructors sailing classes. It could be used to time future food runs to each part of the island and plot accurate courses around island and possibly interisland once Oahu was back on track.

The crew made it to the pier before first light, taking their time through the shallow reefs of Waimanalo. They tied off as planned and dropped the sail to avoid attention in the bay. The crew made their way through the Hawaii homestead neighborhoods with little fanfare. They split up to avoid being seen as a group, having made plans to meet behind the Job Corps building at noon. There was vegetation all over the back roads, and they did not need to look far for cover. They set up two lookouts, one at the farm gates and one at the Job Corps building. They waited and timed the men's shifts. The men would play basketball and ping pong in the hall when not holding their post. There was no consistency, but a mirror was used to shine light on a black target on the wall to indicate when it was time to switch guards. They figured from watching the men that they were not military but must have training. Everyone looked either Hawaiian mix or Japanese mix, but not a haole jarhead amongst them. All carried generation four glock 9mm handguns on their hips. Two guards at the farm entrance had AR-15 assault rifles, and one had a dog. Their shirts were army green, with a small skull which had a snake's head running through its eyes. Army green fatigues with patches were worn by all but one.

They had a task in front of them, as one guard wouldn't leave the post until relieved. The other would have to get down from a narrow watchtower built for one person, and he would make his way not waiting for the replacement. When it was around 10:30 pm, things got quiet in the gym of the Job Corps. The men, quietly, went to the doors and tied two different loop knots around the handles so as to stop them from turning. It would hold only temporarily, but would give them time if the sleeping guards awoke. They sent the boys over to the guard in the watchtower to attempt to distract the guard. They had picked some kukui nuts to throw at the guard as he came down the ladder. The second guard was seen signaling the other that he was headed to the john. He used a candle and mirror to ping light across the farm.

The boys made a nene goose call to start harassing the guards. The guard took two hits in the back before he spotted the boys below. "What, you punks go back to the homestead, you like get shot you fakas."

They taunted him more, and he signaled to the other guard who was in the bathroom. "You boys in deep shit when I get down there."

They yelled, "Ya, whatever monkey. Come down from the tree and catch us." When he hit the ground, he drew his pistol and, as he did, Ha'a came from behind him with his gun drawn and told him to freeze. The other men locked the Port-a-john with zip ties by the time Ha'a arrived. "So, where are the keys to the gates?"

"No chance, brah."

"What if I tip this shitter over? I bet you tell me then."

"Eh, don't tell 'em. Don't do it." The boys started to rock the Port-a-john. "Brah, I getting shit on my shoes. Stop, for real." They kept at it, almost tipping it over. The guard started to gag. "Fuck, the keys are in the tower, on the binos. Let me out of here, you freaking donkeys." They let him out, and the other guard couldn't help but laugh as they zip tied his hands. "How's you, one SWAT officer. You sissy, smell shit and you give up."

Kapu stopped and turned to the other guard. "You guys SSD?"

"Yup, this guy pretty sad though."

He shook his head. "Brah, what you like do with the crops? That's how we been surviving on this side. We been giving out to the people every Monday."

"We thought you were military."

"Well, I'm ex-military, Delta Force, but this guy, he one dog handler, don't think ever drew his weapon."

Ha'a asked, "You local?"

"Ya, Sanoa, our squad leader, was born Tonga, but went school at St. Louis for football. Where you got the rest of us?"

"In the job corp."

"You sure you like steal, these guys no play."

"Ha'a, we are second guessing as we speak, brah. Can you call them down so we can talk? We got a boat at the pier ready to distribute food to the island."

Pomi, the boy's leader, jumped in on the conversation, "Also get one teched out fish pond and Kalo patch, we like help feed everybody." The guard, looking confused, turned to Ha'a.

"Huh?"

"Aquaponics, built it so the fish feed the taro fields and it's sustainable."

The guard laughed. "Brah, Nalo got hundreds of those. All the fish died when the power went."

Ha'a smiled. "We got it covered. We're just trying to prevent chaos until we can get it moved to a secure location with another power source."

"Tough sell, but hey you made me laugh with shitbox over here. You can't be all bad."

They opened the door with guns at their side to a surprised Sanoa and his team standing in the dark. "Sanoa, this guy, he got to speak to you about some things." They came outside, and Ha'a explained more of his plan to feed the island.

Sanoa knew who Ha'a was from his political support of SHOPO, their police union. "Bradda, you caught us sleeping. Good thing, 'cause we may have lit you up and your plan never have chance. What you need from us?"

Ha'a raised his head and talked directly to Sanoa. "Manpower and security is a must."

Sanoa replied, "You didn't do so bad with your team of hood rats but, ya, twelve thick SWAT guys tend to send a message while cruising in high visibility areas." He continued, "Right on. We will organize your path and leave some men to secure what remains in Waimanalo. They got to re-till the land soon, so be nothing to steal once we harvest this last crop. My men will go on the ship around island, could use three guys for the center island route to MWH."

"What the fuck you like go MWH for? You know how many those tap fucks we sent to Halawa? We better gear up and get out of uniform if that's where we are going."

"We cut a deal for safe passage. We should be fine."

"There ain't nothing safe or fine with the MWH."

Back in the valley, Hanalei and Dr. Lightfoot were getting heavy footed from the long walk. The military men were used to this type of strenuous hiking, and made fun of the doctor for his whining. "I see why the other doctor doesn't like you. You complain a lot."

"Most of my days are spent in the lab, or in a controlled field, not walking long distances. What other doctor are you talking about?"

"Dr. Hind, your partner. Or should say your ex-partner? He never complained when we hiked up to the crater."

"So, is that where the system's being brought?"

"Enough small talk, Doc. Keep your eyes forward, and your legs moving."

Kapu made some headway, and could see their torches from a distance. He kept in step with the group, but at a distance, until they were closer to the prison. He had turned on the radio, on and off, during the last two hours of his hike. The only time he would have a chance to guide them towards the prison, off their current path, would be at Kea'iwa Heiau Park. The radio remained on, from this point, which would give away their position to the other radio receivers. Kea'iwa was a burial ground, or Heiau from the ancient Hawaiian times. He felt uneasy about starting a battle there, but knew there was no other way but to light a fire north of their convoy to push them east into the gunfight, forcing them to pass near the prison on their way to Camp Smith. It was nearing 2 AM when he finally passed them, near the tail end of the park.

The ground was damp heading into morning. He was in a great position for stalking the group, but not for creating a diversion fire. Kapu carried with him a box of waterproof matches, but didn't have time to make a fire. He opened up five of his shells from his Ruger .22mm and poured the gunpowder into a large dry tea leaf he pulled from the Heiau. It was wrapped around a rock and he knew this was sacred, but there was no dry kindle in this rainforest-esque area of the valley.

He squeezed some oil from a Kukui nut. He poured another shell down the length of the dried tea leaf as a makeshift detonator. This would give him time to get away from the explosion. He took the oil and poured it over half a dozen more leaves from the Heiau and placed it at the bottom of a rotten banana tree. He knew the dead tree would create a quick burn. The ground he gained past the team had quickly vanished as he saw their torches nearing and heard murmurs of the men. Striking three matches, simultaneously, he lit the gunpowder at the edge of the leaf. He felt uneasy lighting the sacred tea leaves but, with no time to further contemplate, he sprinted back around then, in an effort to flank them, following them from the back of the convoy once again. The SEAL team's leader was the first to see ambers flying in the air, and his reaction was of confusion, not of fear. "What the hell caused a fire out here? The ground is sopping wet. We're in the middle of a freaking rain forest," he said, as he looked at Hanalei.

Hanalei suspected her son was in the area and quickly responded, "Sometimes, hunters don't fully put out their fires when they're stalking boar in this valley. It can smolder and ignite randomly. It wouldn't be the first time."

The SEAL shouted back in frustration, "Frick! Well, that adds an hour. Let's go, boys, but shoot south and then hook back just before Halawa. We'll come up right on the helicopter pad, and enter through the back gate. If you see any hunters, shoot on sight." Kapu was out of earshot, but knew enough to stay clear until they were engaged by the Chinese. Kamai had made it back to MWH, and was not welcomed warmly. He was never shy about rallying people towards a cause but, in this case, the fact that the military was trying to make a run for the control of the island made a good argument for MWH to get involved. The gang leader wanted to know what he was getting his men into before making any commitment.

Kamai had only one objective, and that was to get the system into the prison. "My nephew, he's got one tracking device on his radio. The Chinese are going to follow him straight to the edge of the prison grounds. When the two groups meet up, and I'll light one flare on the Chinese and the SEALs guarantee going to shoot first."

"Oh, yeah? Great plan, sounds like one deathtrap. These giant Chinese soldiers really make me want to help you. Would you put your men up to something like this?"

"My crew went to Waimanalo to take on another group, just so they could feed your people. If they were here, they wouldn't even hesitate."

"Ah. frick! We stay bored anyway. I guess we go." The men started to arm up, grab rations and water for the hike, and prepare for the possibility that they might be held up at the prison for a few days. One of the men threw his hands up in the air and yelled, "Brah! Why the fuck am I going back to Halawa? I made my parole already. Shitty dis gang."

The SEAL team had been disheartened by the setback, wanting to get back to showers and meals. They were off rotation and at home when they got called in, when the fighting broke out. Being that SEALs are used to the shit, this type of mission was nothing more than cutting into their downtime. One of the younger SEALs shouted, "This isn't even comparable to a soft day in Hajiland, can't believe I'm babysitting when I was supposed to be living the good life."

As the men approached, Kapu neared and, to his plan, so did the Chinese. He knew that the radio should not be on at all times, as they could pinpoint the signal. He would turn it on, then off, every five to ten minutes. Once the Chinese were in view, he did not turn it on again. He sat back and noticed they were searching in a grid pattern due to his intermittent signaling. They were similar to the group he and Harold encountered off the Pali. They had heavy gear with a 50 Caliber on one of their men's backpacks. Kapu switched the radios to see if he could sniff out any info from the SEAL team command center, to find out if they were in the vicinity yet. "UCC, come in. This is DEVGRU 1."

"This is UCC Smith. What's your location, DEVGRU?"

"We are due south of the Helipad, two clicks."

Kapu knew from this they were five minutes apart. He swapped the batteries, and started a medium pace towards the SEALs to mimic the march of another squadron. When he hit the SEALs, he laid low in the bush and let them approach. When they were within twenty yards, a noise emanated from his radio. He could only assume it was the homing beacon signal the Chinese must have enabled. A twig broke behind him. Thinking it was the Chinese, he swung with his Ruger pointed at the direction of the noise. It was a young boar, eating guava from the tree line. "Shit," he murmured. Then, another snap. He turned again and, this time, it was a full-size boar bum rushing him. With tusks pointed at him, he fired a shot as he was about to get mauled. Within seconds another shot was fired. He looked in the direction of the shot and saw nothing. The SEALs told everyone to get down. "Hunters, huh? That first shot was a .22, the second round was an assault rifle, and not one of ours. That tracer round, that shit ain't a hunter and it ain't US military issued weapons either."

Kapu bobbed between a set of ferns and kneeled. He saw a large man, black hair. His eyes had no reflection, dark as the night. He knew it was not the SEALs, but he was too large to be the Chinese servicemen. He thought he was seeing a night marcher again, and started to shudder. As he pivoted and turned away, hoping the figure disappeared, he was lifted like a feather from the ground. He opened his eyes to see a giant man of Chinese descent all of seven feet tall, looking more Ox than man. He quivered and eyes widened. "Ke Kua save me," he yelped as the man carried him to the other man. Kapu was frozen. He snapped out of it when he saw a dozen or more similar built men looking as if they were built for war. Knowing he was as good as dead, he reached for his pack and cracked the flare blinding his captor. The light blinded the men, and Kapu fell the ground. The light affected him as well but he ran indiscriminately towards the brush. He thought out loud, "Holy shit! What was that?"

Just as he started to see again, a loud bang with bright streams started to fill the sky. *Bang, Bang, Bang,* followed by a flurry of machine gun fire and tracer bullets in the sky. It took all of his will to head the direction of the flares and tracer rounds, but he knew that is where his mother would be. He arrived at the doors of a fire fight. The Seals were held up behind the Kapu System. Kapu's guts dropped as he knew the system could be in danger out here. His mother grabbed his shirt with both hands. "Get down, boy!" Kapu reached to her and cut the zip tie from her hands. All that was heard was a muffled, "Retreat," from the team's leader. Kapu took his mother and ran. With no sign of the Doctor or Harold, they had no choice.

They kept running until they hit the doors of the Halawa prison. "Kamai, let us in! Let us in!" A sliding window opened. "Ain't no Kamai here, boy. We get one kook we been calling Pele, if that's who you're looking for."

"Just lets us in!" Kamai came from the crowd. There was faint light from torches placed around the yard, where everyone was gathering. "Kapu, what we go get the system."

"We can't, Kamai. It's bad. The Chinese, they ain't Chinese. They something else. It's like they bred with night marchers. Something is wrong. They're giants. They're not men."

"What, boy? You trippin."

"Uncle, I swear. When we left, they were running through the SEAL team. They didn't fire one shot. They didn't need to. They're too powerful. I saw a bullet hit one of them in the shoulder and he didn't move."

"Serious, so we get Super Chang on the island now. First da haoles, now dis."

The MWH gang leader overhearing this. "What den? Lock 'em down, get some guns up in the towers? What the fuck you get us into? Da fuck Kamai? You bad luck."

"Shit, I didn't do anything."

Kapu spoke up. "Look, whatever that was we don't want it here. I got to go back out there."

Kapu's mom smacked him in the back of the head and said, "What's wrong with you, Kapu? You could be killed."

"Mom, they're going to track one of us, not to mention we need to see if the system was left at the site. If the SEALs get back there first, or if the Chinese destroy it, the whole island is going to starve."

With his mind made up, he prepared to set off into the brush again. The MWH leader came to him. "Hey, little man. Take dis." It was a Glock 9mm with five 10 round clips. "This one fell off a boat. We get plenty, get the 10 round clips, hard to find on island. Every banger…I mean warrior should have a Glock."

Kapu looked up at him with a smirk. "Thanks, hope I don't need it." Kapu grabbed two flares, some bread, and dried fish jerky from his uncle.

"I'm not sure what's going to happen. I would lock this place down. If you need to get supplies, you should go soon. I don't know what they were, but they were not good."

The SEAL team made it to Camp Smith, less two men, and managed to get the Doctor and Hanalei to the base with them. Harold was lost during the battle, and assumed dead. One of the team members dropped his weapon and pack.

"What the fuck was that?"

The SEAL team leader yelled back, "I don't know, but you better turn that weapon down range, dip shit! Who taught you muzzle control?"

"Sorry, sir. It's FUBAR. My brain is scrambled."

The SEAL team leader sat down and wiped sweat from his brow.

"What in the hell was that? I have never seen contact like that. They broke through a barrage of fire, and snapped Mason's neck like a twig. They had guns, and didn't even use them."

Another team leader chimed in, "That was not a sailor's death. What the fuck? Who goes for a hand-to-hand option against heavy gear? Why not just shoot at us? They were fucking giants!"

The SEAL team leader put his head in his hands. "UDT Frogmen meeting their match. What the fuck, man? What the fuck?"

The doctor murmured, "The Chinese. They've been testing some weird stuff on humans, DNA doping using the CRISPR system and Myostatin inhibitors. Both have been rumored for years."

The SEAL team leader yelled back, "Speak English, Doc! We're not working on our doctorates over here!"

"Pardon, Myostatin. It's what tells your DNA to not overproduce muscle. It's known as GDF-8."

The SEAL replied, "GDF to a SEAL means Get Down Fuckhead."

The doctor retorted, "Well, in biology it means Growth Differentiation Factor. It's why some people have that ectomorphic body type. They have less Myostatin in their DNA make up."

"Ecto-what?" The doctor laughed.

"It just means you get muscles much easier."

"Or like Gunner over there. He can squat a Sherman Tank."

Another Seal yelled, "That ain't hair cream on his dresser. That's D-Ball! He shoots it daily."

The doctor retorted, "I'm sure those beast of men were chock full of Dianabol as well, and possibly their Germline was run through a CRISPR System to change the core of their DNA at birth."

The SEAL team leader jumped back into the conversation. "Doc, so you're saying there could be an unknown amount of genetically modified Chinese war beasts on island?"

"Well, in layman's terms, yes. That's my hypothesis on what we saw. I couldn't comment on their methods, though. Seems like that didn't use much strategy. I know the other group Ha'a saw was nothing of the sort, much smaller and more bookish looking then superhuman."

The SEAL team leader responded, "You mean like handlers, strategists maybe? Guys in control of the battlefield, not on it?"

The Doctor paused, "Sounds plausible."

The team leader let out a frustrated sigh. "Ya, I had heard the rumors, but they seemed too far off to be true. Three years ago, I was training in Serbia. We were practicing hand-to-hand with some rebel forces for a possible Syrian mission. It was us, the Serbs, a NATO Special Forces team, and some Delta Force. We were training in the hypothetical, on how to get a job done against a superhuman security force protecting Eastern European leaders that would threaten NATO, real I-robot type shit. They even had us go up against some low-tech AI, leverage techniques on robots and GMO soldiers, unorthodox hand-to-hand joint manipulation to give an advantage against a larger opponent and bionic opponents. We all failed miserably, even against their crash test dummies of the real thing. They said we were training for the future of ground fights. They talked about test tube warriors. We thought they meant roided up Russians, but I guess the reality came quicker than they thought."

Another SEAL chimed in, "I heard they were shooting spider silk into the DNA and shit. Is that why they were bulletproof? Fuck! Remote control Chinese Spider-Men. Fucking great!"

The doctor said, while looking at the ground, "Warfare seems to have a weird way of progressing technology, be it biological or AI."

Chapter 5
A Tale of Three Voyages

The boys from the sailing program and the HPD SWAT team were on their way to meet with Nia for their first drop off in Waikiki. Since no communication had been sent prior, they knew that their best bet would be to moor the boat and connect in secret with Nia. They hit the docks at around 12pm, just inside Kaiser's surf break near the Hawaiian Village Hotel. The waves were rolling well over four feet, but with no takers.

Sanoa and the SWAT team stayed on board, and Pono went on to the community hall where he was told Nia would be. It was midday, and the crew kept a tight cover over the crops as they did not want it to spoil with a long trip ahead. Plus, there could be security issues if gangs caught wind of them. Pono reached the hall and made contact with Nia.

Security paid no mind to Pono. He stepped to the middle of the room, "Aloha, my name is Pono. Ha'a sent my crew with a delivery from Waimanalo with crops to help feed town residents. It's not a huge amount of food as we are doing another drop off on the westside."

"Boy, you didn't hear?"

"Hear what?"

"The Westside is a war zone. Ko'Olina is a tourist refugee camp at the resort."

"How you mean a war zone?"

"A mob took over the local family farm lands. They used all kine car bombs. They shut down the Farrington Highway and looted all the stores. You could not pass in or out without getting past this new militia. A lot of people died. Makaha Valley is on lockdown. A large group of armed men seized the gated community and condos up in the Sea Country Valley, secured a pig farm and two produce farms. Supposedly, the workers are being held there against their will to keep them running."

"How is it going here?" Pono asked.

"Not good. We need everything you can give us. Too many people, not enough resources. Canned goods are sparse. We have not distributed anything to the tourist camps, and FEMA rations are drying up. Getting close to our own riots, city checkpoints are abandoned, the workers left to take care of themselves."

Pono looked worried. He thought of the boat, the men, and the food. "So, we should organize quick then. If the public catches wind there is food in the middle of Waikiki, it's going to get bad. We got it in 100-gallon drums but, frick, even fuel could be seen as something to steal even if they can't use it 'cept for to burn."

Nia called for her team to circle around. "Everyone, you need to go back to your houses and get every able-bodied man to the dock at Kaiser's by 1 o'clock. We need as many modes of transportation as we can think of. All the dollies from the hotels, we will use them to get the food to the camp. The rest we are going to need to set up security at the dock's gate for distribution so it can't be stolen. Men will have to help the women get back home safe in some cases. It won't be easy. There are thugs everywhere preying on the weak."

Pono said he wanted to get back to the dock ASAP and left her there.

Pono sprinted back in no time. There was a small group of thugs in the Hotel lobby who watched him as he ran out to the docks. He slowed his pace. Pono could tell they were watching him. When he got there, the men had set up a perimeter on the dock. No entrance besides the gate on the shore line made it easy to secure, and they hid their weapons to not look suspicious. Pono arrived and told everyone to get on the boat and go below deck. Just under twenty men crammed in the cabin, and they left one up top on look out. "Look guys, it's not good out there. Westside is burning, town couldn't be far off, riots could break out here any moment. We have little options. Nia has men coming to distribute the food but it's not going to even touch the problem, but I have an idea."

Sanoa spoke up. "Hey, kid. You making plans? You guys sail the boat. We take care of the tactical, K?"

"That's fine Killa, but I got more intel you need to hear. My cousin, he one syndicate. He works the docks, lets a few containers go missing here and there for Yakimura, mostly insurance scams, theft, and resale online."

Sanoa chimed in, "And how you know dis, boy?"

"I know that's who is securing the food because my cousin liked to talk. Some of his high school friends told me he got promoted at the docks to a 'Crane Operator.' That's code for him moving weight for Yakimura."

Sanoa shrugged. "Guaranteed, they going to sell it to the highest bidder if chaos breaks out in town."

Pono shook his head. "Yakimura's men doing trades, food for bullets. Hundred percent, I'm sure. All the families will give up weapons to feed family. Then they got even more control. Prolley have thirty men running security, maybe more, at the pier."

One of the men spoke up. "Half the dock workers are corrupt longshoremen working for The Syndicate. They pack heat at work, just in case something jumps off. They bury guys that make noise."

Pono nodded and replied, "Pier 19, the cold goods is Pau but the rest they moving any way they like."

Sanoa squinted showing a bit of hesitation. "So, what? We storm da castle? Where we going to put all the food?"

"We not taking the food, we setting up shop. That food is for the people."

"K, big dog. You know how to clear a ship or a container? You ever fire a weapon?"

"Brah, I from Kahaluu. I know how to shoot. I stalk pig, but corrupt Syndicate all da same. Jus' no plug my cousin. Dat's family."

"Right, right. Well, let us think about this. So, what? We offload here and then what?"

"When Nia's crew shows up, we cut the line. They can handle this. We ain't draggin' ass around the island trying to feed a few in a war zone. We can lock down a food depot and get everyone to act right and come to us."

"Good in theory, but then what?"

"We sail this thing to Kewalo Basin, park the boat, go on foot to the Bella Stone building behind the docks. We clock the Syndicate from the roof and go from there."

"Fuck, we go then, Pono. You know, a lot of you halfway kids make good cops."

"I not applying for one job. We pirates out here." The other boys laughed, but were cut off by a yelp.

"Help!" Two men were holding the boy on watch. "Everyone up on deck, or the boy gonna die."

Sanoa pointed at the smallest in their crew, signaling to slide out the port window. "You like fuck with the Syndicate, huh? You know we get ears in the street. We run this town, buleh." Sanoa signaled everyone up onto the deck, putting his finger to his mouth to tell the boys to be quiet. "Put your hand down, Pig. I know you, freaking try bust my friend in Waimanalo back in the day. You da one crush my friend's neck, all for some Pakalolo, ah."

"You mean ice."

"Whatever. Clear, green all the same. We sell 'em if dey buying."

Sanoa shook his head. "You guys fucked upcoming this side, thinking you was gonna be heroes."

In a flurry, two shots were fired from behind the thugs and the men dropped. Pono saw another at the end of the ramp, opening the gate. "Shit, one more!" Sanoa grabbed a rifle from off the railing of the boat, set his sight until he could see the crosshairs align, and pulled the trigger. The man dropped, hitting the sand at the end of the dock.

"See, boys. That's why you don't join a gang." The boy that was being held stood in shock.

"Frick, I thought I was gonna shit right there on the spot."

Sanoa looked at his men. "Well, nothing wrong with a little motivation, huh? Let's muster up, dump these bodies and gear up. We be gone as soon as Nia's men show up." Sanoa paused. "Don't say anything about this."

Pono chimed in, "Loose lips sink ships, boys. No need anyone to know." As Nia's men arrived at the pier, they got busy organizing the crops for distribution. Sanoa met with Nia and told her that they were going to bed down for the night, asking if they could use a room at the hotel. She obliged. They regrouped before leaving for the penthouse suite. As the sun set over Waikiki, Pono brought the boys out onto the Lanai. "Brah, K-bay pirates doing alright. You ever think we see this view from the Hawaiian village?"

Samson, another boy, sarcastically replied, "Not unless you get a job in room service." The whole group laughed at the joke, but the unlit backdrop of Waikiki brought them back to reality.

They wanted to avoid being spotted, so they made their way through the hotel's underground parking structure. Pono was the only crew member from the sailing committee Sanoa allowed to come, as he had an idea of the pier's layout. Fort Armstrong held the lion's share of all-important resources for both foreign and domestic arrivals, otherwise known as Pier 19.

They used the fire escape on the backend of the Bella Stone and Tile Warehouse to get a rooftop vantage point of the container storage facility. 15 armed thugs surrounded the various containers. They were backed up by another dozen men at the front gate, and a half dozen looking out from the boat on the port side of a newly landed container ship. A few random containers remained open and had canned goods in view. Pallets of cans with spam, tomato sauce, and other canned goods could be seen from the outside packaging. There was the strong smell of rotten produce and frozen goods that had gone bad. It was sitting next to a dump. Pono thought he recognized at least five of the 20 or so men around the complex. One of the men was his cousin Pomi, who he relayed was in and out of jail for armed robbery and drug trafficking. "You get on that ice, no chance. Even the boys in blue wouldn't be sitting here with these donkeys." He looked at the Sergeant of the SWAT team.

"I don't judge these guys. Coulda been me. Fast cash, a gun, easy to get one big head."

Sanoa looked at him. "I'm not judging anyone, but I don't want these clowns controlling the food supply either!"

Pono shook his head, acknowledging he was on the same page.

Sanoa raised his head up and said, "Life is about choices, boy. You made one good one, now I need you to make a few more."

They decided the only way in would be if Pono went ahead and tried to convince his cousin and the other gang members to have him work in the shipping the yard. They would spend one more night at the hotel, and come back the same time tomorrow once Pono was inside. The goal was to have Pono lock down as many weapons as he could for a swift siege. They watched as he made his way back down the side of the building, circling back around a few trucks so as not to be seen, before he went up to the front gate.

Pono made it to the gate and shouted, "Hey what, Pomi around? Tell him it's his little cousin Pono here."

A guard jumped up. "Who the fuck are you, boy?"

"I like work, I stay hungry."

One of the guards pointed his gun at him. "Hey, no play around, you like get shot?"

They both turned to some shouting behind them from men playing craps on an empty crate.

"Bango da mango! Gimme your money, clown!" This came from a six-foot-something, skinny tattooed Filipino/Portuguese looking young man no more than twenty-five years old. He grabbed his cash and turned towards the gate. "Pocho, is that you? Should've known you was here. You good luck! I never seen you since I got out of jail, four years already. What? You remembered what I said, huh? You need anything, come to da docks."

Pono shouted back, "Das right, cuz! Stop jiggling those dice, and let me in."

"Ah, good luck you, but not wit da Pochos." Pomi was referring to Portuguese Man O'War jellyfish that Pono had a knack of getting hit by, swimming on the windward side.

"Brah, I never get whacked longtime, cuz, since Hanabata days."

Pomi waved his hands at the other guard. "Eh, let Pocho in. Das my cousin, real kine, bloodline."

Pono crossed the fence, giving the guard stink eye. "What cuz, you like eat? Aunty tell you I was here?"

Pono shook his head. "Not even. I seen your boys from castle. They said you were working the docks down here. You don't see those guys, anymore?"

"Nah, little cuz. Pretty gangster these days, running with a heavier crew."

"So, what about me then," asked Pono.

"I caught a bid for him, so I don't see you staying a problem. Sleep here tonight, you meet him in the morning. They Japanese, like Japanese Japanese, so you better bow. Like for real kine straight FOB, but he da connection for us SYN."

Pono bowed mockingly at Pomi. "K den, where the grinds?"

Pomi laughed. "You're still a clown, cuz."

Kapu had made his way back to the site of the firefight with the Chinese. Besides one bullet hole in the wheel well of the Kapu System, you would have never known anything happened. He could still smell the smoldering trees, in the distance, from the fire he'd set. Not wanting to spend too much time, knowing that this could be a trap, he checked the equipment and made his way back into the bush. He thought about his father being exposed on the highway with the food and limited security, and his mother being detained still, assumably, at Camp Smith by now. He knew that the horses his father got in Nalo, and the transportation flatbeds, could be used to get the system back to the prison. He made his way back to the Halawa by midnight.

Kamai was still up, and greeted Kapu. "Ho, brah! Look what the guys found in the guard shack!"

He looked at his uncle strangely, as he was wide-eyed.

"What's that, Uncle, you OK?"

"Stay good, bud. Found some rev pills. Government funded, medical grade No-Doz. They call it Modafinil. I call it Daffy."

Kapu shook his head in disgust. "You high?" Kamai giggled.

"Nah, I stay on first watch. Was tired, but no more wit da Daffy pills." Kapu looked a little weirded out on his uncle who was a bit manic.

"Uncle, you listening? We gotta link up with my dad. He's out there by himself, my mom's still captive, and the system is in the woods with too much exposure."

"Right on. Let me just grab some more pills and we're out."

Kapu looked at him as if he was crazy, as if he was too easy to convince. "Wait. Who's gonna watch out for you? Aren't you on guard duty?"

"Right, right. Let me go wake up Ronald. He da guy that got me the radio. He's all chronic. He'll love these pills. Guy will be pacing the watchtower."

Ha'a had taken shelter under the Middle Street overpass. He needed to change clothes from the rain, and feed the horses as they were getting fatigued from the lack of water and food. The produce was still viable but, between the weather and the lack of good transportation, had taken some added beatings. Ha'a had daydreamed using it as a moment of rest. His mind wandered, hoping the system was scalable to support the island. Securing it away from hands of the military was only the first hurdle. He was quickly brought back to reality as one of the men shouted in a muffled tone, "Armed men up ahead," as he peeked around the corner.

Ha'a said, without hesitation, "Don't fire unless fired upon." He then took his rifle and ran to the front of the overpass. Looking through his crosshairs, he saw his brother-in-law, Kamai, and Kapu just behind him. As they got closer he put his weapon down. "Kapu, what the heck are you doing? You should be with your mother."

Kapu told Ha'a what happened, how their home had been raided, where the system was left, and about the run in with the Chinese half-breeds. Ha'a was at a loss. "What about your mother?"

Kapu replied, "Dad, she's with the SEALs. I couldn't pull her away during the fight. I saw her taken by them. We lost Harold out there."

Meanwhile, Pono had been working his way through the gang at the docks trying to gather information in the narrow time he had. He needed to find out where the weapons and the gate keys were being held. There were two containers where the men slept, splitting the shifts near either side of the security gates. The men would put their rifles away for the night, but keep a side arm at all times. There would be no such thing as an easy overthrow of the Syndicate. The best he could do was shut down their automatic weapons, and make sure the SWAT guys had the drop on them.

The only way he thought to do this was to daisy chain them through the triggers with a padlock at the end. They had been locking down weapons in a container with a thick gauge chain and lock. Pono decided to prod at his cousin and see if you could extract the lock's number. "Eh, Pomi. What you guys do if someone storms the gates trying get food?"

"Do you worry about that, little cuz? We got a few 44s, forshaw!"

"Ha, no for realz. What if we get mobbed?"

"Eh. You see that container over there?" Pomi pointed down the way, towards the crane. "You see that container? We get enough weapons to take on the Schofield Barracks."

"Ya, but do you got enough guys to man them?"

He nodded. "Well, we just got one more, cuz." Pono smiled, but felt guilty that he was tricking his own cousin. He knew Pomi was no good, but he was still his blood. Pomi grabbed him by the back of the neck and lead him to the container. "Let's get you ready, soldier boy." He opened up the container and removed the chain from the lock. "Here is a revolver for your side piece. It's all we get for right now for small guys. We took all the rest from what the Chinese left when they fled the scene."

"What, you guys know how to use them?"

"It's a gun. You put bullets in, and they come out the other end."

"But how you load them?" Pomi grabbed a clip and pointed the gun at a low, ready position at the ground. "You see this, cuz? Keep the barrel pointed down. I know you like shoot one of us right out the gate. Clip goes here. You spend the clip, you push this little button and pops out. Shells gonna be hot, so don't touch the spent ones. K?"

Pono looked nervous, thinking about how he might have to pull the weapon on his own family.

"So, what if the container is locked?" Pomi looked at the floor, and then back at Pono. "Well, then you open the lock. The code is SYN, use the alphabet, 19, 25 and 14."

Pono looked back. "Roger that, buleh. When can I test one?"

Pomi looked at him with a cautious eye. "Ya, why not? Wake up the neighbors, let 'em know we stay here still." Pono lined up the target at the end of the docks, and lit up a used pallet. Two men came running out from the docked boats deck.

"Eh, what the fuck? We tryin sleep over here. Who the fuck's the kid?" Pono looked at Pomi and giggled.

"My cousin. He da new sheriff in town."

The men went back into their boat's cabin, looking salty from being woken up.

Meanwhile, the team were back at the hotel preparing for an assault. They decided two men would clear the boat, and the other six would storm the entrance when Pono let them in. They would attempt to secure everyone who's sleeping, but there was no way to ensure there would not be casualties on either side. Pono was having a rough time sleeping. He was wrestling with knowing that a family tie would be broken the second that he betrayed his cousin. Pomi was a misguided youth, just like Pono had been, but he remained big hearted even though his actions led him to crime. Pono knew there wasn't a big difference between them besides choices and how they dealt with temptation. Also, Pono was lucky to get caught young whereas Pomi was caught later in life with bigger consequences. Pono decided he would open the lock and sneak back to the hotel that night. He figured the longer he waited, the harder it would be go through with it. He knew that the SWAT team would jump on the opportunity for surprise, plus he didn't want to be there when it happened or wait until after he had to meet the Syndicate's boss. He might even be able to have them let Pomi go, and just send him back to family.

Kapu and his father finished catching up, under the overpass, and came to the conclusion that the only option was to dump the food and alert the locals on the fringe of Kalihi to have at it. They knew it was a recipe for a riot, but they had to get a transport method to move the system ASAP. Kapu went down the road, off the School St. cutoff, to a church that had a faint light shining through the stained glass windows. It was a cathedral building named Saint Teresa of child Jesus. It was an ominous looking building, almost a micro version of Rome's Basilicas. Kapu figured it could be either a place of refuge, or being used as a hold up for miscreants looking for shelter. He entered the property lines only to test a locked door handle. There was a small staircase on the side of the church where the light was emanating from. The lights were from church candles showing twenty or more young children sleeping on the floor. There was a nun in the corner who had a shotgun next her chair. She had a look of sleep in her eyes, and he did not want to startle her and make the gun go off. Kapu lightly tapped on the window to get her attention but her eyes were old and it was clear she could not make him out. She stood and grabbed her weapon and walked towards the door. Kapu took two fingers and made the peace sign. As she made her way to the door, she picked up a candle and cradled the shotgun in the other arm. Once a clear view of the fingers arose in her vision, she lowered the gun and peered through the glass. She could see Kapu crouched under the window, curled in a ball as if he thought the door would stop a shotgun shell. She tapped on the window and cracked the door.

"Young man, we don't have beds for anyone else. This place is for the children."

Kapu looked up, then stood. "I'm not looking for a bed, sister. I have some goods for the church, under the Middle Street overpass. We're not able to bring it any further, and hoped your church could distribute it to the local families."

"Young man, I hope this is not a trick. You know Hell awaits a misguided youth as it does any lying man?"

"No sister, there is a large produce shipment just down the road. We need to be on our way. Can you help us?"

"Praise God! We have hands, but no food. Wait here. I'll get the rest of the staff and clergy."

Kapu left the church staff at the overpass, while the crew packed up for the journey back to the site where Kapu last saw the system.

Pono had snuck out at 1am, first hitting the container to lock the guns. He knew that the only way to really make his plan work was to freeze up the weapons. Just locking the container would not do any good if they had a pair of bolt cutters in the area. There were a dozen weapons laid out across the container on a rack. He went through them, one by one, and removed their lower receivers and put them in his pack while daisy-chaining them. Then he took off around the back gate, where he unlocked the inside latch on the gate and climbed around the fence at the end of the pier. He ended up with his back to the parking area outside of the docks. He ducked behind the loading dock and stayed low behind trucks until he made it to Nimitz Highway and, then, kept a hard pace as he headed back to the Royal Hawaiian Hotel. He snuck past the guards at the hotel entrance. It was better, he thought. He didn't want to alert anyone to what was going on. Less eyes meant less chance of others trying to take advantage of getting into the fort once the SWAT team secured it. A half dozen men can clear a dock, but it can't hold back a mob. The men were still up, planning for the next day's scheduled attempt at securing the pier. Sanoa looked at the door, as it swung open, with his hand on his Glock. "Shit, boy! You almost got plugged." Pono was breathing heavy and wheezing from the run.

"Brah, you gotta hit them tonight! Tomorrow, they're getting reinforcements from the Yakuza. Pomi said the boss is coming to check up tomorrow."

Sanoa shook his head. "So, what? We go now, like chicken shits, instead of take down the big boss same time?"

Pono looked around the room. "All twelve of you, huh? They get twenty easy, between the boats and ground crew. I took out their weapons, just now, but they gonna see it in the morning. Then what?"

A smaller officer looked at Pono. "How? You dump 'em in the ocean?"

Pono threw open his nap sack, and emptied it onto the table. "Negative. I took the receivers out."

Sanoa turned to the rest of the team. "Well, boys. Wake the fuck up! We bumping up the execution. ETA one hour. Frick, boy. I hope you made the right call."

"Eh, it's better than dealing with forty men tomorrow by surprise." The men raised their eyebrows, and nodded their heads in agreement.

Pono said he wanted to hang back. He couldn't see his cousin, face to face, after he sold him out. Sanoa agreed to try and capture him with as little harm as possible but told Pono, "Eh, but if the guy act and pull a weapon on us, sorry boy, he gonna get dropped."

The men geared up and left for the walk back. Pono stayed back, and decided to check on the boat. He knew that he wouldn't be able to sleep. *What a waste*, he thought. "I never stay in a hotel in my life, let alone the Royal Hawaiian," and now he was too ashamed to even enjoy it. He headed back to the docks and, as he made his way up, he saw a figure near the gate. Pono slowed up, as the man had a hood on, and he could not make out who it was. He crossed from the beach onto the dock, and slowly made his way to the gate which was open but with no site of the crew on the boat. Pono tried to make himself known as he approached the man near the entrance.

"Eh, braddah. Howzit? You with Nia's men?"

The man turned to him. "Howzit yourself, cuz? What? You no like work the docks, huh?"

Pomi had followed him back to the hotel.

"What, you faka? You sell us out, ah?"

He had his gun out, and grabbed Pono by the neck. Pono stayed quiet. "You little Aku bird, ratting out your own blood. Who raised you to be one rat? Shitty, Pocho, shitty." Pomi threw Pono onto the deck of the boat, while pointing the gun at him.

"Wake up the crew. We going for a ride." Pono went below deck and woke up the boys. There was no produce left on the barge. They were startled and groggy. "Eh, you little pirate fucks! Rise and shine. We shoving off. Pono pull da ropes now."

"Cuz, I told them not to take you out. You go to let the people access what's left of the food."

"Who said speak? You're shined, Pono. Mr. Yakimura gonna string you up and feed you to the pigs, and to think I was gonna sponsor you into the Syndicate. You had it made, fucking rat."

"Brah, what good you in one gang when your family starving? Brah, I thought you was Akamai, just another hoodrat, Pomi. It ain't about us, it's about everyone!"

"Cuz, shut your mouth before I kick you off your own boat."

Pono went quiet. He pulled the line, and they started to catch the current pulling off the reef formed by the low tide and tradewinds. "Let out the sail, and tack towards the coast so we can come up behind the main tanker at the pier."

Ha'a, Kapu, and Kamai had made it back to site where the system was left. It looked the same, but there was a silence that made them uneasy. It was as if they knew that someone knew they were there. Kapu looked at his dad. "I can turn on the radio tracker and pinpoint where the Chinese are, but then they can see us as well."

"Son, we have two rifles, a handgun, and your .22. From your description, diplomacy is not on the table. If they wanted this thing they would have taken it, and if they wanted to capture us, they could. I don't think they will engage unless they are engaged." Kapu nodded in agreement. Ha'a went on, "If you're right and those men that we dropped off at the base are handlers, those things must need marching orders or to be attached to fight. They may not be autonomous."

Kamai jumped in. "Either way, let's get out these woods before these Asian night marchers get wise and light us up. Plus, I think I need another half a Daffy. This thing starting wear off already."

Ha'a looked at Kapu. "What is he talking about?"

Kapu smirked. "He been reeving all night. He took some industrial strength No Doz pill called Modafinil. He found them at the prison, in the guard shack."

Ha'a yelled back at his cousin, "Eh, you stupid or something? Those things can make a fat man like you have a heart attack."

"Ha'a, I stay sleepy cousin. Can't be worse than a Red Bull."

"How many you take?" "Third one tonight, I think."

"Kapu, give him some water before he overheats. Watch out, Kapu. You gonna become one babysitter, like me, you keep this guy around. That goes for you friend, Harold, too. Is he back at Halawa?"

"He got caught with Dr. Lightfoot. We think they're up at Camp Smith."

Ha'a looked at the ground. "We need to get them. Dr. Lightfoot is essential to the system. Harold is probably safe under military watch, but we are going nowhere fast if the doctor is detained. The system may as well be scrap metal without the doctor and a water source."

"Dad, why don't we just run the system out of the prison? It's secured already, and there's a big yard that can be used for the system. There is a big waterfall at the base of the Halawa Ridge Trail, and we could see if the Menehune Water building has a filter we could use for the entry port. It's two mins from the prison. We hire the MWH to provide security, and we can make this work."

Ha'a smiled. "Always the optimist, Kapu. Let's see, once we get the system back to Halawa and have a plan to get the doctor back."

They finished rigging the system onto the carts, and started their way back towards H1 off the military access roads.

Pomi was high off his rage as they passed Kakaako Park. "Boys, you see Pono, this snitch? You think you all high and mighty because you get a leg up in life, getting on this boat program. You all just like me. Don't you think for a second you better just cause you snitches."

Pono yelled back, "Cuz, fuck you! You got a choice. You made it. I got a choice too, and that's to feed the island. You just looking out for you. How you gonna look at it like it's us and them? We born on this island! Auwe, Pomi, it's all us. Shame on you!"

Pomi looked back at the boys, all looking at him with fear and disgust. Pomi shook his head. "Den what, cuz? We what? Join the pigs? Shake down the Syndicate, the Yakuza? Den what? I just one scrub like the rest of them."

Pono looked at him. "Nah. Then you one man on his own two feet, not one scrub who needs to get scraps from drug lords."

Pomi went silent as they entered near the harbor. They moored off to the dock, and Pomi broke his silence with a whisper, "Ah, you. Gonna make turn into one softy. Frick. What's the plan, then? We feeding the nation den, or what?"

Pono just smiled at him with a look of pride. "Dont got one. You got any suggestions?" Pomi looked back at him as they turned into the pier.

"Rush 'em. I know where they keep the handguns, in the captain's quarters of the boat. I'll go first, then you follow up the ropes and meet me at the ladder at the front of the boat. They not going to think anything of it if I am up there, but they not going to roll over and play dead once we pull a weapon on them."

Pomi looked up at the boat as Pono tied off. Pomi started to shimmy up the rope. As he climbed over, he noticed one of the guards. He shouted, "Eh! You doing your job or what? I just snuck up the ropes without you knowing." The guard looked back, and put his head down. Pomi gestured.

"Ahhh, you're pau already. Go eat with the boys. I get 'em. You look all torn up, no worry."

With the guard going on break, Pomi signaled back over the railing for the boys to start their ascent up the rope into the boat. Pomi made his way to the captain's quarters. He opened a safe that held a dozen Sig Sauer handguns and twenty loaded clips. He filled a duffel bag, and made his way back through the hule of the boat. On his way up the stairs, he heard voices in the kitchen and circled back to check it out. He was careful not to make himself known. He saw Mr. Yakimura, with his inner circle of thugs, standing over a large man who looked beaten half to death handcuffed to the food prep line in the center of the kitchen.

Yakimura spoke, "You guys had it good when we paid you off. Make a vice bust, here and there, to look good and get the white envelope a few days later. One week with no envelopes and you guys trying rob me, huh?"

Sanoa mustered up some words. "I ain't one crooked cop."

Yakimura raised his hand to backhand him. "Don't act like you don't have a price. You're a hired hand. Your captain tells you to jump. You were just working for the wrong captain. This is my pier. Your badges don't mean anything in this new world, my world."

Pomi snuck off to the deck of the boat, where the boys were crouched down watching the security from the railing.

"Pomi, they got the SWAT team handcuffed. There, under the tent." Pomi shook his head. "Ya, they got the big one down stairs. Is he the team leader?"

"Ya, that's Sanoa. Frick. Where he stay?"

"Locked to a pipe down in the kitchen, all bust up by Yakimura's men."

"Well, what now?"

"Shit!" the guard yelled out, as he came back to the ladder. "Pomi, I forgot to tell you. Yakimura is downstairs. He says he need to speak with you."

"K, go get some food. I told you I stay good up here already."

The guard went back down and headed toward the tent. "Eh, boys, you know how to shoot?"

They all looked back with a collective "can do" nod.

"Right. Well, get twenty clips. Grab two each and a Sig. I gonna go down there unarmed. When I say your boy's name, you come in and get the drop on the crew. We get the keys, unlock Sanoa, den we lock up Yakimura's men and walk off the boat to get the other men." They nodded, and made their way down the stairs towards the kitchen.

One of the guards was peeking out the door of the kitchen and saw Pomi. "Pomi, get over here. We need to talk to you."

Pomi signaled to the boys to hold back.

The guard looked back. "Eh, who's with you?" The guard pointed his gun in Pomi's direction.

Knowing he could not get away with a lie, because of the noise, he replied, "I get my cousin, Pono, with me."

"Not a good time, but bring him here. Yakimura needs new blood."

Yakimura looked a bit off at the site of Pomi having someone with him. Sanoa's eye sockets were so swollen, could not focus to see Pono.

Yakimura inquired, "Who's this, Pomi?"

"My cousin, Pono. He's cool. He like join up with my crew. Told him I would introduce him to you."

"So, you like join, young boy? You pack heat?"

"My cousin gave me a piece. I can shoot."

"Well, we got a job for you then."

"That's why I'm here, sir."

Yakimura's men unlocked Sanoa from the pipe, and made their way out of the kitchen. Pomi went first, and signaled the boys to hide. They made their way off the boat and back to the dock, where they encircled the tent. Yakimura took Pono and Sanoa, and put them in the center of the tent in front of the rest of the captives. Yakimura spoke. "So, your leader is one good guy. He never say why you're here, trying to steal from me. He also seems to think he is not in my pocket. If you're not in my pocket, that means you're trash. I don't store rubbish at my shipping yard. We dispose of it." He looked at the men from the SWAT team, who were cuffed together. "You like go out with the trash, boys? It's no problem for me. We good with sanitation work."

The men looked scared. Yakimura looked back at Pono. "You get one chance. You can be recycled, made new on the right side of the equation or you can go out with the trash."

Yakimura motioned for Pono to step forward, and then for Yakimura's men to drop Sanoa in front of the captured men's feet. Yakimura turned to Pono. "So, boy. You like in? Here is your in. Put two in this pig's head. If the others squeal, put two in their heads as well."

Pono raised the gun to Sanoa's forehead. The men looked baffled by the sight of Pono with a gun to Sanoa's head. Pono paused, and looked back. "Eh, cuz, the safety is on this piece. Where it stay?"

Pomi walked over and took the safety off. As he did this, he whispered, "Rush 'em." Pono looked back and caught a glimpse of the boys behind a truck just outside of the tent. Pono punched through the pistol to rack it ready to fire.

Yakimura yelled, "Shoot, already!"

With that, Pono turned and fired on Yakimura, hitting him in the left shoulder. The gun fluttered as it was an illegal setup which had the restrictor disabled, making it semi-automatic. The boys fired on the gang, as well, and Pomi faded back behind the cars. Sanoa and his men were still tied up in the center of the tent as bullets flew by. One man was hit in the leg, and could do nothing but wince with his hands zip tied. Pomi ran from behind the car and cut the ratchet straps on the tent, flipping it into the trade wind towards the gang firing on them.

Yakimura screamed back, "Uragirimono," which means "Traitor" in Japanese.

With the tent providing them a window, they dropped two tables and knocked the men to the ground and cut them free. The boys gave the men their weapons, and a larger firefight ensued. Yakimura pulled back, exiting through the front gate and telling his men to hold down the pier until they could send backup. Under heavy fire they followed suit and fled to the streets of Chinatown.

Two of the boys began tending to the men who were shot, along with Sanoa who had been beaten within an inch of his life.

They knew they had to remove the bullet and seal the wound. "Brah, this guy's messed up. Need some line and a knife fast."

They took a basic fishing knife and popped the round from one of the man's leg. (be more specific. left leg, right leg?) The boys took some fishing line and a small hook to make a makeshift suture through the man's calf. "You gonna get one mean scar, but it will stop the bleeding." The other man had exit wounds high on his right arm, so they took nylon rope and tied a bowline to create a slip knot, making a tourniquet to stop the bleeding. Pono poured lime, salt, and ground up Hawaiian chili peppers to stop infection and cauterize the wound.

Pomi sarcastically asked, "What, you turning his leg into one Corona bottle?"

The boys laughed, making light of the stressful situation. Pono knew that Yakimura's men would be back, and they would need to be prepared for an onslaught from the Yakuza and Syndicate.

Back at Camp Smith, the doctor was being debriefed by the SEALs and, who they assumed to be, a CIA investigator. The man had a scar on his cheek, and wore a blue collared shirt with tan slacks. "So, was this the first you've ever seen of these men? What would you make of it Doctor?"

Dr. Lightfoot responded, "It was a first but, coming from a background in Biology, it's not surprising the Chinese are making anomalies ("creating mutations" might work better) from the Human Genome. Between drones and biotech, why would someone in this day and age fight their own wars when you can make designer battalions with the right tools."

All the men present looked at each other with an air of "Oh shit" in their eyes.

Chapter 6

Shot up in Downtown

The next morning, a food drop-off was held at the tourist encampment. The produce was mixed with what little Nia's men found at the old ABC store warehouse on Nimitz Highway. Mostly macadamia nuts and various sundries, some canned beans, but not much substance was found.

Nia spoke to the camp through an improvised bullhorn. "I am sorry we have had to keep you here. It is for your own safety. There is not much else we can do right now until security measures are taken."

One of the tourists cried out, "Where is the military in all of this? Why don't they come and help us, or send us home?"

Nia responded with a question. "Miss, where are you from?"

"We're visiting from Colorado."

"I'm sorry but to our knowledge, there is nothing viable left west of Nebraska or east of Kentucky. We've been told even our fish could be tainted from the amount of radiation exposure that the world has taken on."

The woman shuddered and disappeared into the crowd.

Nia went on. "We're all in this together. If the hotel rooms were not full, we would place you elsewhere but we don't have a choice at the moment."

The crowd grew angry, and shouting came from everywhere. "We don't need to be held here! Let us fend for ourselves, if that's the case!"

Nia replied, "If you want to leave, we won't stop you but there is no safe haven beyond the zoo. The streets are running themselves, and I can only suggest you stick together as we organize the next move."

Pomi was not able to sleep, fearing a quick retaliation. Pono, on the other hand, was out cold into the early morning. Sanoa was with his crew, organizing weapons, bandaging his wounds, and had been taking small power naps in rotation with the crew. He spoke the men that were awake. "Boys, one gun at a time, strip 'em and clean 'em. Leave the rest loaded and ready, just in case they come back."

Pono chimed in, "You like me reassemble the AKs?"

Sanoa had forgotten about the guns Pono disabled. "Bring the lower receivers here, under the tent, and grab the guns."

Pono grabbed the duffle bag, dropped it at their side, and went to open the container. Pomi followed him.

"Pono, frick we're in some shit."

Pono looked back as he opened the container. "We got control for now. We got weapons."

Pomi jumped back. "We got problems, possibly forty or more of them coming this way."

"Well, we need a plan then. We can't just walk away."

Pomi, knowing the odds, was quick to give his opinion. "Cuz, if we here when they get back, we're dead. You sounded good on the boat, but we no need die for this. We go home, take the boat, fish, dive, grow some Pakalolo. I'm done with this bullshit."

Pono felt heavy hearted. He saw Pomi had his out, finally. No more crime. No more violence. He could be free of it.

"I don't blame you. Go. You don't need this fight, but we going to stand our ground and get this food to the people."

One of young boys was seen in the foreground, trying to open a can of chili. "Brah, I died and went to can food heaven. Chili and rice for life over here."

They all laughed, but it was short lived as they knew the next move was critical. Pono called the boys over to help with the guns. They unchained them, and brought them back to the tent.

Sanoa was looking distressed. "Frick! We got fire power, but no man power. They gonna get our number if we fight head to head."

Pono interrupted, "My plan's been working so far, and I got one more. I say we put your two best snipers up on top of the buildings on either side of the yard. The boys can get to safety on the boat, and sail a load of goods back to Nia and then to Nalo town. I'll hang back with you, Sanoa. The goal is to get them trapped, so they have to listen. If they don't have a choice, they might change their tune." Sanoa shook his head.

"Boy, you so young minded. You think they going to listen to us, the ones putting them in jail all these years? You know they coming for him, too. They not going to let this type of thing slide."

Pono was quick to respond. "Not you, they going listen to me. The past is the past, and it don't mean shit. The here and now is what matters."

Pomi sarcastically interjected, "Sounds great, if we don't get our heads shot off. You tell me how you think you going to get them on our side."

Pono replied, "Yakimura is already on Ha'a's side. They are working together under an arrangement. We might have just messed that up for him. Yakimura is ruthless, but he's not dumb. He knows he needs numbers to keep any control. There's no gang going to take on what he has going on in those hills, with the MWH on his side, but the Military is a different animal. Even if they have limited resources, they are easy 5,000 strong on K-Bay alone." They looked at him and agreed.

Sanoa chimed in, "You know, boy, I'm not sure you know what you are asking us. We are Paramilitary. We're trained in the same way those boys on K-Bay are. Right now, our goal is securing food safely. We not giving up on the US, all of a sudden, just 'cause we get a chance at a new regime. I would prefer to see what's what with the Military before I let more bullets fly or try make good with criminals."

Pono nodded. "You got a point, but who's to say they're going to do a better job than Ha'a? We already know what that style of island life looks like, and it ain't pono wit me."

The SWAT team's K-9 trainer jumped in. "Well, we're damned if we do or don't, so I say let's pin them down first and ask the questions later. If they understand the goal, great. If not, cut 'em loose with their tail between their legs."

They made overnight rations for their snipers and sent them up into the buildings. They had emergency mirrors for signals and a candlestick still from their set up at the farm. Pono took his crew and packed the sail boat with as many goods as it and the flotilla could handle, and sailed back to Waikiki and Nia's crew to drop off more goods.

Ha'a and his crew had made some headway from Middle Street and moved further towards the back gate of Camp Smith. They knew the command center was in the middle of the base, so it was going to be a mission even if their security measures were not functioning. They knew if anyone was seen, it was game over. They were not prepared to handle a firefight with trained Special Forces. It would have to be a minimalist mission.

Kapu and Ha'a began to converse. There was a lot to catch up on. Ha'a asked Kapu what had happened to Harold. "Dad, I don't know. Those things grabbed him. The Chinese night marchers, one of them just threw Harold over their shoulder and walked off. They didn't take anyone else. Maybe they thought he was a Chinese civilian, or mistook him for one of their group."

Ha'a responded, "I'm not sure. The fact that they exist is strange enough. I wouldn't count anything out at this point." They both went on to talk about the Kapu System and what had happened to it.

"Dad, the system is abandoned right now. We need to get it secured at Halawa."

Ha'a thought about what Kapu just said, and it gave him an idea. "You know, our chances are slim if we try to get Mom out of Camp Smith with just us. I think getting the Kapu System is what they want. If they know it's sitting there, they might be on their way back to get it right now."

Kapu was concerned that he was right. "They don't need Mom if they have the system. So, let's bring them to us. We stick to the first plan. Bring the system to the prison. We have men and a fortress. We arrange the trade, and then take them down."

Ha'a laughed. "Son, I'm a negotiator. I don't plan on going head to head with SEALs with your Mom's life in the middle. We give them the system, and I know the General will let us go on about our way."

Kapu snapped back with fierce emotion, "But Dad! What about the plan? What about the people? We need the system to feed the people, and keep the people from another government run by Military force."

Ha'a found a bit a humor in his seriousness. "Son, how many people do think are currently on this island?"

Kapu sat back and thought, "You know, Dad, not sure but the traffic was always horrible coming back from Kam so I know it's a lot."

Ha'a laughed again. "Just under one million, at last I'd checked. That system in the jungle was for the feeding of family and friends. It was a test unit that the agriculture department and the doctors could experiment with, come to the estate and see what worked and what didn't. It was not meant to be used for a mass population."

Kapu was quick to read between the lines of what his father meant by this. "Dad? Are you saying you have another one somewhere on this island?"

Ha'a smiled and responded, "My father taught me to always to do first then talk, never talk then do. What is done in silence is what will be rewarded, just like the bible says."

Kapu nodded. "Makes sense."

Ha'a nodded back. "The ones who talk about what they're going to do already have gotten their reward." He went on to explain that the system would be beta tested at the estate, and then a scalable system would be built in its image on the estate's land at Hale Ikena Valley. Ha'a and the family owned a famous tourist destination at Kualoa Ranch, where many Hollywood movies were filmed. However, he kept a plot in the Ka'a'wa Valley and a storage facility for equipment in an old, World War II bunker the last two months. Ha'a only hoped that the system was kept intact by the thick cement bunker walls.

"Kapu, you also need to understand, we used up the last of the resources on our home system. That pulse fried everything. It will take them months to repair and then connecting it to their grid is another issue."

Kapu inquired, "So, is that why fish are dying?"

Ha'a replied, "Yes, the Talapia needed circulating air to filter through the system. The only fish we have left are the catfish, but the stockpile of Tilapia and catfish at the Molii fish pond are in the hundreds of thousands. We need to get over there ASAP, however, your mother needs to be with us first." Kapu still was confused about why his father would give his technology to the military. They would have everything they needed to keep control of the islands, maybe not now but in the future. They decided to rush transport the system to Halawa, as quickly as they could, but would send Kapu to the base's front gate to make the trade offer for his mother.

The General had been busy at the base, attempting to get information from his Chinese detainees. They were able to get enough info through various methods, most of which would have the US use of waterboarding look mild, but were unsure whether or not the Intel was reliable. The tortured men and Chinese interpreters both had their way of not getting their stories straight. However, if what they had gotten from the men was accurate, there were over three hundred men that had been dropped in remote parts of the island rainforest as a special forces team to back the air and naval onslaught. With the latter neutralized, they still had to deal with whatever threat was still out there. The General received word that the SEAL team had made contact with an unknown fighting force. He questioned the detainees about these men. All the men said, repeatedly, was one word, "Gaiwu," which translated to "Monster." The General was no more intimidated by their lack of detail than if he was to be told there were three nuclear subs lurking in their waters. It seemed the unknown threat was just that. They could be minutes away from a US battalion arriving at their shores or a Military occupation by the Chinese, it was anyone's guess. The General planned on focusing on population control. It was the one variable he knew that had success in US nation building. The first step was to secure the Kapu System on his base and get it up and running.

Pono and his boys made it back to the dock near the Hawaiian Village Hotel and were met with an empty landscape. Tourists in the hotel looked as if they hadn't left their rooms since the attack, while some of the local homeless camped out under the trees were living as if nothing had ever happened. For them, the only difference is that it might be harder to score drugs than before but they seemed to be doing better than anyone else. Surviving without running water is a skill that seems underrated in modern society. The crew stayed back as Pono made a push for the Hall where Nia stayed. There was tension in the room as he arrived. Something seemed to have gone bad in the day since they dropped off the produce.

Pono hung back as one of the men spoke. "Nia, we love you but we can't go on neglecting our families for these tourists."

Another spoke up. "How can we secure food for ourselves against these hoods? They have automatic weapons?"

It became apparent that the food did not make it to the tourist camp and was taken by roaming thugs. There was no order in the city. Waikiki was a tinder box lit at both ends, unsafe and deteriorating fast.

Pono made a move toward the front. "Eh, please listen." The men looked back and waved him off.

A group of locals that had helped unload the produce started to grumble before one spoke up. "The boy was able to get us food better than anyone else in this room. Let him speak."

Pono, caught off guard by the support, spoke timidly. "I need your help. I have something in trade."

The local man looked back at him. "So, speak like a man then."

Pono puffed up his chest and cleared his throat. "Look, this is the deal. I got pallets of canned food to be distributed, but you're telling me you already got robbed. Well, we have the food secured at the docks, for now, but the Syndicate and whoever else they are working with are going to take it back as soon as they can. I know how we can stop this."

Nia looked up from her desk in the corner. "How, boy? How do you propose we stop them?"

Pono was quick to answer back. "Well, they can't shoot us all. There's not enough bullets to shoot everyone in that camp. Plus the Samoans, the Micronesians, the Filipinos, and every local man and women in this city. If we can rally a big enough group, and my guys get them in their sites, we've got a shot. We make a push to show them our numbers and distribute the food in an orderly manner. We have guns but no men. If we band together, we can keep the peace and get people fed, keep some order for the time being."

Nia smiled.

"That's the best idea I have heard in a while."

The local man interjected, "So, what? We just march down Kalakaua all the way to the docks with 5,000 tourists and a couple thousand locals?"

Pono smiled at Nia and responded, "Exactly! If you don't mind, I like carry the Hawaiian flag at the front. If that's okay with you guys? No offense, but dis is Hawaii and all."

The local man who was giving Pono the business replied with a smirk on his face, "You look pretty Portagee to be carrying the Nation's flag down the road but, eh, you get one Hawaiian heart. I stay good with that."

Another local from the group chimed in, "Frick, we all Hawaiians these days. We couldn't send these fakas back if we wanted to at this point."

Everyone laughed, and a plan went into motion. They would rally the displaced tourists, leaving the women and children at the back of the line to protect them from any firefight that they might encounter with the gangs. Everyone seemed to agree, and went back to get their groups together. They would march at first light, hoping that the gangs did not raid the pier prior to their arrival.

Morning at Camp Smith was a desolate version of normal activity. With the exception of Communications and the SEAL team, the base seemed empty. The team was holed up in the rec room they used to decompress and speak freely about past and present missions. Tex, the largest one in the group, turned his head and said, "Ma'am, you holding' up okay?"

Hanalei was slow to comment. She was being held against her will, but with no real restraints. She was not at ease with the men, but safe. These were men of honor with orders. She thought it might be a better situation than being in the valley by herself trying to escape. Her goal was simple; stay alive until Ha'a came looking for her. She did not get into details with the men, what they had planned, who was in charge. From what she gathered, they didn't even have a clue what the end game was, why she was there, or what was next. She thought about it, but she did not want to draw any extra attention. They had been cordial as far as captors went, no need to rock the boat. By the second day, she had been given a nickname. She overheard two men joking, "Eh, go check if Silent Sally is hungry?"

Another remarked, "The Hush Hush Hawaiian got a plate right in front of her, Boss."

One of the men, while giving her lunch, decided to break the ice. "So, you part of that Klein estate by blood or by marriage?"

She paused, and thought cautiously, for a minute before answering. "My husband is a Klein, but I am a Lili'uokalani."

The big gun Tex blurted out, "Like the fruit?"

She laughed. "That's Lilikoi, big guy. You need to go sit in the corner for a bit."

The team laughed. She felt it might be to her benefit to start slowly building a rapport with the men, as they didn't speak much of what they were doing. This made her feel that they might just be on standby with no plan in the works. She was not handcuffed, not in a cell, but she did feel imprisoned like she was a throwback to her ancestors' overthrow. She kept her composure, but she was being oppressed and it felt sickening deep down. The more information she could bring to Ha'a, the better chance they'd have to survive. It seemed, though, that the SEALs knew nothing. She would have to create more opportunities to uncover information. She inquired with the guards, "Could you ask your bosses if I could stretch out in the yard in the mornings, and go for a jog?"

The guards laughed. "Ma'am, there is no boss here. We have the doctor, the DEVGRU team, and that radio that goes to K- Bay. We work direct with the General at this point."

She asked, "So, how do I get to go outside?"

He replied, "I will ask the General, but this place is a fortress so, keep in mind, don't get any crazy ideas."

She raised her eyebrow and smirked, as if to say 'no duh.' "I just can't stand being inside all day. Can I talk to the General directly?"

He looked at the team lounging, reading magazines next to the windows for lights. "Lady, when he calls, we listen. I will ask, but no promises. This ain't a picnic for us either. The whole team was on leave when this shit popped off. I was planning a camping trip, but it was raining. So, I guess things happen for a reason." He laughed.

She queried, "Family trip?"

He nodded. "Taking my son and daughter to Malaekahana, camping for a week with their mom. Get them out of the condo complex she got them couped up in."

She smiled. "Sounds fun."

He smiled. "I guess we're all taking a rain check on our plans. I'll see if we can give you some fresh air tomorrow. I sure as hell could use some."

Ha'a and the crew where rigging transport for the Kapu System to be moved to the prison. Kamai was coming down hard from his pill binge from the night earlier. He yelled for Ha'a. "Come, come. I not doing good. Seeing things, Ha'a, come." Ha'a circled around and was startled by the sight of a Pueo. The Hawaiian owl was encircling Kamai, who just happened to be sitting near a scurrying field mouse. The owl dove towards the mouse, and Kamai swatted at it in a frenzy. The owl backed off and descended backwards, hitting a tree and falling to the ground. Ha'a ran over to the bird just as it closed its eyes. It was breathing, but Ha'a feared it might die right before him.

"Damn it, Kamai! What's wrong with you? You know that's bad luck."

Kamai looked confused. "What? I thought I was hallucinating. That was real?"

Ha'a was infuriated with Kamai. "I'm done with you. Get your act together, or you can find your own way."

Kapu hurried to tend to the Pueo. Kapu knew the Pueo was sacred, that it was a symbol of their ancestors, but he never grasped the mystic about them.

He asked his father, "Dad, what is it with the Pueo? Why is there always such a big deal about seeing them."

Ha'a replied, "They are legend. Pueo are believed to have the power to pull souls back from the Underworld and protect armies in battle. Out of respect, as a Hawaiian, you should not even point at them in awe. However, your cousin nearly killed the one, your tending too."

Kapu took this to heart, and decided he would tend to the owl as best he could as they made a move back to the prison.

Ha'a looked back at him as they started to make their way. "Son, I know you mean well but there is only so much you can do. We have a lot going on."

Kapu sighed and replied, "Dad, it's hard for me to watch an animal we can't feed ourselves with die. Besides, it might watch over us. It can't do that if we leave it here for dead."

Ha'a smiled and nodded. "Kapu, do you have any juice left in the SEAL's radio?"

Kapu replied, "A little. Running the tracking on the other device drained it a bit."

Ha'a gestured for it, and turned it on.

He spoke. "SEAL team, this is Ha'a Klein. Come in." There was dead air.

"SEAL team, come in. This is Ha'a Klein."

A voice came over the radio. "This is Dispatch DEVGRU. Over."

Ha'a responded. "Looking to broker a deal with the General. Do you have contact?"

"We can make contact. What is your message? Over."

Ha'a paused. "A trade. Halawa Prison. The System for Mrs. Klein. Do you copy?"

Dispatch paused, and there was silence for a good minute. Ha'a looked at his son while their men steadily moved ahead of him.

"This is Dispatch. Please confirm again. What time, and did you say Halawa Prison?"

Ha'a wasted no time. The battery light was blinking and the radio was squelching as if there was feedback from low battery. "Halawa Prison. Front gate. Tomorrow at 6pm, dusk. Even trade. We want the General present. Do you copy?"

A pause, as the battery signaled low battery with a beep.

"Copy that. The General is aware. 6pm, Halawa Prison. Over." The radio died moments after. Ha'a stuffed it in his backpack, and hustled up the valley to rejoin his men.

Pono had made his way to the tourist encampment where Nia and her men, along with another thirty locals, had joined in helping with food distribution and security. There was a heavy sense of desperation at the camp. Even the men had a look of despair. One of the camp's residents came to Nia and spoke privately at the Zoo's office. "I know you are doing your best to help us, but it's not safe in here any longer. Some men have been attacking families for food and, worse yet, there have been attempts to attack some of the young girls. Fortunately, some of the others reacted in the girls' defense."

Nia asked, "What was done with these men when they were caught?"

The woman replied, "They've been restrained in the empty chimpanzee cage on the northside of the zoo. We don't know what to do with them."

One of the local men, in his mid-30s, overheard the conversation and spoke up. "Mama, if you don't mind we can handle this situation for you. I'm not perfect, but one thing does not fly, even amongst prisoners is that."

Nia asked the man, "Have you been in a situation like this before?"

He responded, "If you mean have I done time? Well, yes, and what you are dealing with needs to be made an example of, or others will get out of line."

She nodded as if to say, 'have at 'em.'

His men went over to the cages in an uninhabited part of the zoo and made contact with the ones they had separated from the general population. Nia was busy trying to organize the encampment and move to the entrance area of the zoo where there was a small stage. She took a small bullhorn that looked like it was made for a high school cheer squad, and started to address the camp. "We spoke before, and we did not have much good news with the exception of having rations to keep this camp going. However, we have made the decision to forge alliances with the tourists and citizens of Honolulu. We have a large problem with the gang population in Chinatown looking to control what is left of the supplies on this island. Our contact, Pono, is here to explain."

Pono was slow to move to the front and grab the bullhorn. He glanced at the disheveled group of mostly haole tourists looking back at his silhouette, backlit by the sun, squinting and listening for any shred of hope this young local might have. "Look, people, we're all hurting at the moment. We don't have too many options beyond working together. We have a gang that wants to exploit our problems, and not many resources other than our numbers." He paused. "What I am saying is, we need to work together and march on down to the docks as a whole so they can't overthrow what we have temporarily secured."

A man shouted, "How are we going to do this unarmed?"

Pono answered him. "Well, we will be unarmed only until we get to the docks. We have munitions in place. If we pick up more people as we walk towards the pier, from the hotels and streets, our numbers will be too large for them to do anything about the revolt."

A woman from the crowd shouted out, "What about the children and the women?"

Nia responded, "We need every able-bodied person to join in this march to the pier. A distribution of food will begin once secured, and we will discuss the next stage of organizing accommodation for you and the rest. The hope is that the abandoned cruise ships can host families, women, and children. The single men will return to the camp with supplies and set up further infrastructure."

It seemed as if this was enough for the people to grasp onto and a time for action, even if not perfect, was needed. The local men returned, walking on stage with a beaten tourist they had pulled from the chimpanzee cages. The one who had spoken earlier, a man named Erlan, asked to speak.

Nia nodded, and gave him the bullhorn. "To all you who think that society has fallen and you're on your own, please be aware that honorable men will always be there to put you in your place. This is a warning to you and the locals. We are in this situation as one, not separate, and those who do harm will be harmed. It's back to basics. No courts, just justice."

A woman and her child scornfully glared at the beaten man, as if they'd had an encounter with him.

Hanalei woke up at Camp Smith to a small ray of sunlight coming in from the same windows the SEALs had huddled near while reading the day before. She walked over to a gas burner in the mess hall where a tea pot was whistling. She turned it off and, as she turned, she saw the Dispatch operator and greeted him. "Good morning. Any good news about me going out today?"

He smiled. "Well, I hope you enjoy hiking. Your husband brokered a trade with the General. DEVGRU team is peeping to hike you in to Halawa Prison to make the trade."

Hanalei was surprised. "Trade for what?"

He looked uncertain. "I heard mention of some sort of a system, but that's above my pay grade, ma'am."

Hanalei shook her head and thought to herself, *Is he giving up? Is he letting the General get his way?* It warmed her heart to know that Ha'a was putting it all on the line to get her back, but she didn't feel threatened and she wouldn't want her position to offset the course of history. This was hitting too close to home for Hanalei, given her lineage and family history.

Ha'a and the crew made it back just after dark and were greeted by some of the MWH, one of whom was the gang member that had been keeping Kamai hostage until the food drop-off. He called out Ha'a with no hesitation. "I told you! Don't play with the MWH. You like get smoked in front of your son? Your fucking haole side coming out too much. You talk but no do, just like your dumb Portagee brother-in-law."

Ha'a avoided direct eye contact. He did not want to set him off. "Look, there is more to this then you know. Did you know Yakimura is working with the Chinatown Syndicate? I never said anything, but you know he is playing both sides."

Stasi, the MWH leader, nodded. "Tell me something new. A gangster playing the field to his advantage? We no trust the Japanese old fart, but you the one we get issue with. What happened? You never showed up at the projects, and this knucklehead disappeared."

Ha'a responded, "Before you cock your pistols, hear us out. We got hung up under the Middle Street merge, and gave the goods to a church on the fringe of your community. It was the best we could do. We had to get this system out from the open. Kamai, as dumb as he can be, was trying to help. He found a radio in your projects, and was getting signal from Kauai. He brought it back to my estate, and was headed back when I am told he found out my wife had been captured. He came back, spoke to your men, and did the best he could."

Stasi looked at him. "So, the church get the food, huh? So, why you bring this thing here then?"

Ha'a went on. "Well, my wife was taken by the General at K-Bay. He wants this. It's what I was telling you about, the system that could feed everyone and get us off the grid. No need for power, it's self-contained."

With a quizzical look on his face, Stasi asked, "Why give your bargaining chip away? He's not gonna kill her."

Ha'a raised his brow. "Don't think you're the only gangsters on this island. The US Military has been jacking people for a long time before MWH ever existed. Anyhow, this is just a prototype. It's not even functioning. It's a decoy, buy us some time. They'll think it's not running because their grid is down, but we need to get the real system going before they figure it out and seize it on my land."

Stasi looked confused. "Why you telling me all this?"

Ha'a explained, "I don't have a choice. I only went to Yakimura and told him I was bringing him food and the system to store at his property so he wouldn't go looking for us, make him think we were in need of his help."

Stasi interjected, "You mean you playing both sides too then! Why should we trust you?"

Ha'a continued. "I am not going to say more than I am here for the people, for everyone. Not just MWH, not just local Hawaiians. I am doing this so we can all survive with what is left of our island nation. If you help me, you're helping yourselves."

Stasi nodded in agreement. "So, where we at then? We meeting up with a SEAL team at the doors of the prison, give 'em the system, get your girl, and then what? Kiss our worries away? You know Yakimura gonna make a move at one point."

Ha'a looked at the men in the yard of the prison. "You see what you got here? You have community. You call it a gang but, in reality, it's community. Whether good or bad, you can use your community's culture to change things. If it's just me and you, we don't have a shot. We agree on some things, though? To men like the General or Yakimura, that's dangerous. We organize, we win. It's that simple."

Stasi pulled back and gestured like he was confused. "Wait. You want to take on the military then? Yakimura is one thing, the US Military is another."

Ha'a replied, "We're are not taking on anyone. We're organizing. If the public follows one guidelines and makes clear it is not going to follow another, the government forms around the people's choice, not Marshall Law. They could be fully intact, but if everyone goes one way so do the tanks and the bullets. You need a class to rule. You can't shoot your way to a republic."

One of the MWH members shouted, "We already the MWH republic! We run our streets!"

Stasi looked back and put his fingers to his lips to tell him quiet, then turned his attention back to Ha'a. "We run nothing if the military is going to dictate the islands. We just think we do. We control what they let us. We're in, Ha'a. Just keep the Samoans and the locals off our back. We never have good runins with any of the local gangs."

Ha'a nodded, and started to discuss his exchange plan. He explained his goal was to get intel out of the General, to delay the exchange so he could get more time with the General. Ha'a wanted to know what capabilities they had to re-engineer the system with Dr. Hind and get it online. Ha'a and Stasi's men would store the system in the far back of the prison yard, and only allow the General in, at first, to inspect it and call his men to meet them at the gate to move it. They could assume the General would not come in the gate alone, but with the SEAL team or other special forces. Ha'a wanted to be able to light up the area enough to where his men could see the General, but the General would not be able to see Ha'a and Stasi's men very well as he came in through the gates. The prison had two halogen lamp posts that were stored in the boiler room. They were powered by internal generators, very much like those used at a construction site. They tested them, and both had enough gas to run for about three hours' time. They were planning to use these lights to move the system into an uncompromising position making for a difficult haul away. This would give Ha'a's men enough time to secure Hanalei, and Ha'a enough time to talk to the General. They had to assume that if some equipment found in below ground structures was working, that the military must have working equipment in bunkers. It might not be tank brigades, but they could assume the military had been stockpiling for an emergency. Guns and backup generators; they knew the basic weaponry was working but all vehicles, ships, tanks, and the like had been rendered useless if they used guidance computers. If it had seen daylight during the attack, it was a dead bird. However, redundancy was the Marine's way. If one breaks, there's another one ready to move into position during battle.

Pono had sent out scouts from his crew to each hotel and apartment complex to rally people to join the march back to the pier. The locals went up McCully Street and around the Ala Wai to gather up the masses. Even the homeless were excited about the promise of free meal, and said they would march with them. Food was so scarce that even the best of the streetwise homeless were having a tough time finding meals. The Ala Wai Canal was not somewhere you would want to get your meals from but, with not many options, local fishermen were resorting to whatever they could. Rumors of radiation-tainted pelagic fish did not dissuade them from fishing in the ocean. Since the bombs went off, the local reefs seemed to have very little action. Dead fish had been found along the shoreline the morning after the battle, and a rancid stench lingered in the two weeks since the people had been marooned without contact.

Back at the pier, the men had been working in shifts at the buildings surrounding the entrance. With spilt 6-hr shifts, Sanoa would hang back at the tent. He spent his time inventorying the ammunition and prepping the entrance with oil drums so that they would not be susceptible to an easy entrance from the Syndicate or any other unwelcome visitors. Four of the men on security detail were switching shifts on the roof. They caught sight of something coming around the corner down on Nimitz Highway. It looked like a there was a flag floating on top of a sea of salt and pepper, easily a half mile deep and spreading the width of the highway. The men were, at first, petrified. They could not imagine there being that many gang members in the entire city.

They refocused their sights to the flag and recognized Pono, waving the flag as he came down the street with his ragtag band of Hawaiians and haoles. The sentries sent men down to let Sanoa know what was going on. K-9, the officer that got trapped in the portajohn back at the farm told him what he had seen. "About a mile up the road, Pono is walking with an army of people. I'm not sure what he did, but there's not enough rounds in Chinatown to take these buggas down."

Sanoa smiled and replied, "Go out and meet him. Tell the boys to provide cover, just in case someone gets cute, while Pono's leading everyone to the gate." The crowd was passing a stop light, as they approached the pier entrance, when a shot rang out through the air. The light atop the post shattered. In a sudden panic, the marchers dropped down to the ground. Still about one hundred yards out, K-9 heard Pono yell, "Tell your men it's us! Hold fire!"

He yelled back, "That wasn't us! Someone's watching! That was a warning shot! We've got cover in the buildings! Get everyone inside, NOW!"

Pono shouted back at the crowd, "Everyone up! Head for the gates! Take cover in the buildings! We're too close to turn back! LET'S GO!"

The guards in the towers scanned the surrounding buildings across from the pier. There was one that was eye level with their buildings. The rest were older, Chinatown historic buildings with only a few windows. The guards did not see anything that would point to a sniper, but kept on the lookout. They were all too aware that they could a be a target with their heads up looking through a scope. A bullet ricocheted off the CMU block, just missing the head of one of the guards. "Frick, that was close!" The other guard tried to follow the line of the shot. Meanwhile, the crowd kept pushing through street within yards of the gate. Sanoa took the rest of his men and positioned them behind the empty oil barrels with eyes on the buildings.

"I'm not sure this guy alone. The shots came from two different spots. They prolly been watching for the last two days, since we kicked them out. We just moved their plans ahead with Pono's stunt."

Sanoa kept his eyes on the buildings in front, then glanced back to the guards on the pier buildings.

Harold was amidst the Chinese giants, yet, he was oddly calm about it. They would sit in a semi-circle around him as if to protect him. He was not in any danger of being harmed, at the moment, but this was not where he wanted to be. One of the giants tended to Harold's wound, while he slept, after the fire fight. Another would stand guard when Harold went to the woods to pee. It was strange. Harold felt almost as if he had command of these things. He felt not so much like a prisoner but, rather, more like their default leader. They would speak to him in a dialect he'd never heard before. One out of, maybe, ten words he could pick up. He thought if he could only understand what they were repeatedly saying, he might be able to get them to go along with him. He tried signing suggestions to them by looking at an object, pointing, and then waving at them to move it. Nothing. They would go back to their routine of cleaning guns, checking their packs, and building an enclosure. They had finished off a small enclosure they did not use, one of the men grabbed Harold and motioned for him to move into the hut. It seemed so bizarre to Harold. He felt like Pomai from the Terminator movies. Rather than one cyborg from the future watching him, though, he had twelve futuristic Chinese giants protecting him. He just didn't know how to communicate with them. He thought if only Google was working, he could figure the translation and get them to do his bidding.

Besides the communication barrier with his captors, Harold had another issue. These men didn't eat. Well, they didn't eat anything that resembled actual human food. They had gel packs that looked similar to those used by distance runners in an ultramarathon. The giants gave him one. Harold spit it out in disgust. It tasted like salt and battery acid. He assumed it was an electrolyte and protein mix. The men didn't flinch. Harold noticed they would suck one back every two hours. When Harold started looking weak, one of the men forced a pack down his throat. Harold almost puked, but figured he needed the food and who knows what was next if he didn't comply. Conversation amongst the giant soldiers was short and seemed task-oriented, as if their goal was life. Nothing else existed. First it was Harold's wound, then shelter, then food. He noticed the men would use the same word for "Lift" each time they placed a broken branch on top of the hut. Harold, also, picked up on when they would do roll call. The giant with three medals on his lapel would call the others in. Another would point to the men, and signal to come when they needed extra hands. They all would fall in when given the command. It was like they were a computer working together off commands, one source to another, giving and changing orders as the situation progressed. Harold didn't understand how they did not lose focus until the task was done. They finished the hut and a fire pit within two hours. Having gathered wood, the soldiers started a fire in which they forced Harold to sit by until he fell asleep.

Harold awoke the next morning, and went for a proverbial "Hail Mary." He needed to get a reaction from the men. He yelled "Enemy" in the three languages in which he knew the word. Each time he yelled it, the men grabbed their weapons and did a sweep of the perimeter with guns held high at the ready. They would then sit back, with a slight look of disappointment in their expression. Harold noticed they all worked in unison. They all had the same reaction. This meant they understood him, even though he did not understand them. Waiting a bit, Harold thought about testing the giants to see if they would take a command from him in Mandarin. He looked around for a target, something they would attack if they did understand. Harold Spotted a mongoose in the bushes, eating some rotten lilikoi that had fallen from the vine. Shouting at the top of his lungs, he yelled "DIREN," meaning "enemy" in the Northern Chinese dialect. Harold pointed in the direction of mongoose as it turned to flee.

The men unloaded two clips each out of their bullpup-style QBZ-95 assault rifles. Another pulled out a knife and pursued the wounded mongoose into the woods as the men halted their gun assault. Within seconds, the soldier had re-emerged from the treeline, and stood before Harold with the dead mongoose in hand. Harold thought to himself, *Jesus, they must think I'm in command. I might be the only one they can visually relate to as not their own but still Chinese.* He thought about all the bullies at school that he could teach lessons to, and thinking, *Who needs to lift weights when these guys could just do all the work?* A realization hit Harold. He need not be a prisoner. He could be the master of these soldiers. It dawned on Harold that he needed to get to the prison and fast. Using his knowledge of Mandarin, and newly acquired command over these soldiers, he ordered them to the location. After being given general directions, the men set off for Halawa. The high-ranking soldier with the three medals walked over to Harold, picked him up, placed him on his shoulders for the journey, and they headed off in the direction of the prison.

A firefight had ensued back at the pier. Only one member of the large procession marching to the docks had been wounded. Sanoa had his men advance into the streets, away from the people, to draw the fire. One of the men on the roof got a line from a tracer round. He thought for a second, and realized gangs don't carry tracers. These were military snipers firing on them. They must have been commanded to engage. This was too heavy for them to comprehend. *We're fighting what could be our own government?*

Sanoa yelled to the men. "They're enlisted, not gangsters! Look for a perch or the spotter!"

The K-9 handler noticed a scope in one of the windows across the street near Alakea business center. He knew, unless they had communications, the sniper had to be nearby. K-9 took off in a hurry, counting the floors and windows from the street corner, and ran into a parking structure next to the building to avoid contact. He hiked up two flights of stairs in the parking structure, and crossed into the building. Winded from ascending another four flights of stairs, K-9 slowly made his way down the hallway counting four steps for every window he counted on the sixth floor. He was three doors down when stopped. K-9 drew his weapon, knowing he was going in blindly. There was no window, just the door entry. He stood to the left of the door handle, so when he swung open the door he would be behind the door jam and the CMU block construction. K-9 tapped the door handle, ever so slightly, to see if it would make excessive noise. As he did this, he heard a shot fired from inside the room. They were not spray firing. It was deliberate, methodical targeting. K-9 could hear the spotter giving degrees of range to the sniper. He listened for the next position call, waited for the shot, and opened the door without them hearing. He snuck up behind and pointed his gun from a ten-foot distance. "Drop your weapons, boys! That's an order!" They turned as if to fire. K-9 shot the spotter in the leg as a warning. Both men dropped their weapons. He handcuffed the two of them together to a wall pipe. Moving to the next room, K-9 took a makeup mirror off the office desk and started to signal light on a window across the way. He could see another two men looking down on the crowd. The men hit the window with everything they had, and then the firing stopped. K-9 waved a white flag from the window, and pointed to the other window. Sanoa's men spotted K-9 with their binoculars. He was giving the sign for two men, and waved his hand to point the men on the street to go clear the building. Sanoa was behind a parked car laughing, "I guess K-9 can do something without his dog."

Harold had been in the woods now for three days, and had been a bit sick of eating his new buddies' rations. He decided he would pass the Kalihi Ice Ponds on his way to the prison to see if he could catch a mullet, and have his new found army whip him up a fire. The mullet were the only freshwater fish in Hawaii beside Aholehole which were found in the brackish water at river mouths. After thirty minutes with no luck, Harold decided to change plans and hunt for some Lilikoi on the vines hanging from the surrounding trees. If he couldn't find food, maybe he could drown out the taste of the disgusting rations he had been taking in the past two days. While up in the tree, he heard an echo that seemed to be coming from the distance.

"Circle back, boys. You see those branches? Something bigger than a hog has been roaming around here," said the Texan SEAL team member.

Harold looked down at his team and thought he could stay up in the tree and wait for a firefight, or he could test his newfound control further. He hesitated, until he saw the team making steady movement through the woods. He saw Kapu's mother with the SEALs and thought twice about starting a firefight. Instead, he directed his band of Chinese giants to go under the Mangroves, at the water's edge, and hide as the SEAL team passed. The SEALs stopped at the water's edge, as Tex attempted to track the footprints. "Frick, boys, these things are ghosts. Look at that. Straight to the water, and nothing on the other side. Prolley under the water recharging or something." Their leader had the men fire rounds into the depths before they moved on. "Hold your fire. Time to stop chasing ghosts. If they wanted to engage, they would have."

As the team pulled further away towards the prison, Harold descended from the tree. He had the men come out of the mangrove trees and air dry. They marched wide of the SEALs, avoiding all roads, and came up on their backs once they'd reached the gate.

The General made his way over the Likelike. He had a security detail accompanying him, and was planning on taking the roads all the way through to the prison. The SEAL team was to meet them at the Menehune water plant, a half mile before the prison. The General wanted this meeting short, with as little fanfare as possible. There was no need for it. Once they had the system, Dr. Hind could handle the rest.

The prison was not the optimal place for Ha'a to operate. They were safe here, but it did not allow for food distribution to a mass people. It was secure, but too accessible to the major city's population and military which could lead to theft. They needed to be somewhere where they did not have to remain in constant fear of some group trying to take it over. The valley, where the larger system was, had a built-in deterrent. It was far from any major group, military or otherwise. It would be easy to grow but hard to distribute food to the people. If Ha'a could get transportation figured out, it would provide the perfect blend of safety and convenience. If the solar-powered tour group trolleys stored in the old bunker were still functioning, they could load those with food every week to make island wide drop-offs. Members from MWH and Sanoa's boys could provide security for the deliveries. They would have to work in shifts to ease tensions. Ha'a knew his intentions with Mr. Yakimura would be brought to light soon enough. He knew he might become a Yakuza target. Getting security in place at the real system's gate would be key. The valley would buffer them on either side but the front entrance was the security issue.

The SEAL team made it to the Menehune warehouse by dusk and met with the General. "Boys, we're hoping you will just be props on this mission. We have no intention of engaging with civilians. The Kapu System has been agreed upon for the trade of Mrs. Klein. We just need to get the unit back to base efficiently and with as little damage as possible."

The captain of the SEAL team looked at the General. "Requesting permission to speak freely, sir?"

The General looked at him with approval. "Go ahead, son."

"Us boys are a bit in the wind. Our families are not in base housing. We were on leave during the attack, but we are here. What I am saying is we are reporting to you, as the highest commanding officer on island, and we're requesting base housing for our families in exchange for our loyalty."

The General smiled. "Rome fell when they could not offer their soldiers benefits any longer. Altruistic patriotism is not a way I see governing my assets. Your families need protection and, if you're in the field, well then we need to get them on base and safe. Consider this a request approval. Put it in writing as a Naval Joint Task Force request, to the attention of General Kaneohe of the Marine Corps. You will be housed on the naval side of K-Bay, on the Kailua side of Makapuu Road. You can circle back to Camp Smith to get any gear needed for future missions."

The Captain nodded, satisfactorily. "Thank you, sir. Our team stands ready and able."

The men pushed out into the night sky, uphill, towards the prison one click away.

Meanwhile, Ha'a and his team were getting ready for the General's arrival. The lights were hitting the back wall of the prison where the system was stored. Harold had made it to the gates with his new brigade of Chinese warrior giants. "Kapu, Ha'a! Open quick! It's me, Harold…and some friends!"

A few MWH looked back over the wall and drew down on them. "Eh, boy! Get the hell out of there! Why you bring those things here? You like get shot?"

Kapu ran to the front gate. "Harold, get back! Guys, blast 'em! They'll kill him and us!"

Harold raised his hands in the air, desperately waving a towel. "NO, NO, NO! Hold up," he yelled emphatically. They're with me! RELAX! They're on my side!"

Ha'a peeked over with Kapu again. "What's going on? Are those the Night Marchers you were talking about, Kapu?"

"Ya, Dad! I don't know what's going on."

Harold waived his hand. "Hi, Mr. K! You want to meet the boys?" Ha'a squinted his eyes, baffled by the sight of Harold sitting atop a giant Chinese warrior that looked like something off the stage at a Mr. Olympia contest with an assault rifle across his chest.

"Harold, how you know they didn't just use you to find us?"

Harold laughed. "Watch this." He pointed at a spotlight on the opposite side of the guard tower, where they were watching, and commanded, "Seji!" The giants all opened fire, lighting up the spotlight like a fireworks show.

Ha'a frantically told him to stop. "Harold! What the hell, kid? We're about to meet up with the military to get my wife back. Just get inside. Leave those meatheads at the gate." Harold gave them instructions to wait out front for his command. They all pulled a ration from their packs and sucked it back.

The General and his crew heard the shots fired. He paused their march onwards. "Well, I guess contact might be something they're planning on more than we were. I think I might have to throw an audible. Boys, once we're near the prison I want you to hide in the tree line and wait for me to call you forward. Only enough hands to pull the system will come out when called. I don't want them to know our numbers. They will be less likely to make a move if they think we have a few dozen infantry companies lying around the corner."

The men responded back, simultaneously, with a "10-4."

Harold and Kapu where talking about what had gone down, how he could give the warriors orders, how they were trying to protect him, and so on. Ha'a was in earshot. "Look, we might have just caught a lucky break, but are you sure that you are the only one they will listen to?"

Harold shrugged as if to say, well it's working so far. "Mr. K, I thought they were going to kill me two days ago. I don't know anything, but they speak mandarin as well as a bunch of other dialects. For now, it's working. I'm sure if their boss came a calling they might snap my neck."

Ha'a's eyes went wide at the thought of keeping a rogue fighting force around them. "Well, let's just hope we have no one out there that could compete for their attention, Harold. These giants seem to like you just fine for now."

They all laughed. Ha'a asked Harold if he could give them an order. "Can you tell them to meet the General and lead him into the prison with my wife? It might send just the right message."

"Sure! No problems on my end, Mr. K."

The General was a few hundred yards out when the guys in the guard tower spotted him. "Eh, Ha'a, get up here. Your guy stay here, he alone."

Ha'a was surprised when he saw the General walking alone. He shouted down, "Good evening, General! Where is the calvary and, furthermore, my wife?"

"Ha'a, my friend, I travel light. I thought this was a friendly meet up, but I guess those shots fired were just in honor of my arrival?"

Ha'a looked back at Harold and shook his head. "Just some board exinmates letting off some steam."

The General laughed. "I always knew you would poll well with the convicts. If only they could have voted, you may have just had a shot at Mayor, Ha'a."

Ha'a smirked. "So, are we doing this trade or what, General? I don't know what you have laying beyond the tree line, but I know my wife should be somewhere out there or else what are we doing right now?"

The General did not miss a beat. "Spot on. What are we doing right now? Good question. Let's be clear, what I've got beyond that tree line could lay waste to whatever you've got behind those walls. So let's just consider this a gesture on my part, one perfectly healthy loved one for a semi-used system we could have just recreated with a lot less fanfare."

Ha'a spun back to Harold. "Tell team Big C to step out in front of the gate and create a perimeter, with two men escorting the General and my wife back in with his men to carry out the system."

Harold turned to Kapu. "What Big C?"

Kapu kicked Harold's left foot. "Just give them the order."

The General signaled to have Hanalei brought forward. She had a tired and stressed look on her face, having overheard the conversation. The General moved forward only to see six large figures move forward from the security check-in gate. With a slight look of anxiety, the General called back to the tree line, "DEVGRU, fall in! Bring Ha'a's wife, and leave the other men behind," as so to perpetuate the air of a giant army laying in wait of his command. The SEAL team moved forward and aligned to either side of General and Hanalei. They moved through the security check with two members of Ha'a's newly dubbed Big C team remaining at the front while the rest fell in following the General's crew on their six.

Harold looked at Ha'a. "Now what?"

Ha'a replied, "Tell them to leave two men up front, and have the other four follow up the rear of the SEAL team with their muzzles pointed high."

Harold looked confused. "I never muzzled them. They're not dogs. I just tell 'em stuff to do, and they do it."

Kapu snapped back, "Their guns! The muzzle! You know, the thing where the bullet comes out."

Harold quickly responded. "Got it." The giants followed the SEALs to the center of the prison yard. The General waived at Ha'a, and signaled his men to start moving the system onto the flat bed. The General yelled back, "A bit more security than the last time we met up. I guess we should expect that. After all, we did try and take the system and ended up with your wife. I apologize for that. A bit of a miscommunication mixed with some grey intentions on my part. I feel it was justified, you know, for the people and all." As he said this, the faint rumble of an engine was heard and got louder as the General and his men exited the front gate.

Ha'a replied, as the General passed him, "I would be hard pressed to believe anything the US has done wasn't justified."

The General laughed. "You know, Ha'a, being a military man can be summed up in one word. Redundancy. You hear that truck rumbling towards us? Ha'a, that's due to redundancy. For every unit taken away during the attack, we had one sitting in Ulupa'u Crater. I'm a big fan of having things around for rainy days, Ha'a, and boy does Hawaii rain a lot!"

Ha'a smiled. "You know, General, I guess we found some middle ground. Hawaiians prepare for the seasons, and I feel we are going into a Ku season."

The General looked at him as he passed. "Not sure what Ku season is, Ha'a, but be sure it best not have any hostel notions attached to it."

"Ku season is meant for the prosperity of all men and women whether in crops, fishing, or growth of the people. However, how we get to this season will depend more on your intent than ours."

"Ha'a, the mighty eat and the meek, well, they usually end up doing the cooking. At least the military aims to provide a place at the table for everyone. It's just that, sometimes, it's first come first serve in our line of work. You're going to have to put your ideals aside for your people, at one point. We can help. We have the same goals. You just think our intents are not in line with your altruistic view of Hawaii. Nevertheless, the goal is the same; the people fed, the island secured, order restored. We can do it faster than your little Ku season you are planning. Marshall Law isn't a bad thing when everyone is eating three squares across the state."

Ha'a shook his speak aside to attend to his wife. "If you're done, General, I would like to speak with my wife, and I am sure you want to get back to base and get the system to Dr. Hind. He's probably head over heels to know he is getting the project to himself finally."

The General shook his head yes. "You know, military assets are not a bad thing. I see you've got some new ones of your own, but you should check the label. I think yours were made in China."

Harold quickly blurted out, "Well, ya better check the warranty on your assets! My guys almost turned your boys into chop suey!"

The DEVGRU Captain replied back, "We ain't lab rats, kid. Those things are like a Sherman tank with a toddler's brain inserted. I don't know how you got them on your side, but be warned. If we get the go ahead, I got no problem sending those sub humans back to whatever hole they crawled out from. We've got the means. Just say go, little man."

Hanalei hugged Ha'a. Ha'a looked back at the men as they carried the system off. "General, so now that you have what you want, you going to reach out to the people? Give them some hope, or just propaganda?"

The General waived as his troops pulled the system outside of the prison. "We've got to do that Makahiki sometime, Ha'a. I always loved a good war game."

The gates shut, and the faint sound of a diesel truck motor puttered off in the distance.

Chapter 7
Aligned by Alchemy

In the days since the sniper battle on Nimitz, the men at the pier had been able to secure the leftover resources off the remaining boats and unlock containers. The majority of the tourists held at the zoo were moved into the Honolulu business district on Alakea Street. Doctors and nurses set up some small clinics in parking structures, and the offices above were turned into boarding facilities for the zoo encampment residents. Women and children had security measures such as locked doors and private quarters. The team did a sweep through the cruise ships to see if anyone was in need of assistance. The ships were still occupied by those who had docked the morning of the event. The food in the kitchens had spoiled, and the bathrooms were overflowing, to make it a giant funnel of filth. The men assisted getting the families first to the new facilities, and recruited any willing men to help guard the pier as well as the entrances to the holdover areas and buildings. Many of the tourists left in Waikiki were far worse off due to their distance from resources. The men made drop-offs, but the ones who had showed up for the morning distribution of rations were benefiting from their close proximity.

Yakimura had, by now, returned back to his home and contemplated his next move. He knew that he would need more resources, and had heard that a large group of the MWH were holding down Halawa Prison. He set up his convoy, once again, using the last of the juice left in his golf carts which had been stored inside the warehouse facility. A normal, ten-minute drive took two hours. Mocking comments were shouted from the tenement housing as they passed. The sight of ten armed men driving golf carts, it was hard to not laugh. Yakimura and his men rode through the backgrounds of Kalihi. When arriving at the prison, they had noticed the large men at the gates entrance drawing weapons and pointing at them. As they got closer, they slowed. The guards did not make a gesture as to stop or come forward. A shot was fired once the golf carts hit the speed bump, but at the wheel of the lead cart.

Yakimura's men drew their weapons, and hid behind the carts for shelter. "Eh, don't fire! We're here to talk to Kasian," yelled one of his men. Yakimura took a handkerchief from his pocket and waved it in the air towards the prison.

Some of the men were looking down from the guard tower. One yelled, "Get Kasian! Yakimura is here acting all Mahu, waving a flag like one bitch."

His partner smacked him in the back of the head. "Eh, my aunt is Mahu. Aunty Uncs would lick you, brah. Best watch yourself."

Kasian and Ha'a went to the gates with Harold, and the giants stood down. Kasian brought them inside. Yakimura looked a bit perplexed at the sight of Ha'a. "I was not expecting you to be here, Ha'a. What's going on? Making new alliances behind my back?"

Asian interjected, "We not aligned with anyone. We do what benefits us on the day, and our arrangement is still ongoing. I don't see any MWH at your gates burning torches just yet, Yakimura."

Ha'a was quiet. Yakimura responded, "Never mind your arrogance. My men were taken down at the pier. You were nowhere to be found when we went to town. We could have held it down if you would have been where you were supposed to be. Now, we have to hit them head on and, guess what? We're gonna need double the men this time."

Ha'a jumped in. "Who took your men on?" Yakimura looked at Ha'a and squinted at his question.

"So, you're interested in my business now? Ha'a, you better mind your business and part of that business, I thought, was to be filling my warehouse." Ha'a replied, "We ran into issues with the General and my, um, well…just we ran into some trouble."

Yakimura looked angry. "You what? Got into it with the General? You pissing off the military? I told you that's bad for business. I think we're, as you say, 'Pau,' Ha'a. You're too much like your father. What's good for goose is not always good for the gander. I am the goose, Ha'a, and I could give shit about your gander!"

Kasian got between the two. "Look, Yakimura, I get no problem banging some heads for you, but you not gonna be telling me who to do business with. Ha'a got something going and I just assume run some protection for him even if I am sending men your way."

Ha'a pulled back. He didn't want to let Yakimura know he had an idea as to who hit the pier. Sanoa, he was sure, could have been a part of this. It was time to find out what was going on in town before it went dark on the east side of the island. Getting the system up and running was imperative.

Yakimura started to leave. He turned to Kasian and said, "We meet at the Zippy's on Nimitz tomorrow afternoon. We'll wait for nightfall. Bring 30 men." He walked off, looking at the Chinese giants, and shook his head in disgust as he passed the monstrous men.

Pono had been busy reveling in their success, flirting with all the tourist girls, and laughing it up with his cousin. They realized they should get the boat back to Kaneohe Bay at one point, but felt they should revel in their new place in Hawaiian history. The surf had picked up so they took the boat to Kewalo Basin, mooring the boat off an abandoned superyacht, and borrowed some longboards from the Lifeguard headquarters on the side of the harbor. In the lineup, they started talking story with one of the uncles. He was going on about what some UH researcher said to him at the research facility at the basin. "Eh, boy. You not been eating da fish, have you?"

Pono thought about for a second and replied, "Not lately. We should troll on the way back to the pier, though. Maybe get some Ono running."

The uncle went wide eyed. "No, no, boy! Dey get da kine."

Pomi jumped in. "What? Ciguatera no madda. I get the iron stomach."

The man shook his head. "No, boy, radiation! The research lady tell us they getting readings, can give you Cancer quick. We stay in deep shit. We trying survive on one island surrounded by fish we no can even eat. She say the radiation needs to bound or whatever's to organic material like the limu, fish, seaweed, all kine. She said we need eat as little as possible, for now, and the smaller da better. The pelagics stay fucked boys!"

The boys thought back to Ha'a and his system; fish, food, no engine needed, clean water, and so on.

"Pomi, we gotta get going!"

Pomi looked baffled. "I never even got a set yet, Pono."

Pono replied, "I told you about Ha'a, da guy, he is what really going to save Hawaii. What we just did just a drop in the bucket. Getting the containers going was good, but they will be empty soon."

Pomi shrugged. "Cuz, fine by me. Just along for the ride. Not like I got anywhere else to go. Yakimura def not taking me back anytime soon. If you get one posse, I like meet da boss already."

Sanoa was doing inventory with the men, counting the clips, rounds, and weapons after they had deputized some of the locals that helped Pono get everyone from the zoo to the pier. Kapu had left the prison via bike, with Harold, at the request of his dad. They rode their bikes straight up Nimitz with two of the Chinese soldiers Harold was controlling. It would have been comical to anyone who saw, even if the men were packing major weaponry. The two arrived at the gates and caught eyes from the guards. One yelled, "Sanoa! We got something going on up here you might want to come check out!" Sanoa broke from his duties and headed to the front gate. He was taken aback from seeing men much larger than himself. He was used to being the biggest one in the bunch.

Kapu quickly explained. "I am Ha'a's son. He sent me here to get an update, and let you know they are moving with the MWH to the Ka'a'awa Valley. We need men to help us secure the valley and for the trip over the Likelike. Yakimura is not aware we are working together but, between him and the military, someone might take a shot at us on the way over."

Sanoa paused. "Boy, you're going to need to explain these giant men. One, what are they? Two, how did you get them to fit on those bikes?" One of the giants made the bike disappear between his legs, as if there was just two wheels attached to his backside and knees with a handlebar separating the two.

Kapu explained who they were and how they functioned. Sanoa was skeptical but figured if he could keep them inline getting downtown, maybe they were really at the command of Harold.

Pomi and Pono arrived as they had finished up, introductions went down and they caught up to see how they could play a role in the next move. Kapu felt the best way for them to help was to sail off and put the boat back in the bay. It could be used to help transport the remaining fish at Moli'i Fishpond, and assist in distributing the harvest when the scaled up Kapu System went online. After enough stock was pulled from the pound, they would seal the brackish water entry so that pond would not get any organic matter from the ocean and keep the new stocks radiation free.

Pono agreed, but asked if he could keep one of the men for the journey. "It would be good to have some backup for when we pass the base. If they want to, the military could knock us out of the water. Just sayin'. I'm sure they've heard we took out two of their men during the firefight the other day. I'm sure they noticed the ship docked at the pier. They might be onto the K-Bay Pirates already, if you know what I mean."

Kapu agreed. "Best you guys sail past in the dark. We're not sure what's working at the base but, if they do have any systems up, they might spot you on radar and you'll be an easy target."

They decided to leave the following day for the sail. Sanoa opted to send ten of the men they had deputized as security. "Right now, Kapu, this is our priority. Right here, the food that is guaranteed is our priority. I hope your dad can pull this off, but we have our mission. The local boys, and whatever these giant things are, should be able to handle a little road trip to the Windwardside."

Kapu understood. There was too much going on in town at the moment. It seemed like it was a controlled chaos compared to the wild scene they saw the last time they made their way from the estate. It made him think about his home. Was it being taken care of, or if it had been looted? He just wanted to disappear into the woods on a hunt, or into the ocean for a surf, and forget about all the problems the island held.

The General had made his way back to the base. The SEAL team had left to gather their families and move them into housing on base. Camp Smith, without their presence, was now just a shell with no staff and only a bare-bones security patrol. Their new home would be a Forward Operating base they could sink their teeth into. The SEALs were invigorated. They didn't know what the fight would entail, but they knew they were ready to protect their new home and let the chips fall where they may. The SEALs were given three Humvees, each mounted with an M2 Browning .50 caliber machine gun, that were pulled from the crater. It was a familiar feeling, but in a new setting, for the team. They were not the normal grunts who ran convoys on public highway training routes around the island. This was the first time they had been on civilian roads, on US soil, and it made them all have a think.

Tulsi blurted out, "Are we still in America, boys? What is this? I feel like we're running a mission in the tropics, not on leave back in Hawaii." They noticed, quickly, as they ran through the streets that the sight of an armed Humvee driving along the back streets of Pearl City did not imbue the locals with any kind of patriotic sentiment. The Hawaiians were not waving American flags at them. There seemed to be a post-event hangover lingering in the streets, not quite as if a riot would break out but not far off.

The SEAL they called Talon rarely spoke, but when a rock was thrown at the Humvee he let out his query. "Big Boss, what's the game plan? Can we engage friendlies?"

The team leader responded, "These streets ain't ours, from what I see. I think this is a make it up as you go situation. Geneva ain't holding any conventions on our actions, boys. Use your judgement. Don't get us mobbed for a rock in the windshield."

Talon replied back, "Copy that, sir," racking his weapon and putting a sight on a thugged out street kid flipping them the bird as they pulled into secured condo housing on the base near Pearl Harbor and Aloha Stadium.

Sam, the youngest of the group, looked back at the stadium. A large Hawaiian flag had been draped from the side. Spray paint underneath the flag read, "Auwe! Occupation of the Hawaiian Nation no more!"

He smirked, and turned to the boys. "We should just use that stadium as a big swinging dick of a display area. Drop a few tanks and ICBMs in the middle, invite the public down for free cookies, and we can give them a tour of what we got left in that crater back on base. That might calm everyone down a bit, let 'em know who's still running this island. Us driving around in a few Humvees, all alone, just makes it look like we don't have many resources. It makes us look weak. Let's get the transport filled and get the fuck out of here."

The gate was down at the condos, with no guard, but it was stuck in the shut position. The lead Humvee plowed through the gate, bending it backwards towards the guard shack.

Talon joked, "Well, I guess I lost that bet. Aluminum it is. I could've sworn it was wood. Looks like I'll be buying the first round at the Officer's Club tonight."

The other guys laughed. "Great, a round of warm beers."

Talon replied, "Nah, man. I heard they got a backup generator just to keep them taps cool. We going to the promised land! White sand beaches, cold beers, an armory, and not a native in sight!"

Team Leader snapped back, "Eh, boys! The people on this island are Americans, too. Take it down a peg. We got two Irishmen, a Mexican, two African Americans, and Tex. Tex, I don't know what the hell you are, but we got you too!"

The men laughed. Team leader continued, "To my count, that's six Americans all from Immigrant backgrounds."

Tex retorted, "Team Leader, Sir, I am only 90% American. The other 10% is shitkicker. We were that tribe that fucked up all the other tribes up back in the day!"

All the men laughed. The team leader chuckled, then assumed a more serious expression on his face. "We're here. You know what to do. Let's go!"

The team broke up into two three-man groups and went to where their families lived on either side of the complex. Team Leader called the shots on Group One, while Group Two was led by Talon. Talon decided it would be best to go in order of operations, by condo unit number, so as not to play favorites. His house was last in order. The first home they knocked with no answer. They waited 30 seconds, and positioned themselves behind the door jam. Talon hit the door with a door opener, which blasted the door and part of the frame to pieces. His men held position on the door jam. With one man on one side of the door, Talon and the other lined up against the CMU block structure on the other side. Talon cut the corner, peeking out piston and head first, as he pivoted at the hips and cut the angle on the door. He kept CMU between him and frame, between him and the open room, as he started to clear the room. With no threat, he signaled the other two men in and pointed at the couch for cover. Nothing. No sign of their families on either side of the complex. Team Leader and Group One had struck out as well. No sign of them. All that was found was a Tongan family hanging out on their front Lanai on the second floor.

Team Leader shouted up, "Eh, brother! You seen the family that used to live across there in the top unit? They were a military family. They usually hung out with the other military families living in the complex."

The Tongan answered back with a question. "You mean the Sandpaper Gang?"

Team Leader looked confused. "Sandpaper Gang?"

"Ya, that group of military wives always rubbing everybody da wrong way."

Tex laughed. "Yeah. Did one of 'em have a Southern drawl?"

The Tongan man quipped back, "She had a Southern something."

Tex stopped laughing, and pointed his weapon at the man. "Okay, funny man. Where did you see her last?"

The Tongan anxiously replied, "Calm down! Da haole brigade is at the stadium with everybody else. The Hawaii Foodbank is doing their last ration hand out."

Team Leader jumped in. "Why aren't you there, sir?"

The man looked at him. "You ever hear of gout? Well, mine been flaring up. All there is to eat, lately, has been potatoes; Okinawan, sweet, red, all kines. A fucking spud came outta my ass last night! I thought Heinekens was the only thing that brought it on. Learning something new every day, haha. Eh, but seriously though, be careful. It's all G getting the food, but getting out of there with the food? Well, let's just say the Sandpaper Gang ain't the only gang runnin' around that stadium after da handouts."

Tex yelled up to the Tongan. "Hey, thanks! Sorry about, well, you know. I'm just a bit edgy. We got kids. Ya know?"

The man responded, "No worries. I get it. My keiki over der now trying to keep dey fat ass alive. I told 'em no worry, keep da food. I just need water. Finally get to go on that diet I was supposed to ten years ago."

The men smirked, and made their way back to the Humvees. Riley was sent to go get Talon's group. When he found Group Two, Talon was doing a sweep of the last building. Riley shouted to Talon, "We're gone. Gonna go sweep the stadium. The neighbor said he seen everyone head to the stadium for a rations hand-out."

Talon yelled back, "No chance! My family is here. They had two months supplies, a Glock, 50 rounds, and a stack of 5's,10's, and 20's. They're here! Gonna check my house. We can meet up with you."

"Nah, man. We doing this together, as always." Talon nodded. "Well, you gonna help us sweep this last unit or what?"

"Roger that." They came up on the doorway on the second floor.

The door was open, but they noticed a hinge was bent. A faint, "Shit," came from Talon's mouth. As they came up the steps, Talon said, "Check your gear. Rack 'em." They moved fast. Talon barely looked in the room before he entered. He cleared the kitchen, and rushed down the hallway to the master bedroom. "Fuck! God damn it!" Riley came up right behind him.

"Calm down. Don't ever rush in like that, again. What if this was a hot target? We would have been carrying your body out of here."

Talon snapped, "The fucking floor board! Somebody robbed us! Someone has my family, or worse! Fuck!" He started tearing up.

Riley put his hand on Talon's shoulder. "Straighten up, soldier. You're not a detective, but you are a warrior. Let's get to the stadium, ASAP."

Talon took a deep breath. "OK, we're out."

The four men cut through the pool deck to save time getting back to the Humvees, when something caught Talon's eye. There was a blue sundress, three towels, and a tricycle next to the pool chairs. Talon froze.

"Hold up. That's my wife's dress. It looks wet. Something is wrong here." He looked beyond the pool, to the BBQ area around the back of the commons area. There, he saw five kids and two women standing over the burner. "She's here! Let's go!"

His wife turned and smiled. "Oh, hey honey! Where the hell ya been? It's been over a week. What happened to camping?" She giggled. "Just kidding."

He swept her up in his arms and gave her a hug. "What the hell are you girls doing out here? Why was the door kicked in?"

"Well, I've been leaving the door looking like that when we come down here. It makes it look like we've been raided. All the other houses have been getting robbed when no one is home, so I just pulled the cash and the Glock out, and kept them on me while we've been cooking. The food's running low, though. The Sandpaper Gang went over to the stadium to grab some more rations."

"So, you been feeding the girls?"

"Ya, the family's all good. Meat's been gone for a bit, but the pasta lasted until now. No hassles, really, besides the fact I get a lot of comments on my pink Glock from all the gang members. I just remind them the bullets are still hollow point." Tex's wife laughed.

"That's right, sister! She got a twin, too. My man got me one for Christmas. We're Glock sisters, ain't we now?"

Talon rolled his eyes. "Let's pack it in. Grab only what you need. We're moving house, ASAP. We'll send two Humvees to get the girls, and we'll meet at the gate in two hours to get back to base. Can you pack up for the girls, so we don't waste time?"

Tex's wife acknowledged the plan. "10-4, Talon. We kinda been swapping laundry, these days, so I know where all the girls favorite little nighties are…amongst other necessities. Who would have know, Talon? Tex might have a heart attack if he only knew."

Talon was mortified. "Jesus, Clarice! There are kids around. Just pack the fucking bags, you two."

His wife, in a somewhat sarcastic tone, replied, "Missed you too, honey."

Ha'a had been organizing the push toward Kawaa when Kapu and Harold showed up with ten local men who were willing to leave town to help the project.

Kapu went into the security office, where his dad was talking to Kasian. "Look, once we get over the Likelike, your men can turn back to Kalihi. We just don't need Yakimura trying to mess with us while we're on the move. We will run a light crew from there. You can turn back, check Yakimura out, keep him happy so you don't sever ties. I think me and him are done, but he is in your backyard and maybe you guys can get him on board. Remember, it's the military versus all of us. Otherwise, it will just be all of us listening to the General's commands."

Kapu knocked, even though his dad noticed he was back several minutes ago. "Dad, so it's better than it's been in town. They got the tourists secured near the pier, in the office buildings. Sanoa organized the inventory. He said there are two to three weeks' worth of canned goods to keep town going. There are a lot of street fights and disorganization, but nothing new. Pono told us he heard the fish were coming back with readings of high levels of radiation. So, I guess it could get worse before it gets better for the island."

Ha'a replied, "The doctor had warned me that this would be a possibility since there were so many bombs going off. Some were used underwater to create tsunamis on the California coast. The Chinese wanted to be able to reuse the lands once the attack was over. I didn't think it would happen that quickly, but I guess it was bound to show up at some point."

Harold was eavesdropping, and moved in from behind the door. "Ya, Mr. K! I guess some researchers where two hundred miles north of us when it all went down. I heard they were on a catamaran sailboat. They saw flashes in the morning sky, and went above a half dozen large swells rolling east that they assumed were from earthquakes. They stayed at sea for five days after, until they figured the swells were possibly man made. They're with UH. They went to Kauai first, on the way back, and then back to Honolulu. Pelagic fish are reading the highest since the aftermath of the Fukushima Nuclear Power Plant in Japan melted down, back in the day. I think I was like two when that happened."

Kapu nodded. "Ya, Dad. I guess the Maninis and Papio are the issue. The Pelagics always had isotopes in them, but the small fish are the big issue."

Ha'a put his hand on Kapu's shoulder. "Boy, if it wasn't the radiation, it would be the lead. We need to take back the control of our food supply now. All the more reason to pull the fish stocks at the pond and put them into use with the full scale Kapu System. After we get the system going, you two can grab some men and harvest the Ulu back in the valley." Kapu thought for a second. "Dad, so we're not going home for a while then? We going to use the cabins?"

Ha'a had built a retreat he let Kam Schools use for Hawaiian Studies classes. The Hawaii Boy Scouts, also, used it once a year for a retreat. Ha'a always found it strange, although humbling, that the majority haole and Mormon Boy Scout participants would want to be so interested in the culture. He had respected this and put Kapu in the program to learn survival skills. He thought a Hawaiian Eagle Scout wouldn't be a such a bad thing, especially if they were using the land for the purpose it was there for, to sustain the people. Both groups learned to plant Taro and cut down the Ulu. They would go to the fishpond and practice throwing nets and releasing the fish afterwards. The sun was always an issue for haoles in the Scouts. A lot of military kids would join in for the summer programs, and look like a roasted pig sitting around the campfires. The place had found memories for Ha'a and Kapu. Ha'a taught the people about his culture alongside his son. Kapu learned a lot about other cultures in turn, and respected the families that attended. He realized that the men who were committed to their families had a lot in common with the Hawaiian way of life. They just wanted to pass on skills to their sons and daughters. They were not the top tier corporate haoles or cutthroat military leaders you would have thought them to be. They were just men trying to spend time with their kids. Even the ones that would show up hot going on about their week and the drudges of dealing with the Bear market, or the hot stock they just dumped to pay for their kid's college. The layers quickly peeled away once they were humbled by the fact that God's true investment, growing and harvesting food, was not something they had wired.

Ha'a was patient, unlike some of the local fathers who had been burnt by haoles and took it as an opportunity to scold someone that, in the business world, might have had the upper hand on them. Things like, "Eh, haole! You know how to tie your shoes? 'Cause you sure can't tie a knot on that line. Da fish gonna laugh you back to the mainland."

Some men packed it in after run-ins. Others laughed it off, and were quickly taken under the same guy's wing. It was like a badge of honor that they could take a joke at their expense. These retreats were a good lesson for the blow-ins, as well. The transplants and the stationed military kids learned respect for the land, and could translate that to respect for the people.

Once a year, the Boy Scouts and Girl Scouts would meet within the valley and have a Makahiki, a culture exchange. Sometimes, a Kolohe kid from the school group would slap a haole boy and rarely in reverse, but both would be made shame. The Hawaiian boy would be given a test of his knowledge of is culture. Usually, the disrespectful ones could not answer the questions. They tended to be the same kids not paying attention in the classrooms and making trouble. Both sides would answer the questions he got wrong, in unison, as a shaming method. Then, the troublemaker would be given the task of planting a certain amount of Tarro to redeem himself. The haoles that started trouble would be given the same punishment, but when they could not get the answer they were not as ashamed. It was not their culture. They did, however, get asked to relate something that compared between the island and their home. When they were asked what an Ulu was, they would have to compare to something they had at home. The East Coasters would say pumpkins. The West Coasters would say avocado. They all had something to share that in some way made them relatable and more interesting to the local kids. They had more in common than not. Ha'a saw this as a way to show the local kids to be more accepting, and the transplants to have a reason-based respect instead of a force based respect that always led to resentment. He hoped this could bridge the gap and Hawaii's tension would ease with the next generations. However, Ha'a knew that, even with overpopulation and divided family lines, Hawaiians were the most accepting despite the tension of what had been happening to Hawaii.

The so-called progress, the military, and big business that had infiltrated his life since he was a boy had left a line in the sand that had not disappeared after the event. He hoped for cooperation and inclusion but it was not his thoughts, will, or altruism that would shape this new Hawaii. It was the General's, Yakimura's, and any other that would attempt to step into the power vacuum with an opinion, an agenda, or a faction to protect. They pushed off at midday, so both groups could travel by night. Once they split up at the top of the Highway tunnel, that split the mountain range separating Honolulu to the Windward side.

Chapter 8
Stadium-Size Problems

The SEAL team had split into two groups. One was set up with the families to pack and move. The other was heading around the corner with two Humvees to recover the other families, of which there were two wives and four kids between them. Tex went ahead and left his wife with Riley and Talon.

Team Leader was in the first vehicle and had them come around the back gate. They parked in a causeway, under the stadium, that was used to offload concessions to the various vendors during games. Tex pulled a pair of bolt cutters from his pack. "Boys, what do you say we bumrush the tunnel like we're playing for the Longhorns, for shits and giggles?"

Team Leader smirked. "Heads up, boys! We find an angle to scope where they are in here and we move in slowly as if nothing is going on, like we're a security detail for the Foodbank."

The SEALs walked three flights of stairs from the back-gate side to the bleachers. They came up slow, so as to see if anyone had seen them, and scoped the field where the food lines were long and disorganized. Some fights were breaking out at the field level exits. The stadium looked like a prison yard on family visit day. There were kids running around. Big, yoked thugs were shaking down people as they left the stadium. No security team could be seen outside of the staging area. There was a stage leftover from a Pro Bowl football halftime show that the aid workers were using. They had barricaded the stage, and had two men in plain clothes with sidearms at each entrance. These men were not in any recognizable uniform. Team Leader spotted his kids playing with some local boy at the right side of the stage. His wife was in line, ten feet away, with his daughter. "Boys, I'm going to go in solo, and pull them out." He pulled his outer layer of clothing off, down to his dry wick shirt. Using a knife, he cut his fatigue pants into cargo shorts.

Tex jokingly asked, "Is it beach day, Big Boss?"

The team leader responded, "You see anyone with camo and gear on that field? We have three clips each, and a bunch of civilians surrounded by some heavies roaming the entrance way. I'll go inside, light carry with my side arm and knife concealed. You guys set up a cover fire perimeter. Tex, when I get to the line you go start both the cars and get ready to book it when we hit the causeway.”

Tex looked at him with disdain. “The fucking driver? Come on!”

Team Leader nodded. “Just be ready. Get the .50 cal in high ready, loaded on both vehicles.”

Tex quickly responded, “10-4, Team Leader.” Team leader turned. “Boys, use discretion. These are our families we’re extracting. Focus. No emotion. Steady motion.”

The team leader hugged the wall tight until he hit the tunnel where UH football runs into the stadium each game. He quickly moved through the masses, trying to blend in as he headed to the stage. There were not many haole families in the stadium. Luckily, the SEALs had a loose hair and beard code. Team Leader looked more like a local haole surfer that hadn’t seen the beach in a while rather than military. He snuck up on his boy and tapped his shoulder. “Sammy, say goodbye to your friend. Mom needs us.”

The boy looked. “Dad?”

Not even picking up his toy from the ground, he hugged his father. Sam grabbed his son with one arm and hoisted him on to his shoulder.

“You done with work, Dad?”

He looked at his son. “Yes, but let’s keep that our little secret. No shop talk. Okay, son?”

As they were walking towards the gate, a man grabbed him firmly by the arm. Sam grabbed his knife and swung his boy behind him on the ground. “Ho, you faka! Relax. Your boy’s toy. He left ’em,” the big Samoan man said.

Sam replied, “Sorry, it’s been a tense week.”

The man nodded. “I bet.”

The Samoan handed back the toy. “Bradda, eh, maybe you better keep that attitude for now. Dem boys at the gate just looking lay some cracks on a punchy haole. So, best you hide whatever food you can, cause your wife basically just sat in line for those kooks. They gonna jack you, mark my words!”

Sam nodded.

“Roger that. You got family here, too?”

He shook his head. “Ya, your boy was killing time with my boy, over there.”

The team had the Samoan man in their sites. They couldn’t tell if he was hostile or friendly. “Right on. Can you get food out of here?”

The Samoan nodded in response to Sam’s question. “I can try. Why?”

Sam's wife came around the exit of the stage where they were standing. "Hey, honey."

She looked confused. "Hey honey, yourself! Where the hell have you been?"

He raised his eyebrow. "Just got caught in the line to use the porta john."

She winced. "What?" He grabbed her wrist slightly, as if to say just play along. "Where's the rest of the girls?"

She looked over her shoulder. "Denise was two behind me. Maybe she's in the back getting the rations. There was some sketchy guy taking over for the lady when I left, real aggressive for an aid worker. Maybe he's with FEMA. I think he was armed. Her girls are over there, playing with Tonia." She pointed to her daughter and the girls behind the stage.

They heard a yell. "Stop! I said NO!" Sam jumped up the exit stairs behind the stage, where he saw his team member's wife getting groped by a man that did not look like a relief worker.

"Let her go."

The man snarled back, "What? You like get slapped, too? She asked if she could get extra rations. I was just giving her extra."

The man drew his knife. "Don't play dumb, haole. Make nice, or my boys will smoke you."

Sam grabbed Denise by her wrist and retreated toward the stage's back stairs. She walked quickly and got behind him with her bag of rations. She yelled back, "Fuck you, asshole!"

The man laughed. "This ain't no charity, bitch! You see this?" He showed a tattoo that read 'SYN' on his wrist. "Dat means no fucking charity."

The team leader grabbed her firmly by the arm. "Do as I say. Let's get out of here." They walked back towards the exit. Sam could see his wife still talking with the nice Samoan man. They kept an eye on the kids as Sam and Denise walked towards them. "Honey, we need to get going."

She replied, "Okay, but what was that all about?"

The Samoan man jumped in. "Ya, what the heck was that, bradda? You okay?"

"Denise, grab the girls and gimme me your bag. Honey, grab Sam Jr. and give me your bag."

They looked confused, but did what he said. "Hey, buddy, how many kids you got?"

The Samoan paused. "Three, but I get one Hanai kid from my sister. So, four I guess. Why?"

Sam asked, "Think you can do me a solid?"

The man replied, "Brah, nothing funny k? What you gon do for me?"

Sam showed him the two bags. "These two bags. They're all yours. Just give me, ummm, those PopTarts."

The Samoan replied, "OK, den what?"

"Tell your kids we're gonna have a foot race to the tunnel. Whoever wins gets the Pop-Tarts."

"Brah, my fat one she gonna win. She big, but da girl always hungry. Might get ugly. You sure?"

Sam nodded. "I'm sure." The Samoan yelled in a bass-laden voice, "Eh, kids, get ova here! Get one game for you."

The wives brought the kids over, and he explained the rules. As the Samoan was talking, Sam saw the man from behind the stage come out front and talk to a man now guarding the entrance. The man pointed at their group and the men ran off to the front.

Sam said, "Okay, everyone got it? First one to the tunnel gets this box of Pop-Tarts."

The chubby little girl yelled out, "They're mine," as she pounded her chest with a thud. The kids took a step away from her.

Sam said, "Okay, everyone got it? You don't stop until you're in the tunnel. Ready? 1, 2, 3!" The kids took off running.

Sam said, "Okay, let's go." Looking over his shoulder, as the adults walked away, he said to the Samoan man, "Thanks, bud. I'll tell the kids to come right back once their finished."

Sam Jr. was the first one to make it to the tunnel, followed by the other kids. "I won! I won!"

The heavy girl had pushed back the others and was second. They all were in the tunnel catching their breath. She said while huffing her breath, "Brah, you better share or I gonna pound your skinny butt. OK?" He smiled, but didn't reply in fear of her.

Sam looked back as they walked off towards the tunnel. He saw five men coming their way. One was the man that had been harassing his wife's friend. The man yelled out, "Slow up! We need talk to you!" Sam told the girls, "Go get the kids and keep heading down to the causeway. Tell the other kids to go back to their dad and avoid me."

The men had closed the distance, and Sam turned. "Hey, fellas. What can I help you with?"

The man spoke up. "Tell that dumb bitch, and whoever that other dumb bitch is, to get back over here before I shoot your ass."

Sam replied, "A lot of dumb bitches around here. Which ones?"

The man pulled out his weapon. "Don't get smart, haole. I'll plug your ass for fun. Call 'em back." As he pointed the gun in Sam's face he yelled, "Eh, you two! Get the fuck over here before I put a hole in this guy's head!"

Sam yelled back, "Just keep walking. Everything is good over here."

The gangbanger put the gun to Sam's temple. "You think I give a fuck? That's the problem with you dumb haoles. You think we should give a fuck about you."

As he said this, Sam put his arms up and said, "Don't," but before the man could say shoot Sam had moved his head out of range and yanked the gun's barrel down towards the ground and popped the clip out. Then, Sam pulled the gun back towards the sky, racked the final round, and shot the weapon at another man going for his weapon. Sam choked the gangbanger with his own arm by latching his hand around the barrel. Sam drew him towards his knife, and secured a rear naked choke.

"Listen, everyone. I'm not sure if you think this piece of shit's your friend, but you make one move and I will cut him. Then, I'll come choke you out with his limbs."

The men looked like they had just seen a ghost. "Here, take him."

Sam threw the man at the other gangbangers and walked, gun drawn, backwards towards the girls. Jogging backwards, then sideways, he caught up to the girls. He grabbed their heads and pushed them low. "Stay low and run the best you can." The gangbanger replaced his clip, and started running and firing. Sam's men lay down cover fire. Ten men dropped to the ground, bewildered by the sound of machine gun fire pinging the ground.

Sam and the women made it to the tunnel. The men fell in laying one more line of fire, before jumping in the vehicles, so no one would follow them. The SEALs loaded the kids in the back Humvee. Tex pulled out the first vehicle onto the causeway, only to see fifty men coming around the corner with various guns and weapons. He stopped, jumped into the harness on top of the Humvee, and laid a down a line of fire. The second Humvee pulled up alongside Tex. The men he fired at peeked out from behind a souvenir shop. "Just give me a reason! Just sneeze, and I'll pop ya!" Tex pointed the .50 caliber Browning, pulled the trigger, and shot the "M" out of a big sign that said "MAHALO." "Mahalo, bitches! Get some!" Sam yelled back, "Cover my six!"

They pulled back up to the condo complex, where the other two units fell in. They made their way back over the Likelike highway and returned to base. By this time, it was dark and the only lights they could see were their headlights, the lights of the Semper Fi building on base, and the light atop of Pyramid Rock. It was a solar powered light that warned planes and ships of its presence, but now looked ominous as the only blinking hazard light on the island. The base was conserving its fuel resources and energy so much that operations had moved to the center of the base for all night ops. There was security at the gates but, otherwise, you would have thought it was abandoned when night fell.

Ha'a had been at the base of Kamehameha Highway near Kahuhipa Street when he saw the lights of a convoy coming down the hill. "See, boys. They're gaining ground, starting to run convoys. It won't be long before they're patrolling and handing out food for allegiance."

Kapu asked, "Dad, is that a bad thing?"

Ha'a replied back, "If we have no choice, then we have no choice. Right now, though, we still have a choice. One with no strings attached, a Hawaii for everyone."

Kamai, who had been quiet for a while, chimed in. "You feeling guilty, Ha'a. You born into that white bread society with a bit of that haole privilege. It's nice you trying to take care of everybody but, if you want the people to follow you, you better know where you're leading them."

Ha'a looked back. "I didn't ask for this, Kamai, but I'll work with what's left on this island."

Kamai nodded. "Just don't forget us Hawaiians, either. I get the one for all and all for one, but we been odd man out for over a century."

Ha'a nodded, created some space on his desk, and then turned back to Kamai. "Kamai, you remember that book, 'Fahrenheit 451', from high school?"

Kapu interrupted, "I just read that last semester!"

Kamai looked ahead. "You mean the one wit da lolo firemen, burning da books, ya?" Ha'a nodded.

"There is a point in that book where the old English professor tells the firemen, 'Do your own bit of saving, and if you drown, at least die knowing you were headed for shore.'"

Kamai looked confused. "Brah, I not going to drown. I get fish blood in my veins."

Kapu smiled. "Uncle, that means it's better to be going after your goal even if you die trying. At least you're headed in the right direction. Right, Dad?"

Ha'a nodded. "Correct."

Kamai flashed a feigned smile. "Well, I guess let's try to keep afloat until I figure out where your guys shoreline stay, k?"

Kapu took a break and pulled the Pueo from his bag. The bird was making cooing noises. It was white on the breast and off white and brown on his wings. It had a reverence about it, as if the animal carried wisdom that was yet to be known. Kapu gave it water, and the bird looked around in the night sky picking up signals of possible prey around him. It would try but could not fly yet. Kapu secured it back in the bag, so that it did not get over stimulated and try to take to the air. He thought he would need to catch a field mouse soon, to feed the Pueo, because he was starting to run low on the pork jerky he grabbed for the hunt earlier in the week.

They kept moving on, heading down the road towards Waiahole River, continuing in the direction of Ka'a'awa and the ranch. Kamai stayed back with Kapu and struck up small talk. "Kapu, about the Pueo. I'm sorry, nephew. That was an accident. I got chicken skin. I only see one once before, when your grandfather died. Your sister, she was like one rock after I saw the Pueo fly over the house. It was like she seen tutu kane's spirit above her. It wasn't a white one though. What they say again about the white ones?"

Kapu paused. "My teacher had said the Kapuna would tell stories to her when she was young. If you were to see a white Pueo, you were to follow it. It has something for you to see or accomplish."

Kamai looked worried. "Crap! Dis one all bust up. We need to keep that thing healthy so it can show us the way out of this mess."

Kapu agreed. "I think my dad is our Pueo at the moment, Kamai. You know him. He's thinking three steps out, even if he only talking about the one right now."

Pono had pushed off the from the pier with his crew, adding his cousin to their ranks. The wind was steady. They had sailed into Kailua Bay as a wind swell kicked up from the heavy trades. They decided to rest, and wait until the night-time high tide to pass the Kaneohe Marine Corps. Base. Pono had heard a rumor that the base was back online with a generator. If they were seen in the daylight, it would be easier for them to be boarded if the military had and any boats operating. If they were picked up by radar, at least they could lose the military by maneuvering around the sand bars, or dock and run at He'eia Kea Pier.

Pomi was just getting his sea legs again and his stomach was still churning even though they had docked. Pono offered him some Taco Poke, a ceviche-like Hawaiian dish made with squid they found hidden in the reef. Pomi took one look at the dish and almost vomited off the side to the ship. "Brah, keep that stuff upwind of me. I can't even smell Poke right now. My stomach sore."

Pono laughed, and so did the crew. One of the younger boys joked at his expense. "You one tough guy until you get on a boat, huh, Pomi?"

Pomi hollered back, "Brah, you like try?"

The young boy took the bowl of Poke and showed Pomi again. "I don't know. Do you like try?"

Pomi turned and puked over the railing.

Pono laughed but, quickly, got everyone to calm down. "Boys, we need to rally some man power for Ha'a. He said the ranch was their plan, set up shop in Kualoa. We can grab some boys and two ships from the yacht club. The big ones. Split up the best guys to run the new crews, and bring the ships inside Secret Island to meet up with Ha'a."

Pohaku, the youngest who had been poking fun at Pomi, stood up. "Eh, I know where we can get some back up."

Pono looked his way. "I was just thinking we just run through Kaneohe and recruit."

Pohaku suggested, "No need. You just go straight to Kailua Youth Corrections. Half my cousins stay incarcerated there, unless they bailed already. Knowing them, Kawika probably got the guards working for him since the power went down."

Pono decided to leave half the crew on the boat, and had the others go by land and recruit. They would all meet at the yacht club to get more boats the following day. Three boys, including Pohaku, took the dinghy and rowed it towards shore. Pomi aptly giving him the finger as he pushed off from the sailboat.

The following morning on base, there was an assembly to muster both military men and their families. The General spoke over a portable PA system that was mounted to the back of a Jeep. He stood atop a platform rigged to the side of the vehicle.

"Ladies and gentlemen, we have survived the worst and kept the base running smooth. Currently, we have a stockpile of thirty plus operable trucks, two tanks, a Recon Sat plane, and rations to sustain us for another two months. We are sitting secure and ready to head out into the remaining island landscape to unite what is left of civilian infrastructure and restore the proper use of remaining resources. Our goal is to first send our plane inter-island to our sister base on Kauai at Barking Sands, obtain information on how that island is doing, and discern what rations or lack thereof remains. From there we will move, systematically, to the Big Island and Maui to see what remaining security measures have been put in place. To our knowledge, we are the only fully operational base in the state. Soon, we will be sending convoys to pull fuel and guarded resources from our other bases. We will do our best to secure any housing that is still intact. For those on unsecure bases, the remaining servicemen will be offered a home here in order of rank and file. However, our priority will be here on this base and securing our families. We have recaptured the Kapu System, a civilian asset that should lead to this island's food security within the coming months. Other than that, status quo remains. The commissary will be giving rations. If your family needs something, grab a form and put it in writing. If it is an emergency, go through your chain of command. A swift hand will come upon thieves and dissidents. Until further notice, this is a DRY, and I repeat, DRY base. Those caught with alcohol or drugs will be kicked off base along with any relatives. We intend to change this as we head into the holidays, but during our rebuild we need all hands on deck with their full wits about them.

"No domestic issues will be tolerated. Your household is your responsibility, and any actions of ill will from your household will reflect on you and your ability to remain in this sanctuary. That is all. Godspeed! OORAH!"

The men, minus some wisecracks about staying dry, responded positively with a sense of patriotism for their base. The US flag was hoisted but, for the first time, the Marine flag was above the US flag. It seemed that the message to the outside world, beyond base walls, was clear. What once was will be respected, but what remains is Marshall Law and that base had the most Marshall Law ready force going.

Chapter 9
Usury as Usual

Ha'a and his group had made it to Waihole, and stopped to fill up their water jugs. Kamai took them upstream to a source so as not to get any tainted water.

"Eh, Ha'a. Remember back in the day, when we lived in Kahaluu? If the river broke, us eastside boys have no more school."

Kapu chimed in. "You guys must have gotten off school a lot." Ha'a chuckled.

Kamai jumped in. "Das why he moved to the estate, Kapu. Either that, or his dad was gonna start helicoptering his rich ass to Kam. Never like him miss nothing."

Ha'a interjected, "That's one of the reasons we moved. No helicopters, though, Kapu. Your uncle, he likes to remember the old days like he likes to remember it." Ha'a paused. "You know, though, the dam is still pretty finicky. We attempted to pay for the whole thing to be refurbished. We had the money to give the city to get a better system, to flush the water through the valley so it didn't flood the road or homes. All they let us do was divert it with a T junction. It didn't solve the problem, just put a band aid on it. Anyhow, the river still bursts but now there are two streams instead of one big one. Maybe we should try to send a crew back to check on how the system is working, and if there is anything we can do to prevent it from slowing up distribution."

Kapu had a suggestion. "Dad, you could use it for security, too. Pull the pin on the levee. Remove the T Junction from its place, and flush out the river to buy some time if the Marines come looking for trouble."

Ha'a was confused. "How and with what levee are you going to use to charge the direction of a running river?"

Kapu jumped back in. "You said the ranch's warehouse should be operational. They are buried in the caves of the valley. Grab a generator, and have Harold go back with the men and the doctor. Take the Jeeps back with the gear. He is an engineer, after all. Aren't you, Doctor?"

The doctor, winded from the walk, paused. "You know, my focus should be on getting the Kapu System fully functional, not medieval weaponry."

Kapu persisted, "But what good is the system if they can walk right up the road and take it once we're done."

Ha'a agreed. "Doctor, take a mental note of what is needed. Once you give us a plan to get the system started, we'll send you with a team, to secure the dam and get a security function built in."

The doctor acquiesced. "I guess that's the world we are living in, eh? We need to secure it before we even build it."

Pohaku's gang had made it to the Kailua Youth Correctional Facility by dusk. There was a quiet hum coming from the back of the three-arce facility. It was not hostile, it sounded like laughter mixed with teenage shit talking. They pulled around the corner to see a bunch of teenagers, of various ages, playing near a large bonfire that looked newly lit. Pohaku told his guys to hang back. "I'll go look for my cousins. I'll call you when it's okay. These guys pretty thugged out in here."

He walked around the wooded back area, avoiding being seen at first. Then, Pohaku walked towards the group nearest the fire. One guy turned and glanced, just to turn away again, as Pohaku moved through the crowd. He heard murmuring from the kids. "Eh, you seen Veeks dat faka.? Where he stay?" Pohaku thought it was more just teenage shit talking and spoke up. "Eh, you know my cousin Kawika?"

The boy turned around. "Who the fuck are you, buleh?"

Pohaku threw a shaka to ease the tension. "I'm cousin with Kawika. I'm on the sailboat program. Came to check in on you boys."

The boys all turned to him, and the one looked at him straight in the eye. "You one of those sailboat punks, ah? Scared of doing some juvey time, so you bitch your way onto the boat, huh? You gonna be a K-Bay Yacht Club Member when you get done with your time, huh?"

Pohaku shook his head. "Nah, it's not like that."

The boy shoved him. "K den, Popeye. Then show me what it's like."

The boy slapped Pohaku in the face, open-handed. Pohaku shuttered back. His boys didn't rush in. There was a good size mob of kids that would turn on them if they interfered. Pohaku looking around and blurted, "Don't be one kook. Me and you. Keep these other scrubs out of it." The boy swung and connected. Pohaku fell back, and squared back off throwing a quick left jab to his nose. The boy was bleeding but lurched forward trying to wrestle Pohaku down. Suddenly, Pohaku sprawled and pulled the boy back into his clinch. He threw a right knee into the boy's ribs, knocking the wind straight out of him. As he buckled, Pohaku let him down to the ground and whispered, "Name's Pohaku, but you can call me Popeye, kook."

The other boys formed a circle around him, and Pohaku's crew came back around to the end of the fire. One yelled out, "Pohaks, let's go!"

One of the corrections boys responded. "Calm down, you pussies! We not gonna mob you for this kid. What the fuck you guys doing over here? You know we got this place on lock, right?"

Another one of the boys, wearing a bulletproof vest, pulled a handgun out. "We like seeing a good scrap, but you better let us know what the plan is and how you know Kawika."

Pohaku replied, "He's my cousin."

The boy hung his head for a moment. "Too bad, brah. Sorry. He got clipped in the riot by some pig trying to help the Corrections office."

Pohaku looked down. "Then who is Veeks?"

The boy laughed. "He just some portagee haole kid named David. He thinks he's Hawaiian, so he been calling himself Veeks ever since your cousin passed. I think he bailed this morning. The boys been giving him too much shit."

Pohaku nodded. "What's your name, brah?"

"Kona. What you guys doing? Just looking for your cousins?"

Pohaku looked back at his friends. "Actually, we were trying to recruit some thugs to help us save the island."

Kona looked around. "Brah, we got the prison garden and enough dehydrated mash potatoes to last us months. We just got a shipment in the day before this shit went down. We good."

Pohaku quipped, "Then what, you like fight each other for the packet of Hamburger Helper? My guys, they get something going. Something big. Can save this island. We just need some more hands so the military can't get it from them."

Kona looked at him cockeyed. "Oh, ya? Whatever you boys get, it better be fully automated if you fucking with the military."

Pohaku said, "Loko i'a one fish pond but better. Get Tarro on top da fish. The fish feed the Tarro, but enough to feed everyone. Can grow anything, and no need power either. They get some scientist got it all worked out."

"Guess we just need to jump on the bandwagon, huh? Grab a few clips and charge 'em? Nah, we stay good. We'll pass."

Just as he finished, a young boy was seen sprinting with a bag from the kitchen. Kona yelled, "Get that clown!" A group ran from the fire, chasing after the kid into the dark ominous prison yard.

Pohaku turned back around. "Looks like you got your own problems."

Kona agreed. "Ya, these fucking scrubs. They like go to their mommies, and taking what they can as they leave. Kooks. So what, where is this promise land?"

Pohaku was quick to answer. "Ka'a'awa Valley, off the mountainside. Da guy, Ha'a Klein, the rich Happa always in the news. He trying to get a new Hawaiian nation going but the food needs to come first."

Kona smirked. "So, what? We'll be like his ministry of defense or something? We get uniforms?"

Pohaku laughed. "I guess if we help him, we can make it up as we go along."

They both had a laugh and Kona rallied his guys. "Eh, you dumb dumbs, anybody like get out of jail for a while? I been here too long, anyhow. Dis guy, Pohaku, he needs our help. Get one good plan. I let him explain."

Pohaku went on to explain the next steps regarding getting the boats at the yacht club and bringing them to Secret Island. There was a lot to take in, but the jailbirds seemed pretty game for anything once he was done speaking.

Pono had made it to the yacht club and found two boats they would sail around the bay to Secret Island. He thought it would be a good way to kill time waiting for the boys by meeting them up at the yacht club. His crew took the dinghy into the club and pulled right up to one of the hobbie cats docked off their pier. They tied off and headed to the pool.

"Shit, it stay green already. No chance. Let's see if they get any snacks."

Pomi yelled, "How 'bout some beer? You know these haoles drink the good stuff over here. I heard ten dollars a beer at this place. Nucking futs, deez fat cats."

The boys started to rummage through the bar and the club house. Pono noticed an eighteen-foot Boston Whaler coming around the corner into the bay from the windows of the club house. He gathered the boys. "Eh, check this out. The boat, it came from the base. We better find a spot to hide."

Pomi came around the corner with beers in hand. "We get problems. I just seen Yakimura pull up to the club, with his men, being driven in a military vehicles."

Pomi signaled for everyone to get back in the storage area behind the bar. They were crammed in, and Pono had to sneak under the bar to avoid being seen. Out from the pier came the General and his men. Soon to follow was Yakimura. "Greetings, Mr. Yakimura. On behalf of the US Marines, I am glad you opted to take a ride across island. It's nice having real wheels, huh?"

The SEAL team that escorted the General chuckled. Yakimura looked back at the Jeep. "A creature comfort, but a useful one."

The General's men sat around him, with the SEAL team going outside to secure the perimeter. The soldiers were dismissed, with the exception of Yakimura's head of Security, Tomo, and Sam, the SEAL team leader. The General spoke up. "Well, Kimura. Under normal circumstances I don't think you and I would have a reason to meet. It seems, though, that we have a common enemy."

Yakimura shook his head. "I have competitors. Enemies implies it's personal. I am a businessman. I do business as the situation presents itself. There are opportunities in good situations and bad situations. People dislike me because I try to find myself on the good side of very bad things and very often."

The General nodded. "Well, then I think we have a disruption in your marketplace, sir." Yakimura agreed with a head nod as the General continued.

"This disruption will make my men's efforts to stabilize the island non-effective to say the least. Ha'a Klein has already secured the docks you controlled for the better part of a decade. We were right behind his SWAT team buddies, but we had planned to use diplomacy and trade to gain access to your stronghold. Unfortunately, his "movement" got there first, and took out some of our best snipers I might add."

Yakimura took a moment to think. "General, we are talking about the US military here. Correct me if I am wrong, but this is the same US military that ran multiple wars on different continents simultaneously. I have thirty men at my compound and another hundred in downtown at my command. I am slowly losing my relationship with the MWH to Ha'a. What could I possibly offer you in the form of waging a battle against Ha'a and his men?"

The General was quick to reply. "You know the real truth about the US military history is that the best missions, and the men who run them, never really get their time to shine. Maybe fifty years later, we'll hear murmurs and conspiracies but they are generations down the line. Most people just brush them off as irrelevant or, in some instances, agree with their necessity in the long view. If my men brazenly take Ha'a and his movement out of the picture, we are just delaying the revolt while giving fuel to the fire. However, if your men take out the man who is the movement, we can peg it on bad business. Your "agreement" would be spread through word of mouth. A falsified contract you had with Ha'a to store and distribute his goods for a cut of profits based on a trade program of land, goods, and wealth in an exchange for food to the people. We all know he has a socialist's intent but, for our purposes, painting him as a wolf in sheep's clothing will quell any rebirth of this new Hawaiian nation he envisioned with the Kapu System as his catalyst for equal access to food and resources."

Yakimura pondered this proposal. "Two issues I see with this. One, my benefit has not been mentioned and, two, my name is caught up in a negative light killing a man for a business transaction that obviously will not benefit Hawaii."

The General laughed. "Well, now is your time to negotiate. You can't expect us to tell you what you want or need. Aren't you the business man in this meeting? I'm just the strategist. Another man's needs are not my concern until it needs to be."

Yakimura found this amusing. "Spoken like a true military man. Politics. I suggest you have someone put in place for that role, once you secure the bargaining chips this island has to offer."

The General agreed. "That, my good man, will be business as usual once we are finished. I can find an impersonal talking head to replace Ha'a. We'll give them a palace. Heck, maybe give them one of Ha'a's estates as a token. The true new Hawaiian leader will in reality answers to the US."

Yakimura added, "Well, on to what I want for creating this illusion of Ha'a and liquidating his stock with the Hawaiian people, so to say. First, the business deal, the one we are making up for the purposes of Ha'a's unfortunate demise. Well, I want to make it real. However, we are going to transfer it back to a government contract with the US military and its leaders."

The General looked curious. "Go on. Remember, I blow things up for a living. I leave the economic development to the eggheads at the FED and DC."

Yakimura smiled. "Well, that's just it. I want to be the new FED. We will create a central bank for Hawaii. I will mint a new currency that can be used to purchase the goods we currently have, and the commodities we intend to produce with Ha'a's Kapu System. The military will secure for the good of the people fair and free access to market, you see. Well, the illusion of it, anyway. This new Central Bank of Hawaii, my central bank mind you. No one is to know. There will be an appointed board. We will give every household, every single man, woman, and child a one-time allotment to start the market. A flat loan will be given to purchase goods on interest that is so marginal no one will notice. Compounding, however. We'll say .05 percent for the first currency bailout. The people will purchase their goods. We will set the price so that we can predict the level of spending. Those who want to purchase more goods will need collaterals after the first stimulus pack is given to the people. I suggest a values scale from highest to lowest. Property, arms, and all the way down to service."

The General looked oddly amused, but at the same time somewhat off-put. "I get the usury and collaterals of property and arms, but service? Do you mean like slavery?"

Yakimura laughed. "Call it what you want. Ever since I've been old enough to know better, the world has called it a job, work for usury, debt credit economics. Don't act like the empire you work for had done it any other way. I can do it better, quiet the masses, and distribute the needs using Ha'a's system. Provide a system of government and military necessity for their daily bread, Tarro, Poi, fish, and whatever else we decide to produce and control. The debt will make way for the workforce. The workforce will produce the goods, for which we will need your skill set in providing security. I don't need any medals or fanfare. I just want to be the ever-consistent ghost in the machine that runs the numbers, and keeps our public asking for more. For every inch we give, we will take a meter."

The General went slack-jawed. "You know, I must say you are a scary, scary old man. A smart, and to the point one, however."

Yakimura said very succinctly, "General, you see, I am a businessman. I don't need compliments. I seek control. Money is nothing. Money is only real if it is secured by something. We are creating security in trade for our control. The Japanese, Chinese, and even the Portuguese had better trade and use of this archipelago. They had relations with the Hawaiian people as they came and developed this paradise. However, if you know history, the only reason Dole was successful was not because of his use of words and persuasion with the Hawaiian people. It was his manipulation of the US military and word Annex. They spoke it so freely that it became a reality, even if this island was never annexed by the US. Do you remember that term Joint Resolution which was used to acquire Hawaii? This was a term used to step around the system. The people would not know, one way or another, even on the Mainland. Only a treaty could annex Hawaii to the US. The Treaty of 1897 was never ratified by the United States. I assume you never heard this from the look on your face, General?"

The General shook his head. "No, I can't say I have, Yakimura. It's true. What I do know is annexation by resolution is unconstitutional. It would destroy the integrity of the US Constitution."

Yakimura laughed harder. "Ha, your constitution. That piece of paper Washington politicians would have burned if they could. I doubt that when the bombs fell, five percent of the nation had even read one tenth of that rag. History repeats itself, General, just new players come along and rig the chess game in their favor. I'm happy to be the pawn in this move, if I can secretly play King. I am happy for your military to appoint the Queen, Knights, Rooks and so on. We all can be once again be happy with our pretty little illusion and I can fall in line when needed." The General was befuddled by this play on words that made perfect sense, in a sadistic but needed way, to control the masses. They both agreed with a handshake and a bow. A document would not be needed. If there was a paper connection to the two in later years, the conspiracy would have its proof and the illusion would be hard to perpetuate."

The boys all heard this. Some understood. Some twiddled their thumbs, sitting and hoping not to be found out. Pomi sipped shots of Jack from a half empty bottle he found en route to hiding. Once the coast was clear, they all huddled near the center of a ballroom, put some logs on the fireplace, and played rich while they discussed what just happened. They looked like they had just hijacked a businessmen's Christmas party. Pono lit an old cigar as he started to speak. Before he could exhale from his first pull from the stogie, he started to cough to the point of slightly vomiting. Everyone laughed.

Pomi blurted out, "What? Da thing went stale?"

Pono shook his head. "Eh, I never gonna pass as a rich man anyway. Fuck it." Everyone giggled. Pono continued. "Look, you may have been listening. You may or may not understand, but what those educated assholes are planning in short is a takeover, a false story that Ha'a won't be able to defend himself against because he will be dead, and we'll all be back on the tit of high society backed by military thugs. You guys want that?"

They all looked a little confused. One of the boys yelled out, "You fucking crazy, buleh? The only other time I ever been in this place is when me and you was checking door handles and stealing the loose change from the cars at this club." Pomi snickered. "Pussies. Just get a spark plug and boost a Beemer already, kook. Stealing loose change. what kind of criminal are you?"

Pono yelled out, "Not very good ones, any over us. We steal cause we don't see any other way. We're told from these real gangsters to fall in line, work for them, pay them interest on the money they print. Let's get our shit together and shut them down, before these businessmen presenting themselves as the solution steal from the people once again. I would rather die trying than let them do this to Hawaii."

Pomi looked at the ground. "My mother, she inherited our family land. Only had two years left on the mortgage. She lost her job one year in and took a private loan to float the bills. She buried herself in interest. My father was already on the streets. They broke up when the economy went shit. He lost his journeyman job. Looked for work but only found drugs. Sold 'em. Used 'em. Now, here I am, a thirty-year-old crook. Parents gone. My inheritance sold twice since we left to businessmen speculating that the price will always rise for land in Hawaii. You can see from here, near Johnson Road, fucking gone. I'm down for whatever. Let's do something already!"

They all cheered! Pono organized the boys by group to the boats they found still moored in the midst of the bay. The wind was up and they had a mission to get to the Eastside and Ha'a's land in the valley. They didn't know what they would find, but they knew it had to be protected.

Chapter 10
Valley of the Dead

The landscape was always the constant in Hawaii and Nature's perpetual movement around the landscape laid markers for such things as tide, wind, and weather. Ha'a sent the men back in to the Waihole River in clear skies. He had seen the Iwa bird flying off the updrafts of mountains and small islands surrounding the Windward side. Maritime named these birds the Fregit bird, Iwa meant "thief," and they gained this name from stalking others prey. Birds would lose their kill and boats could lose their catch from these split tail scavengers as they dove and flew off at will with other's hard work. Their ease of flight meant there was a steady wind and no more than trade showers would be in the near future. Dead wind meant downpours and sometimes tropical depressions or low pressure upon the islands. Balmy conditions could break away to local flooding and it would not allow for a weaponized dam to be built on the river.

Ha'a had ten men pulled from the ranch along with two of the Chinese super soldiers. Kapu came along as the foreman. Ha'a had few resources he could trust to follow his requests. Harold tagged along as liaison to the Chinese soldiers. Harold, once again, complained about the hike. They had rested at the ranch, but Harold was not one to be left out of a good adventure. He would always tell you how difficult it was, whereas Kapu would suffer in silence. They had a strange but symbiotic relationship. Harold speaking mostly for the two in public settings much to Kapu's disliking, but he handled the embarrassment when Harold spoke incorrectly. He felt it reflected better on him, in the long-term, when dealing with adults and teachers. Harold had a knack for learning languages but his command of his words always seemed to escape him at the most inopportune times.

Harold droned on. "Kapu, how far up the hill do we have to go?"

"About another mile as the crow flies."

Harold looked baffled. "What the heck does that mean, anyway? My uncle always says that."

Kapu laughed. "You see how birds fly, ya? It means to go in a straight line. Well, we got two switch backs to get up that ridge, and I'm sure some terrain that will be peaks and valleys. So, another mile, give or take."

The group of men laughed. "Kapu, I thought your friend went to Kam schools. What they get the short bus over there too I guess, huh?"

Harold shook his head. "Not funny, man."

Kapu laughed. "Na, real funny!"

They made it the T junction where the water would swoop up an embankment on either side of the river then back down to separate cement structures to an outflow down the hill. The old outflow was dry, with the exception of some rain puddles that were nearly dried up from the sun. The outflow hadn't been used in years. It was temperamental and could not handle a heavy, sustained downpour. To get the effect they needed, they would have to reverse the T Junction so it would pour fast and heavy down the old shoot and blow out until the road. They, also, needed to dam up the T Junction to collect all the water they could for a single burst. They couldn't depend on the weather to do the job on the day. They might need to pull the dike and reverse the T Junction to the old outflow. The soldiers made light work of placing cement rectangle blocks above the entryways to the two junctions. They were set in a steel sliding frame, mounted with the ranch's welding tools. They greased the track on either side so the block would slide smooth when the wedged level holding the blocks was pulled out. A rope on either side of the trap was set so it needed two people per junction to be released. Meaning a four-man team would need to be in place and ready for it to work if needed. It was not the most sought-after job, so they decided to leave the two soldiers and two men. The two men would rotate out every two days, bringing food and rations with them to swap out for the next sentry detail. It was a boring necessity to keep the real Kapu System under lock and key. In or out, there was no way to get the system in their hands by land with this fail safe in place. The military would not suspect a man-made disaster. If approaching, this could very well cripple the military attack but also stop them if the system fell into their hands.

Pono, alongside his band of young criminals, turned revolutionaries, had sailed into Secret Island and made their way through the mangroves into the valley undetected. They surprised Ha'a, while the doctor ran tests on the functioning system. Both of them were surprised that there was nearly thirty minors in there, thought to be, secure valley hideaway. Ha'a asked, "Pono, did you even try not to be seen coming in, or is it just that easy?"

The group's laughs echoed throughout the man-made cave. "It wasn't our goal but then again we know these grounds better than most. We hunted here since we were keiki. Your rancher, Uncle Kaimana, he used to let me and Pomi in the back gate to hunt the mountain goats for him. Good meat, and he said you no like them eating all the indigenous plants."

Ha'a laughed. "Oh, so you guys were part of our sustainability program is what you telling me? Ha, I remember you rascal kids I always would turn a blind eye if I saw someone carrying a bow. These days get all kind haole or tourist hunters trying come on the land. We thought we were gonna get sued, so we shut 'em down unless we gave permit."

Pomi interrupted. "Ya, but if we can sneak in here, that means someone else can, too. Maybe not as easy, but you got issues. You got more enemies than you think."

Ha'a replied, "That I can only assume. Do tell, though, Mr.? Sorry. What's your name?"

"Pomi. I was one of Yakimura's men at the docks. My cousin here made me defect. Lucky, too, 'cause your SWAT guys leveled my gang and took the docks. Not sure if you knew that yet."

Ha'a nodded. "I heard something but, to be honest, that was on you, Pono, and Sanoa. They're on their own, right now, until we figure out better communications. I can't say I would have stopped him. Honolulu was about to catch fire if something didn't give."

Pomi and Pono went back and forth giving Ha'a the rundown on what happened in town and how Ha'a's name had been attached to everything from securing the local resources to giving the tourists shelter. Ha'a was astonished to think that he was being tied to all these good deeds. The church that gave out the produce had, also, spread his name as a savior from Nu'uano Pali through Palolo Valley.

Waimanalo had already run with the rumors of a new government for the people being structured. It seemed the coconut wireless had unknowingly built Ha'a's profile, and the work he was doing in the shadows had developed its own movement within the remaining people on island of all race. They told him about the General and Yakimura's plan and agreement to pin Ha'a as an underhanded businessman rather than a philanthropist do-gooder with a real democracy in his goals. Ha'a didn't feel right about his new-found leadership role, nor the fact that he was the target in a ploy to defame his motives and family name.

Kapu had returned to hear the tailend after his first shift was done at the river dike. It was a five-mile shortcut through the woods, two hours at a good pace. He was tired, dropping his bag alongside the ranch dog who was going blind in one eye. The dog barked, not seeing it was Kapu or seeing the bag make the noise. Kapu had grown up going to the ranch and playing with the dog in the valley. He was a great watchdog, and used to be his father's dog for hunting pig. it was a Poi dog, a Hawaiian mut that was supposedly a cross of Bearded Collie and Australian Stumpy Tail Cattle Dog. He had a cataract in one eye, and his left ear was torn but healed from a run in it had at the beach park across the street from the ranch. He got up when he realized it was Kapu, and started cooing and letting out small barks of excitement. Kapu pulled some Jerky he was saving for his owl and gave it to the dog. His father named him Kaipo, after his friend that he lost back in middle school when they were hiking near Manoa Falls. The falls had a flash flood and they were swept into a rock outcropping at the bed of the river. Ha'a was able to hold on to a tree stump, but Kaipo hit the rocks. He was later found down river, lifeless, by Ha'a and a rescue crew.

Ha'a had asked Pono and his crew to do a nightly patrol, and signal with a flare if any boats were coming into their end of the bay. They left two boats inside the bay on opposite sides, so if one was destroyed they would still have another to escape or move the system if the military decided to attack. They stayed within the surf line to avoid any incidents with their boat and ran a grid pattern to avoid hitting the shallow reef towards Chinaman's Hat at dusk before mooring the boat for the night. There was a tropical feel to the weather that was moving in. The winds went slack, cutting off their third patrol heading into their second day at the ranch. The gate of the valley was only secured by a steel gate that would only open outwards when unlocked. However, a tank could blow it right over. It was to keep trucks from heading up in the valley to off-road and tear up the pristine landscape. Ha'a asked his wife to oversee a project to pour cement into the horse's feed troughs. She had the men place the feed troughs every ten feet and staggered them apart so you could drive through but slowly, much like the military checkpoint gate at Camp Smith. The men were surprised that she came up with the design and was not shy of work. She poured cement and replaced the troughs with old koi pond liners that were set to be replaced at the ranch entrance. There was a pride everyone had in their work.

They knew they would be a part of a new Hawaii. Ha'a had opened up his land for the people more than he ever had been able to before, fighting with board members on land use. They hadn't ventured near the properties. They, most likely, were waiting for the government to fix their problems like the majority of the island. It was a race against propaganda, though. There were still enemies on two fronts. The leftover officials were on the base, with

Kimura now under their thumb. Then, there was whatever Chinese military there might be on island or headed this way.

Ha'a was laughing to himself as he played with a HAM radio he grabbed from the offices. He used it to pick up any boating issues on the Coast Guard and police chatter in their area, so if an emergency happened it would not affect tour groups visiting the valley.

The doctor was quick to comment. "Did you pick up someone on the radio, Ha'a, a comedic trucker making radio calls into the abyss, maybe? That looks like a pretty powerful recover antenna I saw up there."

Ha'a, seemingly lost in thought, responded. "Oh, hey. No, I was just laughing at the financial advice the estate was getting prior to the attack. Buy silver. Buy gold. Hedge your bets. The Chinese were manipulating their currency, setting up the biggest crash of all time."

The doctor grimaced. "That doesn't seem very funny to me."

Ha'a laughed. "Perspective, Doctor. They were telling us to hoard metals of no value. They can't be traded in small denominations for food that does not exist. And who is going to use it for bullets? We would have been sitting on shiny happy nothings. The world killed for gold, started wars for oil, but cut down trees and decimated farmlands to put up malls. Aren't we just the smartest bunch of apes going, Doctor? Had it all figured out, didn't we?"

The doctor shook his head. "I see the irony, but back to that radio. Anything?"

Ha'a replied, "Some fishermen on sailboats, trying to get back to shore, talking about bad weather approaching. Tropical weather. Sounds like we should let the boys at the river know we're in for some good rain squalls. Maybe test the dike, and see if we can redirect the water."

The doctor retorted, "If it's all the same, I'll let you plan the security, Ha'a. I would like to stick to getting the system up to high yields. I think if we have enough nitrate, we could have a full crop in three weeks and another hatchery of catfish. We could cycle the tilapia in, and give fish out with the first batch of reens and so on."

Ha'a smiled. "That's great, Doc."

The doctor lit up with excitement. "I think I have figured a way to produce rice, as well. We just need to stick to the Nutrient Film Technique, and the DWT with the deep-water troughs for the fish until the nutrient base is extremely high. From there, we would add iron chelate to the filter. We can switch to the rice field, and run the greens off the secondary filter we are prepping as the backup system. If we can start doing grains, this will revolutionize the use of the Kapu System. Energy will be greater, so using the river might be something we need to figure out for hydroelectricity. Even if we store solar, the filter pulls so much energy to flood the field for grain it would need to be something more substantial."

Ha'a smiled. "This is really coming along, Doctor. Since we were on the subject of security, how can we protect it from another EMP blast?"

The doctor paused. "Well, Ha'a, I really don't field well in the art of war. Electrically, we could put protective magnetic sheathing on all the exposed wiring, from the grid to the system. It's a long shot and, the reality is, if they let off a radioactive EMP, we have big problems off crop contain inaction on Island. The grid attack on the docks was to leave this island in semi-working order. The Chinese had planned on setting up shop. This was not a level and move on operation. They knew the value in these islands, just like every other nation did."

Ha'a nodded. "That was my guess. Whoever is left out there might be still thinking the same thing. I would not say the enemy on island is the only one we may ever encounter."

Back in Honolulu, a calm of sorts had been instilled. Talk of Ha'a's mission to feed the masses had quilted the mass fear of future starvation. The lack of toilet paper and where to put waste was an issue everyone welcomed versus a famine. The bullets had temporarily stopped flying. Families were seen at the beach. Rations were given out at the docks every second Monday with a system of last names and times set up to avoid lines and riots. It seemed to be working. The SWAT team had deputized some men. Some former police and EMT joined in the efforts. Any person caught stealing would be dealt with quickly. Sadly, body disposal was becoming commonplace at the docks. Feeding the fish with the remains of fighters from the event and swift justice became part of an everyday routine at the docks. The central island communities were not faring as well, with FEMA abandoning the Stadium and the SYN taking over what was left of the rations they had been handing out. Trading bullets for boxes, they were bartering with any public holding weapons for dry goods and canned food. Little were the gangsters aware they were starting an economy that Yakimura had planned to lock down with the military's aid. The Westside farms, and thus the people, had been controlled within days of the event. Some tried to leave, others fell in line, and others revolted. However, with very little military presence and a non-existent police force, it was an "every group for themselves" scenario. Hunters fled to the mountains daily, and overhunting island wide was slowly becoming a reality. For the first time ever, feral pigs were not keeping their populations up. A once over breeding problem now could not keep up.

Yakimura was given a vehicle, fuel, and some weapons for his men. He remained at his complex while his men went out to check on the stadium operations armed with a .50 caliber M2 mounted on top of a freshly painted Humvee. It was now jet black as if to give off the effect they had stolen it from the military. It struck fear into the locals. The military would be welcome at this point. Seeing weapons fall into gangster hands was a scary image. Even if they had been given the equipment, the aura of chaos was in place and the SYN was a new authoritative presence.

Yakimura told his men, "We don't explain ourselves. We just do. If you think it benefits my business, you act. If it helps us gain a foothold of control, you do it and I will reward you. If you explain why you are doing something, you have already lost the public's respect. If they get used to our control, they will grow to accept it. Then, they will expect it. Eventually, they will come to yearn for it." He spoke this to his inner circle that ran the thugs that were controlling various streets. "We need to regain control of the docks, not for revenge or for the leftover cans of food, but for control. A movement is only as good as their momentum. People, internally, love their slavery and I am happy to give it to them. Small acts of strategic violence done by ordinary men leads to extraordinary control of other men. Feed fear, control the currency, control the goods, and control the people. It's for their own good, mind you."

Then men were half-tempted to start fearing the old man themselves. He had a way about him that was so callous and calculated, it was hard not to respect him but it was also easy to hate him for his sheer brazen assumption that men needed to be led for their own good. Part of the men agreed, which led them to commit horrific acts on the streets in the name of Yakimura's future view of Hawaii. This, essentially, was all that was left functioning in the world.

Ha'a had rallied his men, and sent some back-ups to the river. He let them all know what Yakimura had planned. He said that a war was coming, one way or another, and that anyone not willing to pick up and fight should leave the premises. He asked each person from a different part of the island to venture back and tell men that would want to live in the valley to fight when the time came. They would be fed and their families could come with them. They had weapons, but asked they first recruit gun owners and people with combat experience whether it be military or in the streets. They needed numbers and, with Sanoa guarding the pier, they would not have that side their movement to help if they were attacked.

Ha'a closed his speech to the men helping secure the valley. "Men, I know we would all like to go back to the way things were. I could not think of anything that would make me happier. However, we are here at this junction with not many choices. If we don't care about what happens to the system and what happens to our new Hawaii, then I don't know if anyone else will. So, if they are coming for our future and our food source, Hawaii must push back as one. My intent was to help unite us all but there are agendas at play, none of which include unity. It is your call. Without your help, I am a man sitting in a valley with a hunk or equipment. Do your best, and come back with the best resources you can find from your ahupua'a."

The men ventured back to their regions and started the process of searching for the best that were available and could leave their families to fight or farm depending on their skill set.

The General was with his translator at the cells of the Chinese captures. The men had been treated well for POWs. They were fed, given beds, and were not abused. The General asked his translator, "Ask them if they feel as if they have been treated fairly?"

So he did, and no one answered. "Ask them which one is their leader?"

Again, none answered. They acted as if small talk would be treason, their lips were sealed.

"Ask them if they prefer hot meals to torture." The translator looked at him as if he was off in the head but then relayed the question. The prisoners all looked up at the General.

"Let them know, I like doing things that work. If what is going on now is working, we stick with it. But if it is not, well then we just try something else."

The men looked at each other, fearfully, and then one finally spoke up. He spoke to the translator who relayed who was the leader and he went on. "We were here as a first strike team. We had planned to meet our commander once the fighting had finished. We had taken over the harbor and island. We don't know where anyone is at the moment."

The General nodded. "So what about the super soldiers? Are there more than the six that were taken?"

The translator relayed, and the commander replied. "Six in our team. 10,000 in the Army, but not here. Maybe on a boat headed to the mainland, or killed in a plane, or headed here. I do not know. We do not know anything that has happened since that day."

The General asked, "Can you control them?"

The translator relayed. "Only my men. We are handlers. We are with them from birth. We take them from their surrogate mothers. They are like loyal dogs, they listen to the master, and they imprint on the next master if he is killed."

The General paused. "They may think that you have been killed. Wait! Don't translate. I wonder if they will follow his command if we put them together, but we give the actual commands. Tell him this. If he wants to continue their stay with us, the comfort and food and all the amenities, they will have to give allegiance to me. Not the USA, but to me. For all we know there is no China, no Russia, no Mainland USA, only this. Hawaii. So, his best move is to get past previous tensions and work with the new controlling force."

The translator relayed once again. The Chinese commander took the information to his men and relayed back, "We will control them on your behalf if we are given our own wing of the base to stay, remain separated from the general public, given food, and granted asylum on this island."

The General grasped this. "Tell the men it's done! We will even give them a letter of war asylum."

The message was relayed and the Chinese leader replied, "No, we are now war refugees of this island, not of the USA. We cannot make deals with your nation, but if your nation no longer exists we can make a pact with you as a representative of this island and the controlling power."

The General worked over this statement, which made him mill over the actual situation he found himself. He was in command of the remaining portion of what was the US military, but there was no such thing to their knowledge. They were representing a wasteland to their knowledge. He stood as an independent entity by default, with no regulations nor chain of command beyond himself, and thus he responded, "I am asking you to be a wing of this military force, which is to be dubbed the United Republic of Hawaii, and we are its security force. You will be a part of a new island nation and have your requests."

The translator did his best to relay verbatim and the response was a head nod in agreement. The General decided to call Yakimura to the base for one last meeting to give him a weapon that they could pin on the attack. He would give Yakimura and his men the handlers and translator to turn the super soldiers on Ha'a and his men. They would be defenseless once the giants defected to the General and Yakimura's side.

The boys came back to shore after docking the boat inside of Secret Island. Leftover props from film projects littered the beach. The boys made the shanty homes from a movie set their base camp. A tropical depression had started making its way ashore. Humid air and winds from the east had settled in, and the ocean surface was torn up outside the protected bay. Torrential rains could be seen on the Ko'olau Mountain Range. Waterfalls with heavy, steady streams were being produced as the storm pulled into the island and hugged the mountains, making the peaks disappear into the ominous grey clouds. The Koʻolau Range was created from volcanic activity and sheers of its cliffs from earthquakes. Geologists still assume it could one day erupt, even though it ceased being active thousands of years prior. When you looked at its vertical peaks, it had a calming effect, especially when its waterfalls billowed over from heavy rains.

The General and Yakimura met, along with their men, at the Heʻeia Fishpond. The General relayed what needed to be done to break up the faith in Haʻa's movement and following. "Yakimura, you need to be there, and it needs to be documented. We need to have a way to prove that he was killed and with reason."

Yakimura replied, "Dead is dead. We can do the talking for him once he is gone. Documenting will be worthless with no media. We need to spread the rumor, and keep spreading it until it becomes true. My popularity will decrease with his name. So, I intend to retreat to my home and stay out of your way until it is time to release the new currency on loan to the people. Even then, our meetings will be in secret. I will have final say on who is appointed to be my proxy in the marketplace."

The General nodded in confirmation. "I am giving you the translator to recover the Chinese men and the SEAL team to run reconnaissance and set up a sniper outpost. If I know Haʻa, now that he is in motion he won't be easily drawn to a position where you can shoot him, or be stupid enough to let you bring weapons into his premises. The goal is to have him allow you inside, show him your change of heart, and that you want to help. Let him show you what he is up to, gain his confidence, and draw him to the gates to see you off. Once you are leaving the valley near the gates, we will have planted a sniper on one of the goat trails near the entrance. They will go by boat, ahead of you, and situate themselves in the night."

Yakimura laughed. "You're coming at it from the wrong angle. Haʻa does not trust me. He never did. All he was doing, by asking for my help, was buying time. He knew if I thought he needed me, that I would not take him as a threat. The only way to do this is an assault, using whatever means you give me. The only mouths that will be left to speak about it will be us. No one left to tell the tale of Haʻa and his movement. If we control the story, and spread it the way we see fit, the seed he planted will die. If we kill Haʻa and it is rumored he was taken out in a coup by the military, you will have a revolt and give credence to his legend and movement. You hurry it for good, and write a new history."

The General, seemingly impressed with Yakimura's callous nature and disregard for anything that got in the way of his goals, took a moment. "Well,

Yakimura, you're talking about annihilation of a would-be regime. The US military does this well, but that means Hawaii's new history can't have holes in it. Can you stomach the fact that you would be killing a lot of innocent people? Ha'a, essentially, is doing the right thing. He just should have let us do the right thing on his behalf."

Yakimura smiled. "The problem with democracy is that it is democratic. Your USA loved to hold ceremonial elections, and then let the nation squabble while the banks implemented monetary policies. The people knew it was really a back door for the gangsters on Wall Street to tax the public's bank accounts through fees, service, and advice. They loved their systems and false hopes. This was all well and good, but let's take it a step further and make it cleaner. Let's take it from the guise of financial security as the motivation for the public's participation to the food security on loan with interest. You see, General, humans crave routine. From birth, the patterns are the only true control. Break the pattern, and the children throw a tantrum. Missing a nap leads to missing a meal which leads to chaos. The people have lost their routine, General. I just want to give them something new to hold on to. Someone will come along and put them into a system. The question is who and when. When will determine the level of chaos reached in our current state. Who, well, that's not really theirs to decide. That is a matter of will and means. Together, we now have the elements to be that invisible guiding hand.

"Ha'a has the will of a good doer, an altruistic view of the way the world should be, but that is not strong enough for the people to grasp. There is no regard for man's true contempt for other men in his plan. Nature will always beat nurture. Nature is a jealous beast. Nurture can subdue nature's true self in dribs and drabs, but when scarcity leads to jealousy, the have-nots will eat the haves. Even if his system took hold, there would be conflict within his new socialistic tribe. How do you make the tough decisions to keep control of this perfect society? No man wants to be equal. There will be a rival to his system. If he is the designer, he is a target. He will weaken himself with each comer. They will call him a tyrant, a controlling oligarch. He controls the food, and everyone deserves equal share, but what about him? Does he not have more than the ones he passes on the work to? No, a person cannot guide the people.

"The system needs to be the actual guiding hand with no conscious, no choices, just a market and a debt all men owe to the system. A market for which people buy, sell, work, repeat. Everyone a cog in the machine, everyone bound to a routine that keeps them within the boundaries of the law of compounding debt, which will lay the track to a law-abiding society in which you, General, and I can write the laws. Yes there will be haves and have-nots as there has always been, but in this new version of capitalism the usury starts at birth, born with a bank account they did not earn but will have to pay back with interest. As in prior times, you needed to do things through politicians and lobbyists to find a voice box for the banks. In a shadowy dance, now the bank and government will become one, with no reason to think of living any other way. Everyone knows it, and everyone needs it. An intern wants it, and depends upon it for every life decision that crosses their consciousness. This will be reflected back to their government-backed financial accounts. We start in the physical, in notes, and move back to digital as soon as the grid is repaired. You will be my sword and debt will be your shield."

The General still, truly, did not understand how it could all play out. "By what method do you expect the people to use currency they have never seen before. Why would they trust it?"

Yakimura countered, "Well, that's the easy part. Control the food and you control the people. Laws will only allow government to produce food and goods. However, it will also print the money used to by all of the above. A wholesale slavery in which the seller is the bank and the bank is the government."

The General took a step back. "I never really saw myself as a financier but, hey, if it means a peaceful society that looks to us for security, then I guess we're on track to rebuilding a society I can live with. If we crack a few eggs during the process, all the better to show the public who they should be betting on."

The two men parted, with Yakimura taking the Jeep in which the SEAL team leader sat beside him. The two barely spoke a word as they rounded the turn towards the Waihole Hegenic store.

They were in the second Humvee in a convoy of three, all of which were painted black. Sam, the team leader spoke. "I'm no social engineer Mr. Yakimura. I'm a soldier that was sent with you one for your protection, and to take out a target. One issue, though. We have ten men. They have thirty, from what I gather. Ha'a may not have any trust in you. Are you still planning on trying to drive him into our sites, and if not, why are you here? We could just go in at night, clear the target, and be back by dawn."

Yakimura leaned back in his seat which was facing back towards Sam. "Good soldiers follow orders and don't ask questions. So what's your excuse?"

Sam's shook his head. "SEALs are taught to think, sir, on the fly and with reason. We are target-oriented, not a mass of men sent in as a wrecking ball. We are tactical and reasoning is something that comes along with it. The more I know the better I can do my job."

Yakimura was happy with the answer. "Well, as you may have heard me say to the General, it's best that this is seen as a business deal gone wrong. I can have him taken out and everyone hates me. At the same time, if everyone hates the military then the stability of the island runs parallel with the hatred and we lose order. I have been hated for years, so this is nothing new. If I can transfer this weight of hatred partially on to Ha'a by being tied to me in his death over business, he is guilty by association with no opportunity to speak and defend himself. That is, if you do your job correctly."

Sam understood. "So you paint the picture. We draw a target on it, and shoot the eyes out of it. Can do, but can I make a suggestion? We are getting close, and I think Ha'a may have more eyes than you think. So, if it is all the same to you, before the river, drop my team off and we'll hike in across the backside of the valley. Given it will take us two hours to get to a suitable vantage point, take a rest as you get to the river. Hang back for an hour and then proceed. We need you to draw him out of the cave into the fields where we will have a perch setup. It needs to be a single shot as he walks alongside you. This might be the only way to get a shot off."

Yakimura had no issue with the plan. Having Ha'a out of the picture would benefit him. Yakimura's men pulled off, leaving three SEALs at the end of a side street. They had a long hike in front of them to reach the valley.

Ha'a had left the doctor to run with the system now that they had finally gone fully operational. Moving on to security, he appointed the boys as his Navy. The waters seemed to be the easiest to defend as the Marine base had limited capability in maritime warfare. There were two boat operations, both motorized, but the current seas would not allow them to enter through anywhere besides hugging the channels inside the bay. He knew the boys at the river were his line of defense for any military attacks by land, so they set up a checkpoint at the He'eia Pier with cement roadblocks. Communications had been attained with solar charged walkie-talkies that had a three-mile range. It was spotty, but they set up a 10-code system of their own to avoid confusion in bad communications or weather-related signal disturbance. With no cell or radio, there was a fairly clear signal even though they were bordering nearly seven miles in a line of sight to the valley.

Ha'a sent a crew, with a newly charged set of radios, to the river in which he and Harold were on the second day of their third shift. The boys had been taking turns sitting in a tree stand, off the utility road that lead to the river's T junction. They had set up a trap for pigs that would eat from a pile of strawberry guava. They collected a pile each morning and set them down in the trench off the side of the road. One would go down each evening and sit for an hour before dark. They had a view of a portion of the road, just at the edge of the roadblock. The radios that had been brought up to them were connected to the two-man team at the roadblock. The cement dividers that blocked the road were pulled from a 7/11 parking lot that was under construction. There were two large excavators parked behind them that were out of commission from the event. Harold had been moved to the roadblock with his soldiers, who moved the road dividers by hand like an Ox in the field. There was no effort. They moved them with ease and, once done, the one giant was given an order to remain at the blockade and to shoot if the men gave them the signal. Which was a finger waived in the opposition direction. Simple visual codes were easily understood by the men, but what to do after was an issue. They could fire and decimate, but to get them to stop was tricky. To get their attention in attack mode was not something they wanted to test unless needed. A simple tap on the head of the commander is all that it would take but getting them to look at you was the issue when in a gun battle.

Yakimura's team stopped at the Hygienic Store to give the SEALs some time to position themselves. The men smoked clove cigarettes while checking their weapons and rounds. They knew that they might be disarmed, so Yakimura had a failsafe in the form a sharp metal blade the shape of a credit card. It was something he carried with him in his wallet for protection. It had identifying numbers on it but was metal, not plastic. It looked every bit like a credit card but if you ran your finger along one edge, you could feel its blade and would cut you with ease. The hour went slow. They knew there was a small journey left, and wanted to get on with the ordeal. Yakimura was patient. He knew that this was his play, and that his place in Hawaii would be attained. Even in the shadows, he could have the leverage he always desired. He could improve upon his predecessors, controlling a food supply in a sustainable system that was based on debt. A debt that he ultimately controlled.

Kapu sat perched one eye on the feeder and alternating the other back out toward the base of the utility road. He could see Harold coming back up the road with the other soldier and, in the distance, the three men at the roadblock. The sun was setting, and there was no action on the feeder. He was about to climb down when he saw a movement on the edge of the utility road. There was a rustling, and it was moving towards Harold. Kapu grabbed his binoculars to see if he could get a closer look. By the time he could see anything, Harold was off the road, gone. The soldier was paused, scanning in circles for a half a minute, then disappearing into the woods. Kapu kept searching with the binoculars, but nothing. No sign of Harold or the soldier. He looked back at the roadblock in the distance and saw figures walking towards the security blockade.

A radio call came over the channel. "Ha'a, I have Yakimura and his men at the blockade. He is asking to speak to you personally."

Ha'a took a minute to respond. "He is more than welcome to speak to me on the radio."

The man held out the radio to Yakimura. "All yours."

Yakimura went on. "Ha'a, can we speak in person? This is not something for open airways or anyone else's ears."

Ha'a shook his head, "Can you give me a hint to the subject? I'm sure we can work it out over the radio."

Yakimura responded, "The General, he's planning something. He asked for my help."

Ha'a felt like he was being played, as if Yakimura knew that Ha'a already had knowledge of their arrangement. "Tell me how you know what you know, and I can make my decision."

Yakimura didn't hesitate. "Well, treason in short. I sold you out, Ha'a. He requested a meeting to discuss breaking our agreement. I had thought about it, since you picked up and moved your operation to the valley. I thought about it, and gave him my terms but they would never last and I knew this. Might will always make right. I can set up anything I want, a social project that would restructure this island, but they have the manpower and the weapons. All my men wouldn't last more than a day if they turned on me."

Ha'a knew Yakimura would play any hand that suited his needs and survival. He was old and only was as strong as his perceived power and his control over others through his accumulated wealth. "Yakimura, you're welcome to come up but leave your men at the blockade. We'll send out food for them with our vehicle to pick you up. The men will search you, there is no other way I can let you into the valley."

The boys in the bay had made their way to the valley. With the weather pushing in fast, they felt it was a good time to ease their sea legs and pick up some supplies. They went in by way of the valley itself, avoiding the roads. They could hunt for Lilikoi and fruits on the way to touch base with Ha'a. Two of the boys stayed back to guard the boats, one of which was docked just off shore. On the way over the second ridge, they spotted figures heading over a hilltop. They noticed they were all armed except for an exceptionally large man and a young boy. They decide they would track them. They had never seen this group before. The boys knew the trails well and were able to make headway within a few yards of the group, three heavily armed men walked behind the boy and the large man. As they arrived, about a quarter of the way down the windward side of the mountain, heavy rains began to pour down. Both parties disappeared into the brush to find shelter.

The General, while back at the base, had been busy organizing his own mission to the valley. The SEALs were aware there would be a swift boat in the area, if they were in need of an extraction just in the case they had to fight their way out the front door. He equipped the boat with a Marine squad of four, and the handler in the case they were able to secure the Chinese warriors from Ha'a's control. They were delayed due to the weather, but had launched on the back end of the squall. A tank and a squadron had been prepared for a land-based attack to secure the base. Yakimura was not aware of this, but the General had his apprehensions about working with Yakimura. Not that his plan was far off, but he could enlist a number cruncher. The General didn't need Yakimura to be the guiding hand of a new monetary debt-based system. It would be a bonus if Yakimura could pull off removing Ha'a for him without any involvement. It would be much easier for the military to memorialize him as a figure in the new Hawaii rather them actually work with him.

Yakimura arrived at the gate at the mouth of the valley. He looked out to see, as if he was scanning for something, and the men noticed it. It was like he was a fisherman accessing the weather before setting sail for the morning. He looked at the cloud line pushing off the ridges from the NW. The storm had fully bared down on them by this point. They continued beyond the barricades, meeting Ha'a at the base of the large cave.

"Welcome, Yakimura. There's been a lot going on since last we met."

"Yes, Ha'a. Is the prison still in your control, or has the MWH moved on?"

Ha'a smiled. "I'm not too sure what the MWH is doing at the moment. They gave me a few men and that was that for now. They were given all the resources we had promised and were supposed to bring the remains to your dry storage."

Yakimura responded, "Ha'a, let's be honest. I know you were throwing me off your scent. There was no deal here, just a time grab. I just don't know why you think you needed to waste your time. I was not seeking you out. You sought me out."

Ha'a shook his head. "Your wrong, Yakimura. I do need you. I need you to realize we're in this together. You playing your hand with everyone, and seeing where it takes you, just makes you weaker. You alone can't control this new society. It might not know where it's going, but it does not want to be ruled. That I can be sure of! We were getting so close to a world where the vote was populous based in America. The electoral was hanging on by a thread.

You're not going to be able to structure this society to fit in a box now that it has been let open."

Yakimura paused. "Ha'a, we have different views of the world. You have one that has faith in human self-government. I have one that is aware that all are here for self-preservation. I have never met a person that, given the opportunity, did not use their power, deeds, or status to better their position over another. It is the human default. You will be their hero, then someone will come along and do it better and they will defame you for not progressing. Then, the next will eat that one and the following. It's the fuel of progress, but to contain that progress one needs to cap its exponential growth. I have been open with my process. Debt, we all carry it. If you feel you are born debt-free, a man will create his debt to God to fill the emptiness. Whatever the religion, there needs to be a debt; debt for sin, debt for blessings, a burden and reason for your plot. If you don't have religion, a government will give you your burden to carry through life. If man felt he was deserving of all the earth by birthright, it would be never-ending war for resources. They would all want more, more than the next. You see this with governments, a justification by size. The bigger the empire the more access to resources. They go hand in hand. We are the biggest, so we need the most. We are the smallest, so we are in debt to the biggest.

"You think you can evenly distribute what you have produced in that field? When the time comes, you will see them want your head. My family is bigger, I deserve this. That family did not help, they don't deserve that. If you curb their greed with a debt they owe, and are able to grow or shrink by their work and merit, then you find their worth. If give a self-determined even amount, you will develop a great thirst of entitlement and an unchecked greed with no resources to satiate their want. Human nature runs counter to this. Also, one with no master serves no purpose besides their own. Do you think if you give equally, all will give equally back? Welfare for all leads to warfare. Everyone wants to be at the top with no one at the bottom to carry the weight."

Ha'a looked out onto the field as the sun peaked around the corner. "Well, you made your case. Can I make mine while we check out the progress of the Kapu project?"

Yakimura agreed. "No harm in taking a look. If technology can change the human condition, I wouldn't oppose it."

Two SEALs were guarding Harold and the Chinese soldier in the brush, while the other searched for a clear vantage point into the field. They needed to be within range of 500 meters to make an accurate kill shot with the long gun they carried. The SEAL had a 30 ought 6 sniper rifle with a laser scope. A simple solution with a 5-round cartridge. Harold knew Kapu would be looking for him. It had been over two hours, and they were running low on light. Kapu, unarmed, had decided to call in the threat via radio first but needed to get within range as the weather was throwing off the signal. He got within a mile from the guarded road. "Kapu to Guard Shack 1."

"Guard Shack 1, reading you clear." The guards walked down away from the men at the trucks. "Kapu, what's going on?"

"I have three armed men on the ridge. They captured Harold and one of the Chinese soldiers. Can you relay to the basecamp? Let my dad know to stay out of the fields for now."

"Copy that." The guard tried to relay but got a squealing sound in response.

Ha'a and Yakimura made their way down the track to the Kapu System. Rain was bearing down on the roof of the open-sided vehicle.

"You see where the stream feeds into the basin? It's flowing well with the storm. It moves the turbines for one generator while the wind turns the backup battery. There is a solar component charging the batteries that are off the grid and stored in a secured area for bad weather. If both break, there is a backup to keep the water filtered. If we can store enough energy, we will be able to grow rice fields in the same manner. The added rain water will keep the leaves green at the surface without having to worry about adding a spraying system. We are using vinegar that is produced from the spoiled crops to spray as an organic insecticide. There will be enough produce and fish to feed the island within a month's time, with a second system online by next week."

Yakimura could not help but be impressed with what he saw. A static came over the radio as they hopped out the side less tour bus. Nothing clear enough to understand but Ha'a grabbed it and put it in his pocket as the radio squelched once more.

"Let me show you something else, Yakimura. Something you never put into your equation." The men left the road and ventured off into the field. "You see that fence line? That renders currency and trade useless. If it can be scaled out to that fence line, we can produce enough food in this space to feed the entire island chain with surplus. Where would a system of currency be needed if our needs were covered, our family's fed? Greed, hate, and scarcity would be things of the past."

Yakimura responded, "You have out done yourself, Ha'a. You have miscalculated some things however."

Yakimura reached for his wallet and pulled out the credit card. He drew closer and pointed at the fence line. "Your scale is measuring consumable goods and taking into account this island's human need. You see this?" He pointed to the credit card. Ha'a nodded in confirmation as he went on. "This is just a manifestation of greed-based debt. No one is satisfied with one's equal position to another. They can use it to project themselves above another, even to their own demise. Debt, the master of greed. You've given them two Taro plants, a fish and a goat for milk. They will want a cow, corn, and a new table to eat at. Why? Well, their neighbor has one. Coveting is a uniquely human flaw. I'm sorry, Ha'a. Take a good look. This is the fate of your new world. It has gone this way throughout history. Amor Fati. Love your fate. Embrace it, and if you're wise, expose it to your advantage in this savage landscape."

Ha'a stared at the credit card as Yakimura moved to put it back in his wallet, trying to stall at the same time, as he signaled for the sniper team to shoot. Nothing came. He looked around but nothing. The sniper had not given much in the way of notice or position.

Two men sat atop the hill on the southeast corner of the valley. One spotted through the rain-filled binoculars and the other set his scope between the two men below, water droplets splitting the two. The third SEAL watched over Harold who was bound and gagged. The Chinese soldier lay dormant, arms bound around a tree facing the men. Kapu was tracking them and was two ridges away. He saw a broken brush line, and assumed that's where they entered and were lying in wait for something. He hugged a steep ledge and used a goat trail to cross to the next ridge without exposing himself. He stayed under the treeline. He crossed under an Ulu tree and grabbed an unripe breadfruit from it. As he approached from behind the treeline, Kapu saw a snippet of the spotter and the SEAL guarding the captures. He paused, and pondered his outnumbered position. Three on one; two distracted aligning a shot into the field below. Kapu didn't know what they had their sites on, but he aimed to distract the guard. He took the Breadfruit and lofted it high over the trees, trying not to hit on the way up. It came down twenty feet away, hitting branches and making noise. The shooter yelped, "Check that out! If it's a pig or a goat, drop it. No distractions."

The sniper and spotter turned back to their sites. The guard went into the brush with his Sig drawn from his chest mounted holster. Kapu ungagged Harold, but the guard had circled back to grab his rifle. They heard him entering back the way he came. Kapu hid behind the tree, and started cutting the rope off the hogtied soldier with restraints.

The SEAL grabbed his long gun and turned, saying out loud, "Might need more than my Sig for a job."

Harold nodded as if it was a question and replied, "Good idea."

The man drew close and pointed his weapon. "Where the fuck is your gag, boy?" He put the Sig to Harold's temple. "You're all quiet now. Speak up."

Harold yelled, "Bahou," or protect in Chinese as the ropes fell from the Chinese soldier. He was shot twice, in the leg and arm, as he approached but grabbed the SEAL and folded him backwards, snapping his spine and killing him instantly. The men scouting the shot down below turned to see what was going on. They couldn't make out what had happened. Kapu, in a frenzy, grabbed the Sig handgun and told Harold to follow him with the soldier. The soldier chased after Kapu. He was not sure if he was a threat. Harold pointed to Kapu, and commanded the soldier to stand down and head towards the two perched soldiers. Sam turned his sniper rifle and shot right into the chest of the Chinese soldier.

Down below, Ha'a looked up after hearing shots fired. He was unable to pinpoint the echoes of the valley. Ha'a turned to Yakimura, "Let's get moving." As they jumped into the cart, Yakimura looked up at the ridge line to see one of the men being thrown from a ridge by one of the giant Chinese soldiers. He looked at Ha'a. "I see your son. He's on that ridge line."

Ha'a pulled over immediately. He could see a body hunched over the ridge. "There!"

Ha'a looked up. Yakimura pointed with one hand as he pulled out the fake credit card from his wallet with his other hand. He sliced Ha'a's throat just below his neckline. "I'm sorry Ha'a. Business has its casualties just as with war."

Ha'a tried to grab at Yakimura, but he kicked Ha'a out of the cart and took the wheel. Yakimura pulled out a green military EPIRB that the General had given him. He pulled the tab to give the emergency swift boat a location signal to meet him at the front of the valley where it met the ocean. He took off towards the gate and stopped at the two security barricades. He shouted at the men, "Ha'a is hurt! Jump in and drive! I'm wounded." He pointed to Ha'a's blood on his sleeve. Yakimura grabbed a small Ruger .22 and pretended to get into the back of the cart. The men turned to speak to him, as they took off, but he was perched at the cement barricades. He shot out the back tires, and then shot at the men striking one as he fled towards the mouth of the valley. The men went over their radios.

"Ha'a is hurt! Yakimura is fleeing with a weapon." Kapu heard this clear over the radio and started sprinting down the goat trail. As he hit the clearing, sniper fire rained down around. Harold ordered his children to take out Sam and his scout. Sam was struck hard by the Chinese soldier and rolled down the hill, falling into a gulch with his rifle. He fired upwards until his clip was empty. The soldier threw Sam's partner into the gulch, his neck already broken and weapons gone. Kapu made it to the valley and saw his father lying lifeless in a pool of his own blood.

The boys back at the cove saw a boat moving fast inside the wind line heading towards the valley. They recognized it was the same one that they saw pull into the yacht club earlier in the week and something must be going on. Quickly pulling anchor, they pushed off and hugged the coastline at half-mast in the stormy conditions. As they approached the valley they saw the swift boat beach sliding up onto the shoreline. Three armed men ran into the valley. Seconds later four men embarked on the boat, taking off past the boys, heading in the direction of the base.

Kapu made it to his father, but there was nothing he could do but try to put pressure on the wound. He reached into his backpack for a cloth. As he did, the wounded owl Kapu had been nursing took flight. His father gasped his last breaths. Watching with tears in his eyes, as his son called over the radio for help. Ha'a grabbed his son's hand and, with his last bit of strength muttered, "Ku Season," as the white owl flew towards the mouth of the valley.

THE END

www.ingramcontent.com/pod-product-compliance
Lightning Source LLC
Chambersburg PA
CBHW061515050726
47593CB00002B/587